HARD HATS

HARD HATS

Edited by
Neil Plakcy

CLEIS
PRESS

Published in the United States.
Cleis Press Inc., P.O. Box 14697, San Francisco, California 94114.
Printed in the United States.

Cover design: Scott Idleman
Cover photograph: George Shelley/CORBIS
Text design: Frank Wiedemann
Cleis logo art: Juana Alicia
First Edition.

10 9 8 7 6 5 4 3 2 1

Contents

| INTRODUCTION

I spent five years working as a project manager on various shopping center construction sites, and the hardworking, hard-bodied guys I saw around me every day were the subject of some of my most intense fantasies. From the shirtless carpenters to the beefy laborers, there was plenty of guy candy.

I loved their macho posturing, and after a few months I was able to give and take with the best of them. I always had an eye out for a handsome guy, and for a secluded corner of the site where we could get together.

That experience inspired me to put together this collection, asking some of the best writers of gay erotica to turn their attention to the hard-hatted construction workers who had provided me with so much inspiration in the past. There's just something about a guy with a tool belt that turns me on, and I hope you'll feel the same way about the men in these very hot stories.

Take a trip to the top of a high-rise under construction, or down into the belly of a mine. Hang out in the backyard with some hunky landscapers or roofers, slip into a construction manager's RV or into a storefront under construction. Wherever you go, you'll find sexy, men-loving men who are turned on by their buddies' tools. In this world, the hats aren't the only things that are hard!

Neil Plakcy

HAMMERED AND NAILED

Rob Rosen

It was my first home. Well, condo, to be exact. Ten stories high, overlooking the ocean—if you leaned far enough over and craned your neck, anyway. At least that's what I'd been told. Still, it was all mine. Mine and the bank's, that is.

Okay, mostly the bank's.

In any case, it was going to be spectacular. High slanted ceilings, a massive window line, state-of-the-art everything, luxurious bathroom—you name it, the bank was paying good money for it. And all I had to do was make a few decades of easy payments.

I was thrilled at the prospect, hence my visit that day. Honestly, I couldn't wait any longer to see how it was progressing. Visions of stainless steel and marble tile and ash-blond hardwood floors danced in my addled mind. Plus I already had a key, which had been burning a hole in my pocket for several weeks.

So I snuck inside the vacant building. It was a Sunday. Naturally, no one was working. The place was eerily quiet. No construction crews, no hammering, no welding, and, sadly for me, no electricity, which meant a ten-story climb. Ten stories in the middle of summer, no less.

Still, with a buoyed spirit, I sprang up the stairs—my spring giving way somewhere around the fifth floor. Luckily, I was smart enough to wear my shorts and sneakers. The T-shirt came off on floor number six. That's when the silence turned from spooky to sexy. I was alone. Utterly and completely alone. I could've heard a pin drop. Only, instead of a pin, it was my shorts dropping.

Then it was just me in my undies and sneakers, lumbering silently up the stairwell. By the eighth floor, fairly exhausted, I stopped to catch my breath. Fortunately, the small window I was standing in front of, with the magnificent city view, had yet to have the glass installed. A somewhat cool breeze flowed through and over my sweaty, nearly naked body, sending goose bumps across the nape of my neck and down my arms.

Then, of course, my nearly naked body became totally naked.

I figured by then I had earned it. That, and I was getting hornier by the second. I climbed a few more steps until my midsection was at window level, then pointed my cock out toward the city. Quickly, it jutted up, rigid with pumping blood, greeting the teeming masses below.

My panting filled the stairway. I turned and slapped my prick against the railing, sending a pinging sound in all directions. A drop of precome slid off my mushroom head and stuck to the metal. I wondered if my come was the first to land in all that marvelous empty space. It was a heady thought. And a hot one. My dick grew even wider, eager to burst.

But not there. Not yet.

Newly invigorated, I climbed the remaining stairs. Then, slowly, I opened the door to my floor. Still silence. "Hello?" I whispered into the hallway. My voice echoed down the unfinished cement corridor. I left the stairwell and proceeded forward, my cock bouncing, my sweaty, heavy balls swaying with my stride as I approached my doorway. The key proved unnecessary, though. I still had no door. It stood inside, leaning against the pristine white entryway wall.

I pressed against the knob with my back. The metal was surprisingly cool to the touch. I stood on tiptoe and rubbed it against my fuzzy ass. Then I spread my cheeks apart and let it press against my asshole. What the hell, I figured it was mine to do with as I pleased. Well, again, mine and the bank's, but what they didn't know wouldn't hurt them.

I walked inside the vacant space. The walls had been put up. Gaping holes, where appliances and light fixtures would soon be, stared blankly at me. The place was big and stark and empty. I roamed around, stroking my cock with my spit-slicked hand. I couldn't wait to spread my seed on the bare floor.

And that's when I spotted them: a pair of electrical clamps, small and metal and vivid red. I walked over and lifted them off the floor, breathless in anticipation. I spread them open and then clamped them down one at a time, slowly, gently, on my rigid nipples. A rush of both pain and pleasure filled my chest, and traveled down to my belly and my pulsing cock. I yanked on the wires that hung from the clips. My body quivered and quaked with a rush of internal electricity.

I walked farther into my new home, into what would be my bedroom. The flooring boards were stacked about two feet high to one side. I placed one foot on the stack and squatted down several inches, pulling on my hefty balls as I did so, and still slowly working my seven, upturned inches, occasionally pulling down on the clamps, each time moaning as I did so.

Luckily for me, the clamps weren't the only things the workers had left behind. On the end of the pile of wood sat a finishing hammer, its base as wide as my prick, as phallic an instrument as ever there was. With my cock and balls and nips getting stimulated, why not my asshole?

I reached over and grabbed it, then looked around for some sort of lube. My answer lay in the almost finished master bathroom. On the sink sat a small, open tub of grease remover, its white, gloppy filling beckoning me.

I dipped my hand inside, engulfing three of my fingers in the slick goop. The trio quickly found their way to their intended goal, gliding around and then slowly inside my puckered hole, lubing it up, stretching it out, getting it ready for the object that now rested on the soon to be installed toilet.

Once my asshole was adequately prepped, I spread a layer of the lube up and down my shaft, then reached for the hammer, also slicking it up before placing the wooden base flush against my hole. It would be a unique way to christen my new home.

The solid wood slid in and up and back, sending a shiver down my spine and a flush through my stomach. My asshole clenched then gave in to the pressure of the unbending tool. My cock thickened and precome dripped from the tip. I sighed, and slowly, rhythmically, fucked myself with the end of the hammer.

I was too preoccupied, or too far in the belly of my home, to hear the approaching footsteps, but I did, however, hear this: "Um, I think that's my hammer you've got there."

I froze, with half the tool buried inside of me, and my hand gripped tightly around my dick. My eyes, which had been shut tight in rapture, suddenly popped open.

A man in denim shorts and a tight, white tank was staring at me, grinning as he stood there, arms akimbo. He was tall, lean, ruggedly handsome and, much to my relief, amused at my present state.

"Um," I coughed. "This is my house, er, condo."

"And, as I said, that's my hammer," he laughed, and a blush crept up my neck and across my cheeks.

"It's a good hammer," I thought to reply.

"Seems as much," he replied. "Never tried that with it before, though. Mostly, I use it for, uh, hammering."

"Multipurpose," I said, sliding it out and placing it in the bathtub and out of sight, removing the electrical clamps and setting them to the side.

"Apparently." He stepped backward and let me exit the bathroom, my cock, in its mortification, quickly withering down to its normal size as I passed by him.

"Sorry. I got overstimulated. First home and everything," I justified.

"No need to explain. I mean, it's your home. Not like I don't do the same in my own. Minus the hammer, though." Again he smiled, his sapphire blue eyes twinkling, causing the skin around them to crinkle around the edges. "Name's Greg, by the way."

He stuck his hand out to shake. I did the same, then thought the better of it, what with the grease remover still on my hands. "James," I said, with a nod and a smile as I glanced around for my shorts.

"They're in the kitchen," he offered, obviously aware of my discomfort. "Gonna be a nice kitchen, by the way. That's why I'm here, actually. Can't work tomorrow, so I thought I'd get the floor done today. Keep us on schedule, so you can move in on time."

"Much appreciated," I replied, moving out of the bedroom and toward my clothes. "I am eager to move in. Obviously."

He snickered. "Yeah, so I saw." I laughed as well, mostly out of nervousness, then bent down to reach for my shorts. "By the way, does that grease remover make a good lube?" he asked. I froze, yet again, my hand an inch way from the khaki waistband.

I'd heard the telltale catch in his voice, and looked back over to him. The smile on his handsome face remained, though something else was behind it. Something searching. Eager.

I left the shorts where they were, stood back up, and turned to face him. "Surprisingly, yes. Slick without being sticky. And it keeps its, um, *lubiness*, quite well."

"Lubiness, huh? Don't think it mentions that on the side of the jar."

I followed his train of thought and walked back to the bathroom. He trailed close behind. I lifted the jar up, returned to the light of the bedroom, and read the label. "Yep," I said. "Says so right here. *Good for removing grease, grime, and soil. Especially good for the occasional jacking off.*"

The smile on his face wavered for the briefest of seconds. I handed him the jar, brushing my fingers against his hand. My dick twitched at the sensation of skin on skin. He scanned the label. "Must be in the small print. Too bad I left my reading glasses at home. Guess I'll take your word on it."

I hesitated about saying what I was thinking, then realized I had little to lose. After all, he'd already seen me at my most vulnerable. "Why take my word on it. Try it yourself."

It was less of a dare than a come-on. He looked at me with curiosity, the now familiar smile returning to his handsome, stubble-darkened face. He paused, for a brief moment, as if to gauge my sincerity, then grabbed for the edge of his tank top and pulled it over his head. He was thin and ripped and covered with a fine, blond layer of hair, not to mention numerous scars.

He saw me staring at them. "Nature of the beast," he said. "Carpentry's sometimes a dangerous trade. Sharp, heavy objects and thin skin don't always go hand in hand." He ran his fingers over several of his more obvious accidents. "Worst one's here." He pointed to his behind.

"Really? Let's see." He looked at me uncertainly. "Fair's fair," I added, waving my hand up and down, referring to my obvious nakedness.

He paused and nodded before loosening his belt. Then he unbuttoned his shorts and dropped them down to the ground, revealing well-defined, equally hairy legs and calves. Not to mention a pair of tight blue boxers. Pausing again, contemplating what to do next, he quickly turned around and slid the boxers around his legs. His ass was stunning. Taut and white. Like granite. With just a thin blond trail down his crack. I gulped at the sheer perfection. Then I spotted the inch-long, thin, pink scar.

"Ouch," I said.

"Yep, ouch," he echoed. "Fell backward onto a nail. Thirty stitches. Hurt like a motherfucker."

He stepped completely out of his shorts and boxers, and turned back around, holding his hand modestly over his crotch. Not that he could cover the obvious, though. He was already semi-hard, and he had two of the largest low-hangers I'd ever seen, stretching down several inches beneath his thickening cock.

"Um," I said, motioning to the jar in his hand, as a reminder.

"Oh, yeah," he said, with a mischievous smirk. He sat on the ground, with his back up against the drywall, and placed the jar to his side. Never taking his stunning blue eyes off of mine, he reached in for some of the white goop, and then slid it over and down his cock. I stared, mesmerized, as he stroked it. Watched it grow and grow, inch by widening inch, and begin to curve upward, until the thick head was pointing at his fuzzy belly. "Yep. Good lube. Go figure."

"Told you so," I said, sitting down in front of him. I grabbed for the jar and slathered more of the stuff on my already rigid prick, matching his rhythm, stroke for glorious stroke. He was a beautiful man with an equally beautiful cock, and I watched in stunned silence as his massive balls slapped against the hard concrete floor. "Doesn't that hurt?" I asked, pointing at the dynamic duo.

He looked at me and winked, then jumped to a squat and grabbed for the hairy, dangling pair, yanking them away from his body. "Nope. I like 'em pulled. Twisted. Um, played with."

It was my cue.

I leaned in and slapped at the bottom of them while he gave a tug. He moaned, appreciatively. "Harder," he suggested. I obliged with one, two, three fluid flicks of my wrist. His balls bounced up, as did his hefty tool. "See," he said, in a rasp. "They like it. Now pull down." Again I obeyed, grasping the fleshy base and tugging down, slowly and evenly. The skin stretched until his nuts were now a couple more inches away from his body. His moans reverberated around the room. It was a joyous sound that completely filled the empty space.

"My turn?" I asked, hopping up and matching his squat.

The impish grin reappeared. "Well, I am on the clock. Might as well get your money's worth."

He leaned in and caressed the long hairs on my ball sac, then gave a tentative pull. "Actually, it's the bank's money," I said. "Of which they have a lot." The pull grew harder, firmer, until my balls were stretched to their limit. I winced, but otherwise retained my balance.

Suddenly, he let go and reached for my cock, gliding the slick lube up the shaft. A wave of intense bliss spread through my body. I groaned, released his balls, and stroked his cock too. He crabwalked in closer, so that we were inches apart, our hands moving up and down, our faces in breathing distance of each other.

"You gonna kiss me or what?" he asked, his eyes unblinking, staring, pleading; intense blue on muddy brown.

I closed the gap, pressed my lips softly on his, and felt his tongue slide in, around. The kiss grew firmer, more intense, and still the eyes stayed open, eager to see what was to come next. We crouched there like that, stroking, swapping some heavy spit, and moaning with abandon for several more minutes. Eventually, he broke away and said, "I hear the view outside is nice."

"So I've been told," I said, reaching down for a final yank on his mammoth nuts, then a glide across his hairy asshole.

"I've never been finger-fucked ten stories up," he whispered into my ear, before biting down gently on my lobe.

"No time like the present," I replied, jumping up and walking him over to the sliding glass balcony door. I grabbed the lube on our way, and then we were outside. "Man," I gasped upon first sight of the tremendous view. Mine was easily the tallest building around, by far. No one could see us, and the balcony was encased so that if you leaned over all someone from the sidewalk would witness was your torso—and from our extreme height, barely that.

Greg reached for me, pulled me toward him, engulfed me in his sinewy, strong arms, and hungrily kissed me. The sun caused his irises to twinkle, like stars in the heavens. His cock pressed hard up against my stomach, and mine on his. His hands caressed my back, working their way down to my ass and eventually my hole, which he flicked and rubbed and fingered, slowly, in and out, in and out.

"They say you can see the ocean from up here," I said to him.

"Really?" he asked, breaking away from me and leaning over the balcony. I watched his lats and triceps tense as he grabbed the edge and looked over the side. "Wow," he said, with a low whistle.

"Wow," I repeated, bending down and spreading his legs apart and then his fuzzy cheeks. He had a perfect pink hole, surrounded by fine blond hairs that circled it like a halo. The musky aroma drew me in, and my tongue gave an initial deft lick, then two, before sliding inside of him.

"Here," he said, pushing his balls between his legs. "Pull on 'em while you're down there." I tugged, hard. His knees buckled a bit and his stance widened. I pulled the balls up and rubbed them against his hole, then alternated between sucking on them and his sweet spot, all the while stroking his thick meat with my free hand. Soon, I was sucking on his hole like it was his mouth, kissing it, sliding and gliding my tongue inside of him, back as far as I could, and never letting go of his balls and his cock, working all three zones at once.

The lube was by my side. I reached for it, then sat on the ground and looked up at him. The sun made his blond hairs seem even lighter. His body was dense with them. They wound around his thick calves, circled his worked thighs, made their way up his beautiful crack, and splayed across his lower back. Even the scar on his ass was picture perfect.

He reached behind him and spread his cheeks even farther apart, winking his hole at me. "It's not gonna fuck itself," he joked, sliding one of his fingers inside for example.

I spread some lube on his bulbous dick head, then slicked down the length and breadth of his prick with it. He stroked his cock as I pulled and yanked and twisted his balls with one hand and worked his hole with the other.

One finger easily slid in, up and toward the muscular aft. I reached for more of our makeshift lube, then two fingers glided in and up and back, then out, then in, repeatedly, over and over and over, until his ass was bucking into my hand.

"Three," he groaned. "Come on, three, James. Work that hole. Yeah."

And so two became three. Three digits grouped together as one. Three long, tapered fingers that fucked him long and hard and deep, until they were battering up against a rapidly hardening prostate.

"Oh, man," he groaned as he quickened the pace on his cock, aiming it downward as I gave one final thrust. I stared intently between his legs as stream after stream of sticky white come sprayed my once pristine balcony. His whole body shivered and his back arched as one long, low moan erupted from his lungs and rode the wind out to sea. With a final tug, the last of his juice dripped down and pooled around his feet.

Then silence, except for his ragged breathing. Then, "Your turn, boss."

Music to my ears. My cock was about ready to burst by that point.

We traded spots, with me leaning over the balcony and him on the ground. He spread me open and licked me up and down. I leaned farther out. "Hey, the ocean," I shouted, glad that I hadn't been duped. To which I quickly added, "Hey, a finger." And, soon enough, two, then three, piston-fucking me from ten stories above the city.

My cock was as hard as it had ever been. I quickened my pace on it as he quickened his inside my ass, until we were both in sync. Waves of intense pleasure traveled up and down my spine, through my stomach, and burst inside my cock like fireworks.

"I'm gonna come, Greg," I moaned, for all the city to hear.

"Come, boss. Come," he ordered.

I gave my dick one final jack and shot my heavy white load. Rope after rope of salty jizz erupted from my quivering, slick cock, and joined his on the concrete balcony. I held on to the ledge as my entire body spasmed, trying hard to catch my breath.

Then he stood back up and hugged me as we both stared out at the magnificent view. "Welcome home, James," he whispered into my ear.

"Thanks, Greg, for making it feel like one," I whispered back.

One final kiss, one final stare into those pools of blue, and one last hug before I cleaned up, dressed, and was out of there, leaving him to the job of finishing my floor.

Oh, the joys of home ownership, I thought to myself as I made my way out of the building.

I returned several weeks later, this time for good. The door, by then, had been set in place. With a feeling of reverence, I unlocked it and made my way inside. The bare walls were now painted, the living room was now carpeted and the appliances were all in place, as was a gleaming, marble-tiled bathroom floor. In the kitchen, the ash-blond hardwood floor had been beautifully finished.

Almost finished, that is.

One small strip was missing, and in its place sat the jar of grease remover, plus a little note for yours truly.

Sorry, it read. *Guess I'll have to come back and finish the job, boss.*

I laughed as I made my way to the balcony. Two stains were still evident on the cement. I opened the jar and dropped my shorts. "I think I'm gonna like it here," I said, lubing up my already rigid shaft, this time aiming it at the sky as I stroked and coaxed it to eruption. "Watch out below," I shouted to the city that spread out before me like a veritable buffet. "Here comes a big one!"

DEMO DOGS

Dale Chase

The house has to come down. Old and stately, twelve rooms on two floors, it's been neglected too long to reclaim and besides, I have ideas for a compact rancher that better fits the hilly terrain. My contractor friend Jeff has taken the job of building me a new place and because I want to watch the whole process, I've moved into a large trailer on a bluff just uphill from the site. I even had Jeff add a little deck out front.

Now that I'm settled in, with work about to begin, Jeff finds me there. "Lotta money just to spend your days watching men."

I laugh. "They're just icing on the cake. C'mon, it's my dream house. I want to see it born."

He tells me he's hired an outfit called Demo Dogs to do the teardown. "Big job," he adds. "That old place is solid as hell but these guys know their stuff. They'll demolish it, clear away the rubble, even clear the additional land we need for landscaping and the hot tub."

"Sounds good."

"They start tomorrow. Probably wake you up."

"Not a bad way to start the day."

Jeff shakes his head. "You're incorrigible."

As I watch him drive back down the hill I consider what I've taken on: selling my San Francisco mansion and dropping out of the high life in favor of semirural quiet. I'm still only twenty miles from the city, can still get over there if the mood strikes, but for the most part I'm going to live in the woods—with amenities.

Next morning it's just as Jeff said. I awake to a powerful engine sputtering to life and men shouting. Lying with a hand around my stiff dick I'm tempted to get off but something holds me back. There is promise afoot, after all. Surely there's a Demo Dog who might like a little action.

It's late June so I know there will be lots of bare chests. I put on nothing but cutoffs and take my coffee out onto the deck to stand watching as a bulldozer rams the big house's front porch beam.

The guy driving this massive yellow belching beast wears a short-sleeved chambray shirt that looks about to burst at the seams. Beneath his white hard hat he's deeply tanned. Even at this distance I can spot a chiseled jaw and rugged good looks. As his dozer chews into the old house with slow, persistent attacks I think of him doing that to me, knowing there's gotta be a fat dick in those jeans. After a while when the porch overhang has collapsed, he backs up, pauses, and looks my way. Still at the deck railing, I wave. He nods, then goes back to work.

Others drive Bobcats and clear the rubble he creates. Some glance my way but when they stop for what appears to be a morning break, the dozer dude comes up the path.

"You like to watch," he says.

"Like to do more than that," I reply because my dick is hard and I can see he's interested. "Why don't you come inside," I suggest.

He nods, rubs his bulging crotch.

As I go through the trailer door he grabs my cutoffs and pulls them down, shoves me to the kitchen table, not bothering to shut the door. Grinding against my ass as I bend to him, he gets a rubber on in record time, then shoves his dick into me, giving me a full-out fuck that I swear sets the trailer rocking. He's got the fat prick I imagined, totally reaming me, and I'm ready to shoot but then he lets out a few grunts, slams into me, and I know he's letting go. When he's done he pulls out, utters a "Shit, man," takes a couple deep breaths then flips me around and sucks my throbbing prick into his mouth. I shoot like I haven't gotten off in days.

When he's swallowed the last of my jizz, he sits back and blows out a long sigh. Standing up he simply nods, zips his jeans, and departs. He hasn't taken off his hard hat.

Satiated, I decide to get some sun on the chaise. I change to my Speedo, slather myself with suntan oil, and stretch out to the accompaniment of demolition.

The house doesn't go easily. It lets out mighty groans and screeches as walls are torn apart, awful wrenching sounds that, with my eyes shut, conjure a terrible dismemberment. I can't fall asleep with all the noise but I soon find I enjoy the men's calling out to each other with raucous shouts that most often include the word *fuck*. I'm also pleased that a breeze blowing downhill keeps the dust off me.

Lazing into midday, I hear work stop again and figure it's lunchtime. What I don't figure is another visitor.

"Hey, man," says someone close by. I open my eyes to see a handsome young Latino standing over me. His dick is out.

"You want it?" he asks.

"Hell, yes," I say and when I start to get up he says, "No, here." He pulls a condom from his pocket and readies himself. I glance toward the house but see no one. "They're down at the trucks eating lunch," the guy tells me. "Roll over, get your ass up."

I toss the Speedo and do as I'm told. He straddles the chaise, grabs my ass, and eases his prick into me. "Fuck, yeah," he says as he begins. He doesn't seem in any hurry, and sets up an easy stroke, the chaise squeaking beneath us like some old four-poster. I think about the scene should any of the crew finish lunch and come back to the site. But this guy doesn't seem to care. He's more interested in giving me a good long fuck and I, greased and sweaty, wallow to the fullest.

Finally, however, the inevitable: "Okay," he says as he kicks it up a notch. "Okay, okay," like he's commanding a spigot be turned on. His strokes are urgent, fast, faster, then his moans climb the scale until he's into a near wail that is finally overcome by a strangled silence.

He immediately pulls out and climbs off. I roll over to see his dick disappear into his jeans. As he heads back down the path I wonder if word is out.

The demolition takes much of a week, probably longer than necessary due to all the fucking—because word has indeed gotten out and I am blissfully had several times a day. The Demo Dogs just can't get enough ass.

After the first couple days, I begin to sunbathe nude. Lying greased and glistening, I get hard in anticipation and soon one of the men is on the deck with his dick out, ready for action. One of them surprises me by slipping a condom onto me and climbing on. I lie watching him bounce and squirm on my cock, this tanned hulk taking it up the butt, and I get off big-time in his furry ass.

A voyeuristic game soon develops, with the crew often stopping to watch the on-deck action—which, as a result, becomes ever more bold. One blond bear of a man strips naked and does me standing at the railing, my hard cock pointed at the spectators. Looking down at them as I get pumped by the biggest of all their cocks, I am so crazy with the scene that I shoot my wad unaided, spewing spunk while he drives it home up my rear.

That evening when work is done this same guy comes back up the path, takes me inside the trailer and does me again, only this time it takes hours.

He sucks my dick as I stand naked, then puts me on the bed and sucks still more and when that's not enough he rolls me over and eats out my ass. He works himself into a frenzy back there, slurping and growling as I take his tongue deep. He's frantic finally and flips me back over, shoves his cock halfway down my throat and comes in a gusher, me gulping jizz as I feast on the fat salami.

When we're done I'm thinking he'll take off but he does no such thing. He stretches out beside me and starts licking my tits while he gets a couple fingers up my ass and I lie there feeling like some toy beneath a lion's paw. Soon it grows dark and he tells me to get up, get into my shoes. He puts on just his boots and we walk naked down to the site where a half-moon shines on what remains of the house.

"Up here," he says, moving to the seat of his dozer. "Fuck you up here," he adds as he climbs into the seat. He's brought a rubber and has it on by the time I reach him and he pulls me into his lap, drives that big dick up my chute, and sits holding me at the hips as he grinds up into me.

"Tomorrow when I'm working, I'm gonna think of this," he says. We're like this for a good long while, him squirming inside me until he finally lets out an "Oh, hell" and rams home another climax.

When I finally climb down from the dozer my knees nearly buckle.

"Hey, you okay?" he asks.

"More than okay. Ecstatic, if you must know, but you guys are wearing me out. Talk about demolition."

"Too much?"

"No, never too much."

Next afternoon I'm happily put to the test. It's hotter now, all the men are shirtless, and I remain naked from the start. I now have no hesitation in walking around on my deck wearing nothing, enjoying both the freedom and the anticipation. At noon I'm dozing on the chaise, awash in sweat, when I feel a hand on my dick. My eyes open to see not one but two of the men—the cute Latino and the burly blond. "Let's go inside," says the blond. We've never exchanged names and I realize that's best as anonymity makes for great sex.

"He's gonna fuck you," the blond says as he strips.

"And you?"

"I'm gonna watch."

His drooling dick says otherwise but I go along as the Latino knows how to use that little plug of a cock. Soon I'm on the bed, him riding my ass while the blond sits stroking his dick and taking in the sight.

They're all into my lube now and we're soon awash in the stuff, the fuck giving off that squishy slap, me full of juice and looking for more. He's giving it to me thoroughly and I am riding his dick because there is never enough, and I'm so turned on I'm thinking I might come unaided again but then I see the blond is rolling a condom down his honker. And then he gets up and, swear to God, climbs in behind my guy and apparently shoves it up the sweet boy's ass so we've got a three-way fuck train going. "Yeah, man, yeah, yeah," the Latino says, and I feel him adjust his stroke to that of the blond ramming dick up his ass. And soon the fuck slap has a grand rhythm, double timing as two cocks work in sync. It feels like they're both doing me.

Finally the Latino goes crazy, starts spouting off in Spanish, pounding me while the blond growls "Do it man, 'cause I'm gonna," and both are then lost to the familiar grunts and moans of unloading in a friendly ass. I, of course, with such a powerful rear assault, shoot into the bedding big-time.

I pretty much collapse after this. While the Latino pulls out of me and the blond pulls out of him, I don't move. Lying flat and totally, happily, wasted I get a "You okay?" and all I can do is raise a hand to wave an answer. I sleep the rest of the afternoon.

The place looks odd when the house is down. The crew works at clearing the site and as truckloads are carted away, I see the hillside like it's new. Trees and shrubs once hidden come into view and only then do I accept the fact that the Demo Dogs sex party is near an end. On the final day, as they clear the last few scraps, I stand nearby fully clothed, reminding myself there's a larger purpose here. This wasn't about sexual services even if it seemed like it much of the time. It was about old making way for new.

I shake every man's hand when they've finished, noting I've fucked them all. Nobody says they'll be back, it's not that kind of thing, and I almost feel jealous of their next customer, who I hope discovers the real talent of Demo Dogs.

When Jeff comes by later to go over the construction schedule he asks what I think of Demo Dogs.

"Great guys and great work. They were wonderful."

"Well, you'll have the construction crew here Monday morning. I hope things go as well with them."

I smile. "I hope so, too."

70s PORNA-PALOOZA

Stephen Osborne

When Eric Satterfield's boyfriend of six years broke up with him, he was devastated.

He found solace, however, in porn.

Eric had never really been into porn before. He'd seen a few movies here and there, of course, but he honestly couldn't see the fascination some men had concerning it. Why bother with images on a television screen when you could have the real thing? Several days after Mike had left him for someone else, though, Eric found himself incredibly horny. He toyed with the idea of going out to a bar and picking someone up, but the thought of going through all the motions of chatting someone up left Eric cold. He just wanted to get off. Quickly.

His Internet connection was still on dial-up, so online porn wasn't an option. Instead, he found himself outside of Nighthawks Video Store. It was late but there were still several cars in the lot. Finally mustering the courage to go inside, Eric pulled the collar up on his jacket, hunched his shoulders,

and forced one foot to go in front of the other.
Inside he was surprised at how bright the place was. Shouldn't
it be dim, so faces couldn't be seen? The guy behind the counter
nodded at Eric. He seemed like an everyday guy. Not a sleaze-
ball at all. Patrons (all men and all looking exceedingly normal)
browsed the aisles, occasionally picking up an item for further ex-
amination. Eric found the DVD rack and located the gay-themed
movies. One entitled *The Delivery Man Has a Package for You*
caught his eye. The two guys on the cover looked hot. It would
do. Eric snapped up the DVD and took it over to the counter.

The cashier nodded with approval when he saw Eric's choice.
"This is a pretty good one. I've lost many a load watching this
one myself. Will that be cash or charge?"

"Cash," Eric said nervously. Did people actually buy porn
using a charge card, with their name embossed on the damned
thing for all to see? Hell, for all Eric knew the FBI tracked sales
of gay porn and had a master list of "deviants." Eric didn't know
what the hell the FBI could possibly do with such a list, but
he wouldn't put it past them to have one. He took his change,
grabbed the bag the clerk handed him, and rushed back outside.

Safely back at home, Eric lost no time putting the disc into
the player. He settled back onto his couch and got comfortable.
He had his jeans shoved down and his engorged cock in his hand
before the opening credits had even finished.

The film lost no time getting to the sex, which was fine with
Eric. If he'd wanted a plot, he would have rented *Casablanca*.
On-screen, a man in maybe his late twenties (slightly younger
than Eric) was vacuuming his apartment when the doorbell
rang. Opening the door, he found a brown-uniformed delivery
man standing there.

"I've got a package for you," the man said in a horribly stilted
voice. Acting was not the guy's strong suit, apparently. Eric didn't

care. He just wanted to jerk off watching some hot fucking. He began pumping his cock in anticipation of what was to come.

The apartment dweller eyed the man's crotch lasciviously. "You sure do!"

Seconds later the door was shut firmly behind them and the delivery man was groaning as the other guy deep-throated his nine-inch dick.

Eric came before the bad porno music had even begun.

He returned to Nighthawks Video the next day and purchased a DVD entitled *Kentucky Bone and the Temple of Cock*. It purported to be a spoof of the Indiana Jones movies but ended up not even being good on a camp level. The sex, what there was in it, was badly lit and the actors really didn't seem to be at all interested in what they were doing. The guy playing archaeologist Kentucky Bone was particularly bad. In one scene, where he was butt fucking his native bearer, the guy had a distant look on his face, like he was thinking about what he was going to have for dinner. The hot man bucking underneath him seemed a mere side note. Eric turned the movie off in disgust. Within an hour he was back at Nighthawks.

This time he came away with two films from the 1970s. One of the actors on the cover caught his eye and he thought he'd give it a try. The other he bought simply as a precaution. He didn't want to return for a third time in one day if he ended up with another disappointment like *Kentucky Bone*.

He needn't have worried. Within minutes he had a crush on the star. Checking the box, he found the actor's name was Kip Noll. Luckily Noll was in both 70s DVDs he'd purchased. Eric jacked off six times before going to bed.

During the next few weeks, he bought every 70s porn film he could find, especially if they had Kip Noll in the cast. He rushed home from work every day to jump onto the couch and grab the remote. Eric wasn't sure what it was about that decade's porn that fascinated him; maybe it was the innocence of the time. AIDS had yet to rear its ugly head, so fucking seemed so much more spontaneous. Sure, the videos were often poorly lit, had horrible camera work, and boasted the worst acting on the planet, but they made Eric forget getting unceremoniously dumped. After Kip Noll his second favorite was Jon King. He wondered briefly if they were still alive and what they were doing nowadays. He toyed with the idea of looking them up on the Internet but decided against it. He didn't care what had happened to them after their porn careers. They were alive and young for him on the screen and that was all that mattered.

Having become a regular at Nighthawks, Eric no longer slunk around between the aisles. He strode in with his head high and waved a cheery hello to Max, the guy who always seemed to be behind the cash register. Max often suggested movies for Eric to purchase.

They even chatted about their favorite scenes in the films. Max noticed a pattern in what Eric enjoyed most. "You like those chance encounters," he said, nodding. "You know, the plumber comes and fixes more than just the pipes, the carpenter uses the tape measure to measure more than just wood, or the pizza guy delivers more than just a pie. That happened to me once. For real, I mean."

Eric's eyes widened in amazement. "You're kidding?"

Max grinned at the memory. "Kid came to the door bearing the pizza. He was just too hot for words. I gave him a hefty tip, looking hard into his eyes the whole time. He set the pizza aside and gave me *his* hefty tip. He fucked me in more positions than I knew existed." A frown crossed Max's brow. "Pizza was cold when we were done, though."

That evening Eric ordered a pizza.

He envisioned opening the door and seeing Jon King standing there with a pie in hand and a huge bulge straining to escape his tight jeans. When the doorbell actually rang, Eric rushed to the door.

The young girl who brought his pizza in no way resembled Jon King, although she did have a slight mustache.

Over the next few weeks, Eric tried everything he could think of to get his porno fantasies to come to life. He called in electricians to put in new lighting fixtures. He had cable installed. The cable guy was quite a fox and seemed a nice guy, but he had been totally oblivious to the overtures Eric made. Eric hovered around as the guy worked, licking his lips in what he thought was a seductive manner and finding excuses to rub a hand over his crotch. Nothing worked. The cable guy left after smiling broadly to Eric and wishing him a pleasant day.

Eric thought he'd struck gold the night he'd ordered his sixteenth pizza in a row. The delivery boy was in his early twenties and had that hungry I-really-need-the-money look to him. He wasn't Eric's ideal, having a bit too much of the skater-punk look to him, but he would do. Eric took the pizza, fixed the boy with a steady look, and put a twenty dollar tip into his hands.

The boy's eyes lit up. "Hey, thanks, dude!" He began to retreat.

Eric took a step forward, saying, "Wait a minute. Isn't there something you want to give me in return?"

The kid thought a moment. "Did you order bread sticks too?"

After the delivery boy was safely gone, a frustrated Eric put the pizza aside and paced around the living room. These scenarios worked for guys in the porno films. They even worked for Max. Why couldn't they work for him? The more he thought about it, the angrier he became. Was it too much to ask to have one of his fantasies come true? After all, he'd suffered enough from his breakup with Mike. Didn't he deserve a little pleasure? Eric went into the bathroom, intending to splash some water on his face in an effort to calm down. Standing before the freestanding sink, however, he found his fury only deepening. He got only as far as turning on the taps when he found he couldn't take it any longer. He growled and kicked out his left leg angrily in an attempt to vent some of his frustration. Unfortunately the kick connected with the bottom of the sink, which separated from the wall by nearly an inch with a sickening crash. The pipe under the sink burst, sending forth a spray of water that hit Eric right in the face.

Sputtering, Eric sat on the floor, dejected. "Ah, shit," he said aloud.

While Eric waited for the plumber to arrive, he popped in a porno film and began to whack off. There was no use pursuing his dream of a porn scene coming to life. Those things never really happened. Max had most likely been fibbing about his experience. No, the closest Eric would come to having a hunky carpenter nail his ass would be through watching *Nailing Studs* or, one of his personal favorites, *Hammer My Ass*.

Eric was getting close to his climax when a loud knock sounded at the door. "Shit," he muttered, shoving his swollen cock back into his underwear. He took his time pulling his jeans back up and doing up his fly. After all, the plumber would end up being some out-of-shape, grizzled straight guy who would have no more interest in fulfilling one of Eric's fantasies than any of the other carpenters, cable installers, or electricians that Eric had called over the past several weeks.

"Coming," he said without enthusiasm in response to the

second knock on the door. He opened it and his mouth fell open.

Standing there, wearing the blue uniform of Caspian Heating and Plumbing, stood a young man who bore more than a passing resemblance to Kip Noll. Eric found himself looking for the man's name on the patch over his right pec, half expecting to see KIP written there in red. The name there was JED.

Jed smiled and said, "You're having some problem with your bathroom sink, I understand."

Eric realized he was staring. He gulped and managed to force some words out. "Yeah. Had a bit of an accident. I sort of knocked the whole damn thing off the wall."

"It's easily done. If you'll show me the way, I can check out the damage and give you an idea of what we're dealing with here."

It was several moments before Eric realized he hadn't ushered the plumber inside. "Sorry," he said. "Sorry. Please come in. I just wasn't expecting…"

"Someone this young?" Jed finished. There was no animosity in his tone. "I get that all the time. I'm older than I look. Honestly. Usually I work with a partner, but he's out with the flu, so you just get me. I can take care of your problem, though. Don't worry about that."

Eric tried not to look at Jed's crotch. He bit his lip and tried to stare at a spot on the far wall. It didn't work. His eyes wandered and eventually lit on the plumber's hip area. Eric blinked. Did he see a bulge there? He did. He was sure of it. It wasn't the type of bulge caused by a very large but limp cock, either. This was a full-blown bulge. Eric could even see the outline of the head of Jed's dick showing plainly through the fabric of his blue pants.

Eric shook his head. He was imagining things. He had to be.

"Care to show me where the problem is?" the plumber asked.

He even sounded like a young Kip Noll. After Eric realized a question had been asked, he blurted out, "Right down the hall here." He led the way, trying to control his breathing. *Just show the guy the bathroom and get out of his hair,* Eric told himself. *He's not interested in your porno fantasies or your Kip Noll obsession.*

Jed nodded when he saw the damage Eric's outburst had caused. "This isn't bad. I can fix this in a jiffy. You've got the water valve turned off, I see."

"Well, yeah," Eric said, blushing in embarrassment. "Otherwise I'd have drowned by now."

The plumber set his toolbox down. He got down on his haunches and looked under the sink. "Piece of cake, this. I've seen this happen all the time. The job will go quicker, though, if you wouldn't mind helping out a little."

Eric blinked. "What would you like me to do?"

"If you could hold the sink up so that it's back against the wall again, that would be great."

Eric did as instructed, trying not to look down at the plumber's splayed legs. Jed shifted around so his head was under the sink. Eric heard some metal on metal as Jed worked a wrench around the water pipe. "This won't be difficult at all. Just have to reattach the sink to the wall, replace this bit here, and we're all set."

"Just let me know whatever I can do to help," Eric said. His voice sounded small, even to him. He hoped the plumber was oblivious to his nervousness.

"Actually," Jed said, setting the wrench down on the tiled floor, "if you could come down here and hold the sink up from the bottom, I'll be able to get a better look at the situation."

There wasn't a lot of room in the bathroom, so Eric moved a little awkwardly. He chuckled uneasily as he squatted down next to Jed. He managed to keep the sink in place, but being so close to the hot plumber caused a thin line of sweat to form on Eric's brow. "How's this?" he asked.

Jed raised his head a little. "You can let go of the sink, actually. It's not like it's going to fall completely off the wall or anything like that."

Eric slowly released his hold. The sink slid once again away from the wall a few inches, held by the pipes. Jed was right. While it looked precariously askew from its normal position, it was obvious the sink wasn't actually going anywhere. Eric bit his lip and gave a tiny shrug. "What is it I can do to help, then? I don't really know anything about plumbing."

Jed smiled up at him. "You don't need to." He was stretched out on the bathroom floor with his work boots pressed against the wall. His head was nearly touching the opposite wall. Eric thought it looked terribly uncomfortable, but the plumber seemed totally at ease. In fact, he brushed a hand down his pants in what seemed a leisurely fashion. The action seemed innocent, but in pushing down the fabric of his pants, Jed's crotch became accentuated. Eric could plainly see the outline of Jed's cock through his pants. Instinctively he licked his lips. It was one hell of a nice-looking bulge.

Eric shook his head to dispel any thoughts of Jed's privates. "You want me to just hand tools to you or something?" he asked.

Jed laughed, his eyes twinkling. "I don't really need you here at all. This is such a simple job I could do it blindfolded."

"I don't understand, then. You said the job would go quicker if I helped out."

The plumber ran his hand over his crotch again, this time slower and more deliberately. "I don't really need help with the work. I just meant it's been a long day and I could use some relaxation before tackling another job."

Eric started to speak, but no words came out. He tried a second time but only managed to say, "What?"

Jed grinned and took hold of Eric's hand. "Sheesh, do I have to spell it out? I'm all wired and tense and could use some release." He took Eric's hand and placed it over his crotch. "I was hoping you could help out by sucking my dick."

Eric wanted to pinch himself to make sure he wasn't dreaming, but he didn't want to remove his hand from Jed's lap. He could feel Jed's hardening dick through the fabric.

In his head he could almost hear the *wonka-wonka* strains of 70s porn music. "You want me to..."

"If you wouldn't mind. Honestly, it will make the work go so much faster. I'll be able to concentrate, and..."

Eric didn't need to hear anything else. He quickly undid the thin brown belt and unzipped Jed's pants. Jed helped out, shoving his underwear down, allowing his thick cock to flop out in all its glory. Eric barely paused for breath. He swallowed Jed's cock in one swift motion. With a sharp intake of breath, Jed raised his hips slightly off the floor. His fingers tangled themselves in Eric's hair.

"Oh, man," he said, groaning, "you know how to suck a cock."

Eric took his lips off the plumber long enough to run his tongue up and down the length of Jed's shaft. He glanced up to Jed's face long enough to make sure he hadn't invented the guy's looks in his head. No, Jed looked every inch the young California dude, complete with sun-bleached curly hair and weathered skin. Eric went back to bobbing up and down on Jed's dick, not believing his luck. Finally, after he'd given up all hope, his porno fantasy was actually coming true. Not only was he sucking the dick of a hot plumber, the guy even resembled one of his favorite stars. The only thing missing was the cliché language so

prevalent in the porn films of that time. The "surfer guy" talk
that nearly all of them used would make the picture complete.

"Oh, man," Jed murmured after emitting a long moan.
"Yeah, suck that dick. Oh, dude, that feels so good!"

Dude! He said dude! Eric's heart began to race. He let Jed's
cock slip out of his mouth so that he could attack the young
man's balls with his tongue. He slurped one hairy testicle into
his mouth and felt Jed tense as the shock of pleasure ran through
his body.

"Fuck, yeah!" The plumber squirmed and his fingers tightened, tugging slightly at Eric's hair. "You're driving me crazy!"

Eric gave a final loving suck to Jed's testicle before releasing
it. He ran his tongue back up the rock-hard prick and resumed
the blow job. Jed began to lift his hips to meet Eric's hungry
mouth. They worked as one, Eric's mouth taking in Jed's meat
with increasing speed as the plumber bucked beneath him. They
reached a fever pitch and Jed's hands held Eric's head in place as
the plumber began to face-fuck Eric with a savage intensity. Eric
could feel the thick cock begin to throb. He knew Jed was about
to spill his sweet juice. Finally with one last thrust of his hips Jed
groaned. Eric kept his mouth tight around the base of the plumber's cock and was rewarded as a huge wad shot down his throat.

Only when the last drop had drained from his balls did Jed
relinquish his hold on Eric's hair. He groaned and laughed at the
same time. Eric looked up to see the pleasure in Jed's face. "How
was that?" he asked.

The plumber chuckled. "Do you have to ask? It was fan-
fucking-tastic, that's what it was. Just what I needed."

Eric wiped his hand across his mouth. "It was a dream come
true for me, let me tell you."

Jed raised up on his elbows. "I feel bad, though, dude. You
haven't gotten off."

Shrugging, Eric replied, "It doesn't matter. I've been wanting something like this to happen for so long that…"

The plumber picked up his wrench. "Hey, dude. You're my last job of the night. Give me a few minutes and we can have another go. I'll get this sink back in place and we can give it the Test."

"The Test?"

Jed smiled. "Yeah. That's where you bend over it, gripping the sides, and I fuck your sweet ass so hard that neighboring states will complain. If it holds up to that, we know the job's done correctly. Am I right?"

Eric nodded, unable to keep the grin off his face. He fished around in the plumber's toolbox, hauling out as many tools as he could grab. "Just tell me what you need. After all, we want to make sure we use the right tools for the job…"

Jed laughed. "You've got that right."

"Come to think of it," Eric said as the plumber began to work on the sink in earnest, "I think I've got some other problems that need fixing. The bathtub has a slow drain, and the kitchen sink leaks every now and then, and…"

The plumber raised his eyebrows. "Sounds like this might take several nights."

"It might at that."

"Good," Jed said with a smile. "Our company likes the customer to be satisfied, so whatever you need, I'm here to take care of it."

Eric's DVD collection went untouched for weeks.

LIVE-WIRE DELTA

G. Russell Overton

I finished changing a faulty main breaker at my first service call around ten thirty in the morning and radioed in to let the dispatcher know I was ready for my next job. I was a journeyman with Oklahoma City's largest electrical contractor, and most of our work was in running service calls. He responded, "KTK Base to KTK five thousand, come in."

I picked up the microphone and said, "KTK five thousand. What have you got for me, Richard?"

"I need you to take a quick service call at the Burnished Oak Apartments. They have a bedroom light that's not working, and a new tenant is set to move in this weekend. They have to clean the carpets this afternoon, so you need to get in there ASAP."

The Burnished Oak Apartments were one of our best clients and one of Oklahoma City's largest apartment complexes. I typically had a service call there at least once a week. I told Richard I was on my way. "I'm ten-eight to 6215 Northwest Expressway."

Richard closed, "Joe, you need to see the manager, Tim Michaels."

I smiled. Tim was a hottie, about my height, slender, with a dark head of hair and a full, short-trimmed beard. He was in his thirties and unattached as far as I could tell. When I had been there a week earlier, I had exchanged some rather suggestive eye contact with him. He had not seemed offended.

I parked my truck, strapped on my tool belt, and took my stepladder off the top rack. The leasing office was buzzing with prospective tenants, but Tim stepped out of his office after only a minute. "Joe, thanks for coming on such short notice. I'll take you over right now."

We walked out to the courtyard, past the swimming pool, to apartment 1217 on the first floor in the D building. Tim explained that the fixture had worked intermittently before quitting completely. They had tried changing lightbulbs several times without success.

I set up my ladder and took the globe down. Busy as they were in the leasing office, I was surprised that Tim stayed with me while I worked. He chatted on about all their new tenants. I handed him the globe to set in a safe place on the carpet. Next I loosened the two screws holding the fixture to the mounting bracket. While holding the fixture in one hand I removed the screws and instinctively wedged them between my lips.

Tim asked, "Would you like me to hold those screws for you?"

I looked over my shoulder and mumbled, "Naw, I guess I'm just used to sticking things in my mouth."

Making direct eye contact and with a dead-serious face, Tim said, "So am I."

Realizing the significance of his comment and my own culpability in leading to it, I nervously went back to work. The problem with the light had been nothing more than a loose wire. I secured it with a new wire nut and refastened the fixture base.

Tim handed me the globe off the floor. I returned my linesman pliers to the front center pocket of my tool pouch, and I felt Tim's left hand cup my upper left thigh. I looked over my shoulder, and he said, "I thought you were about to lose your balance."

I smiled and said, "Thanks."

His hand did not move, but his left thumb gently stroked the inside of my left thigh. I continued returning tools to my tool pouch and cleaning up the debris on the top of my ladder, slowly. I let out a faint "Hmm," approval of the movement of his thumb. It moved up into my butt crack and stroked a few times. I sighed approvingly again. Tim's right hand reached around to my front and began stroking my crotch. He rubbed my hardening cock, and I turned around on the ladder. He was eye level with my inseam.

In an instant my navy blue work pants and striped boxers were around the ankles of my spit-polished black boots. Tim buried his nose in my crotch before taking my cock in his mouth. His skill was evident. He knew just the right way to bring me to the brink of shooting before backing off to let me regain a sense of control.

I thought I should try to reciprocate and started to step off the ladder. His right hand firmly pushed my torso back against the ladder, and he pulled off for just a second. "Stay put, Joe. This is exactly how I want it."

It was exactly how *I* wanted it, and I relaxed with my back against the ladder and my heels dug in against the second rung. My hands ran through his hair and stroked his beard. I never took my eyes off his handsome face sliding up and down on my cock.

Tim could sense when I could hold out no more. He pulled

his own cock out and began stroking it while he continued sucking mine. I began to pulse. He shot off in short powerful bursts. One stream hit the third rung of my ladder; another missed the ladder and sprayed the carpet.

He helped me up with my pants and shorts, and I stepped down off the ladder. We embraced for a moment. I could taste my cum on his lips and licked off the small amount that was clinging to his mustache.

Tucking my shirt in, I said, "Now I know why you wanted me here before the carpet cleaners."

Tim signed my work order, and I left for my next job.

The spring and summer of 1988 opened a new world for me. I started to toy with the idea of fucking just for the sake of fucking. My encounter with Tim proved that the straight men in the office, who were always bragging about how much pussy they were able to score on the job, weren't the only ones who could get some on-the-job action.

I began to carry condoms and lube in my tool belt. There were a few encounters with customers, and I could always depend on Tim for a great blow job a couple of times a month, but most of my tricks were with other men in construction trades.

The summer turned out to be a scorcher, with record temperatures from the middle of June through September. Our shop even took the rare step of stopping attic work after noon each day. We still had plenty of opportunities for working in dangerous heat.

I started a remodeling project at a high-rise office tower in early July that would take several weeks. It was almost all rooftop work. The first part of the project was to install new air-handling units and rooftop security systems. The interior work would not start until winter.

Marvin, the shop manager, picked me for the job because he knew I was the best man at running conduit and was one of the few competent to work in a three-phase delta panel. A three-phase delta system can be dangerous and tricky. It differs from most home and office systems by having three hot wires. The third hot wire, typically called the "high leg," runs at 208 volts to ground instead of the standard 120 volts. Any mistake can fry expensive equipment or cause serious injury. Marvin only let the most talented and skilled electricians live-wire a delta panel. I felt honored to have the job.

Workers from several trades were involved on this project: mechanical contractors, roofers, painters, and me, the electrician. It was miserably hot on the roof. All of the other tradesmen wore T-shirts, tank tops, and shorts. I was the only one dressed in a starched and pressed navy blue uniform. After the third day I asked Marvin if, for the duration of the project, I could dress more appropriately for the location. Being the conservative ex-Marine he was, Marvin emphatically said no. He insisted that proper uniform was the only appropriate attire while I was on any job.

After the first week I had all of the security system lights and horns installed, and I was mostly there to hook up and test out new equipment as it was being set. From that point forward I had a lot of downtime while I waited for other tradesmen to complete their tasks. I still had to stay on-site and on the roof most of the time.

On Tuesday of the second week I could stand the heat no more and took off my shirt. I kept it hanging nearby in case Marvin made one of his unannounced visits. It seemed like the painter and the mechanical journeyman did a double take when I strutted by with my bare chest. Johnny the painter said in a sarcastic tone, "Aren't you afraid Sergeant Marvin will throw you in the brig or something?"

I laughed. "Sometimes we just have to take chances."

Johnny looked me over again and said, "You look like you work out. What do you do?"

I said, "Kind of a basic routine. I run six miles each morning and lift at the gym about three or four times a week."

Johnny raised an eyebrow and said, "Impressive."

He filled out his tank top nicely, and I commented, "You look like you keep in shape."

He said, "Yeah, I lift some and play racquetball." He stared right at my crotch and said, "There's nothing like banging some balls really hard after a tough day at work."

I returned the glance and said, "Yeah, maybe we could get together sometime and slap a few balls around."

His paintbrush was starting to get crusty out of the bucket, and he needed to get back to work. He walked off and said, "We should get together soon, real soon."

Gary, the mechanical journeyman, had been working nearby. I wondered if we had been too brazen. Gary smiled at me when I looked his way. He was wearing a T-shirt and cutoff jeans. His legs were hairy, just the kind I liked to have wrapped around my neck. I imagined that his tight little butt was as hairy as his legs.

Gary stopped me and said, "You know, I'm a runner, too, though I don't do six miles a day."

I knew he had heard every word. Now I had to find out if he had picked up on anything. I said, "Really? You certainly have the legs to prove it. Maybe we could go for a run together some weekend. On Saturdays I either go up to Lake Heffner or one of the other reservoirs around here and do an eight- to twelve-mile run."

Gary nodded, "Wow, that sounds aggressive. I wouldn't mind trying something aggressive like that sometime."

I had to take the bait. I looked down at his legs, then up slowly at his crotch. "I could show you just how aggressive I can be."

Gary smiled out of one corner of his mouth. "Maybe later."

The next day was the hottest yet. By 9:00 A.M. the temperature was ninety degrees. Gary and Johnny were the only other workers on the roof. I knew Marvin was tied up with a project in Norman and would be there all day. I took off my shirt right away. Gary and Johnny did the same. Hairy-chested Gary was a stud in his skimpy cutoffs. Johnny was equally nice in his white painter's shorts.

The three of us took our ten o'clock break together. We found a semishady spot on the north side of a cooling tower. Gary and Johnny both commented about how hot I must have been in my navy work pants. I told them I was miserable.

Gary said, "Why don't you bring some shorts and change once you're up here on the roof? We're up high enough nobody can see us anyway."

I shook my head, "I would be busted for good if Marvin ever came up here and saw me in shorts. At least if I keep my shirt handy, I can grab it quickly if I get wind of him paying a surprise visit."

Johnny asked, "Is there someone in your shop who could warn you if he were coming? You would have time to change back."

I said, "Yeah, Richard, our dispatcher is cool. He would two-way me."

Johnny said, "There, problem solved. Why don't you take off your pants?"

I knew where that was going but was a little too uncomfortable stripping out in the open. I said, "I don't have any shorts with me."

Gary asked, "What are you wearing underneath?"

"Boxers."

Gary said, "That would work fine. Even if someone saw you from a distance, boxers would look just like Johnny's painter's shorts. No one would think any different."

It was time for us to go back to work. I said, "Maybe after lunch. I'll think about it."

The sexual tension combined with the oppressive temperature made the roof nearly unbearable. I was running conduit for a compressor Gary was still assembling. Johnny was only a few feet away painting a railing. The three of us were quiet for about half an hour, but eye contact was continual.

Gary broke the silence. "Joe, you sure do look hot. I wish you would just take those damn pants off."

I smiled. "I'm still thinking."

Johnny increased the pressure. "The problem is you would probably look even hotter with your pants off."

"Yeah, Johnny and I wouldn't mind the view," Gary agreed.

I said, "Maybe I would be more comfortable if you guys did the same thing."

"I'll do it," Gary said. He stood up and started to unfasten his cutoffs.

Johnny spoke up. "Wait, I'll do it, too, but I've got an idea. I need to paint the steps coming out of the roof access. It won't take very long, but no one will be able to go up or down for a few hours. I was going to wait until the end of the day, but I could do it now. I'll put a sign and a barricade downstairs so no one will be able to come up this afternoon."

Gary and I went down to our trucks and gathered up any parts and tools we might need for the rest of the day. We grabbed our lunch boxes, too. I double-checked for lube and condoms.

Johnny barricaded the roof entrance and started painting the steps. I stood next to the compressor unit facing Gary. Gary said, "Okay, I'll go first." He unfastened his cutoffs and they dropped to the ground. I could tell that his cock was already semi-hard.

I had to take my work boots off first, and the roof was too hot to stand barefoot on for even a moment. I had to do one boot and one pants leg at a time so I could put my boot back on immediately. Johnny saw what we were doing and apparently noticed that both Gary and I were fully erect. Johnny yelled over, "Hey guys, wait for me. I'll be done here in thirty minutes."

I said to Gary, "We really should finish hooking up this compressor before lunch."

Gary agreed, and we went back to work. Our erections went down while we focused on our job. Gary put the initial charge on the compressor. I just had to switch over the power disconnect so we could fire it up after lunch.

Johnny laid his last brushstroke on the steps and came up to where Gary and I were working and said, "Okay, it's my turn. Are you guys ready for a show?"

I made a final turn on the faceplate screw of the disconnect. Gary and I looked over and Johnny performed a playful strip-tease. He had a nice body, muscular and lean with a perfect six-pack. He was mostly smooth but had a nice treasure trail running down his navel. He started dancing like one of the strippers at the Nail (one of Oklahoma City's cruisy bars). He unfastened one button at a time while he danced and rubbed his abdomen.

Johnny finally got to the last button, and I looked over at Gary, squatting next to me in front of the compressor. He was mesmerized and completely unaware that his cock had grown fully hard and was poking out of the opening of his boxers. I reached over and stroked his cock. Johnny dropped his shorts to reveal a jockstrap.

Johnny strutted over, walked up between us, and faced Gary. Gary mouthed Johnny's jockstrap. I buried my nose in his butt crack. It was sweet and musky from sweating but was otherwise clean. He obviously had prepared for the encounter. He pushed back against my face and I used my tongue to open him up. Gary whispered, "Yeah, Joe, that's the way he likes it. He's really hard now."

Gary pulled Johnny's seven-inch cock out of one side of the jockstrap and began sucking on it. I kept eating Johnny's butt while I fumbled in my tool pouch for a condom and some lube. I stood up and dropped my boxers, kicking them to one side. Johnny bent over enough for me to push inside but not enough to interfere with Gary's blow job.

I kissed Johnny's back and licked the salty sweat from his shoulders, neck, and pits. A few moments later I whispered, "Are you ready?"

A squirming Johnny said, "Fuck, yeah!"

I massaged some lube into his butt and smeared a little on the condom. I held his triangular lats while I pushed in. He sighed, "Ahhhhhhhhh."

We had thirty minutes for our lunch break, and I wanted to use every minute of it fucking Johnny. I made sure to fuck him slowly enough so as not to set off an early climax. I told Gary to take it easy on his end. Gary alternated between rubbing my legs and Johnny's. I continued kissing and playfully biting Johnny's shoulders while at times rubbing his torso or Gary's head.

I pushed in as far as I could and stood still. Gary pulled off of Johnny's penis and twisted his head in between our legs, licking and biting at both my balls and Johnny's, which were slammed up against each other. Gary slipped his tongue in between our nuts and played with the base of my cock. His bushy mustache made every nerve ending on my scrotum tingle.

We were all dripping with sweat, but it felt like a cool spring day. Gary could feel my groin start to quiver, and he went back to work on Johnny's cock. I started fucking again, slowly at first, but with a gradually increasing pace, so much so, that Johnny grabbed Gary's head to hold it still. The force of my thrusts jammed Johnny's cock into Gary's mouth with equal power.

I knew I could hold out no longer. I whispered, "Are you guys ready?"

Gary mumbled, "Mmm-hmm."

Johnny moaned, "Yeah, I'm gonna explode."

I pulled back to where the tip of my dick was barely still inside. Then I jammed it back in hard and fast. That was it. My body shuddered. My groin pulsed and I could feel Johnny's load gunning for Gary's throat. Gary was yanking at his own cock and shot up between my legs, coating my balls and the front of my thighs.

I pulled out and tossed the condom off to the side. Gary stood up and the three of us embraced. Our lips smashed together for a three-way kiss. I could taste Johnny's salty-sweet cum on Gary's lips. I said that I would like a turn at Johnny's dick on the next round.

I put my boxers back on and strapped my tool belt around my waist. I spent the rest of the afternoon running conduit. I had two more compressors to hook up over the next two days.

Johnny made it a point to barricade off the steps around noon each day for the rest of the job. He brought a drop cloth we could lay out on the north side of the cooling tower. We tried almost every position imaginable.

On the last day of the project we took an hour and a half for lunch. All we had left was to finish picking up our tools. We fucked for most of our lunch break but saved enough time to stretch out on Johnny's tarp. I watched thunderheads build in the sky for a late afternoon storm. We dressed, picked up our stuff, and shared one final embrace on the rooftop while heavy raindrops fell upon my brow.

Back at the office the next day, Marvin was happy with my work. "The same client has another job with a live-wire delta situation," he said. "They're putting the same crew from this job together over there. Think you can handle it?"

"Think so," I said.

HIGH-SPEED CONNECTION

Dalton

work from my home office as a freelance graphic designer and writer. Most days I wake up, roll out of bed, and then head into my office for a day of email, design work, phone calls, and so on. Ever since my wife left several months ago, I've been in a mixed state of lonely, horny, and hopeful.

Our sex life was always decent, and at times, quite imaginative. I'd told Jan about a gay relationship I had while I was a junior in college. She listened as I described how my college lover and I would spend long hours in bed pleasuring each other as only two horny college guys can. When I described how much I enjoyed it when he made love to me, she asked if I wanted her to do the same.

She enjoyed our role reversal where she was the aggressor and told me what to do and what she wanted. I enjoyed being her bottom, especially when she wore a nice big strap-on cock and used me like her little fuck toy. I had always missed the feeling of a hard cock inside me, and while a strap-on will never replace the real thing, I have to give Jan credit—she became so good at using it, I sometimes forgot and almost believed I was with another guy.

Some nights, she'd turn out the light, make me kneel down in front of her, and drop her jeans to reveal the thick cock jutting from her slim hips. She'd leave on a heavy flannel shirt that totally obscured her small breasts. She'd stand before me with just the shirt on, her voice deep and commanding, and tell me to suck her cock. I'd open my mouth, gazing up at her dim profile and her short haircut, and suck for all I was worth, taking inch after rubbery inch into my mouth, forgetting at times that it wasn't a real cock.

After a few minutes of my frantically sucking her, my own cock would be rock hard and straining against my jeans. She'd order me to strip for her and then tell me to lie on the bed and grip the posts of the headboard. She'd tie my wrists to the bed and then lift my legs up onto her shoulders. She'd lube me thoroughly and then slip into me while her lubed hand glided up and down my aching cock. The strap-on had an end that pressed into her vagina so the more she thrust into me, the hotter she got. By the time I came, she was usually coming, too and screaming her head off. I would shoot all over myself, my body shaking, my arms straining against the ropes that bound me until I slumped back in a sweaty heap, totally used. The only thing I missed was the exquisite feel of the cum leaking slowly from my ass afterward.

Jan and I played this fantasy out over several years with many variations and toward the end, we rarely had straight sex at all. On the day she was to move out, she finished packing her things, took my hand, and led me to our bedroom, now half empty. "Jeff, could I fuck you one last time before I go?" she asked, tears in her eyes. I nodded and for the next hour, we played our game, this time with me on my hands and knees while she reached underneath and jerked me off.

As we stood on the front porch watching the sunset she smiled up at me and touched my cheek. "Maybe you should find yourself a nice guy and settle down," she said softly.

"Maybe you should find yourself a nice girl," I responded. She smiled, kissed me, and drove away to her new job and her new life out on the West Coast. That had been almost four months ago, and every time I went out with friends her words bounced around in my head. Women who heard Jan had left kept stopping by our table at restaurants and bars to say hi and offer themselves, sometimes not too subtly, to help me with my loneliness. But I just kept begging off, saying I wasn't ready.

Truthfully I *was* ready, but I had no idea how to find what I wanted. I was a responsible adult looking for another adult, and I had no idea where to begin. Luckily, a responsible adult found me.

It happened the day my Internet connection went down (no pun intended). I woke up that day and was trying to get my email when I noticed that my cable modem wasn't lit up. After checking my connections, I called the company and they said they had a private contractor who specialized in troubleshooting complex systems like mine and they'd send him over in an hour or so. I looked down at myself and smiled. I was sitting nude in my office and figured I'd better put something on. Since Jan left, I spent many days without ever getting dressed as I'd always enjoyed being nude, given the chance. Working from home, it didn't matter what I wore or didn't, so I indulged myself.

I took a quick shower and stared at myself in the mirror with a critical eye. My five-foot-nine frame was slim and well mus-cled, thanks to a routine of running, cycling, and lifting weights at the gym. My dark brown hair hung halfway down my back, and I usually held it back with a small silver tie that I'd bought in Arizona. My eight-inch cock hung down low and my large balls in their heavy sac were even lower owing to the summer heat. I slipped into a pair of thin running shorts and a tight T-shirt and tied my hair back. I looked at my face in the mirror, and saw that my smooth, tanned skin went well with my hair. I carefully trimmed my mustache so it looked neat and saw the tiny wrinkles at the edges of my dark brown eyes crinkle as I smiled at myself. "It's like you're getting ready for a date," I said to the mirror.

Maybe I was. The doorbell rang an hour later and I went to answer it. I opened the door and gaped. The man who stood there simply took my breath away. He was almost exactly my height but slimmer. He wore thin khaki pants that fit like a glove and a red polo with the company logo on the left breast. He carried a computer bag, and he was smiling at me. He was young, maybe midtwenties and had a full head of gorgeous blond hair gathered back in a short ponytail. He was totally clean shaven and had the most beautiful green eyes I'd ever seen. His lips were full, soft, and sensual, and his voice was rich and medium deep. "Hi, I'm David. I'm here to help you with your Internet problem," he said, offering a clean, well-manicured hand. I took his hand in mine and felt gentle pressure and heat that rushed through my whole body right to my cock.

I stood there a second too long holding his hand and then came back to my senses. He smiled at me again, an interested look passing across his eyes for a second. "Uh sure, let me show you what's up," I said, releasing his hand and turning to lead the way to my office, hoping he didn't see the bulge in my shorts. As we walked, I could almost feel his eyes on my body and my cock grew even harder. When we got to my office, it was his turn to be impressed.

"Wow, this is some serious hardware. I see why they called me," said David, his eyes traveling around my large, well-lit office. My office had countertops on two sides and shelves on the other two walls. In one corner were a fax machine, copier, and two large laser printers, one a Xerox color and the other an HP monochrome. My main workstation was an Apple tower with two thirty-inch flat-screen monitors, and my writing station was an Apple Powerbook seventeen inch with a twenty-inch second screen attached. I also had the usual scanner, digitizing tablet, and wireless keyboards and mice. It was a nice setup.

David opened his pack and pulled out a small Apple laptop and hooked it to my cable modem. I watched him move, my eyes drinking in his fluid, athletic build. He was graceful, confident, and very competent. I watched as he quickly determined that my modem had failed and I'd need a replacement. "Let me run out to the car and get a new one. I'll hook you up, call the change in to the office, and then you'll be all set," he said, standing and turning to me. The bulge in my shorts was now getting out of hand, and I could feel sweat breaking out under my arms. I smiled weakly as I saw his eyes dart downward for just a second but then my hopes soared as he smiled and his eyes locked on to mine.

"Sure, I'll just be down the hall, call if you need anything," I said, heading to my bedroom as he turned to walk out to his car. I went quickly into my bedroom and stood next to the bed, taking deep breaths. Without even thinking, I tugged my shorts down to my knees and freed my straining cock. I gripped it and sighed at the contact. I closed my eyes and stroked it very gently, trying to picture what David might look like without his clothes. Suddenly I heard a noise and opened my eyes. David stood in the doorway, a cable modem in one hand and a broad smile on his face.

"You sure do have some beautiful hardware in here, too," he said, his sexy voice low and his eyes glued to my straining manhood. "You know, I'm very good with that sort of equipment, too," he said. He set the modem on a table and moved closer to me.

"Do you offer this sort of service to everyone?" I asked, suddenly wary, but still frighteningly turned on, yearning for his touch.

"No," he said, suddenly looking a bit sad. "I was with someone for the last five years, and he left me a few months ago. I've been alone since then. What about you? I see where you had a ring," he asked, eyeing my left hand.

"My wife left a few months ago after five years. It's okay, but I've been alone, too. Until now," I said, pulling off my shirt and stepping out of my shorts. He moved into my arms, and our lips met in a soft tentative kiss. He tasted of mint and smelled wonderful, like he'd just stepped out of a shower. His lips were incredibly soft. His arms came around and his soft hands moved down and cupped my naked ass. I groaned into his mouth. I felt his warm tongue probe my lips, and I opened my mouth allowing him in. My tongue touched his and we stood like that for long, endless moments, kissing and each getting more turned on by the minute. Finally, he broke the kiss with a moan and stepped back. Wordlessly, I watched as he stripped with quick, smooth movements until he stood before me, a young god bathed in morning light.

His slim body was lightly tanned and all smooth, evenly muscled, with just a gentle dusting of blond hair on his chest and a thicker patch above his erect penis. We gazed at each other's bodies until, with a yearning sigh, I sank to my knees and leaned forward until his penis was an inch from my hungry mouth. With a shaky hand, I reached out and ran my fingers over the soft, smooth skin of his slender, beautiful, seven-inch manhood. His penis was like a piece of sculpture, perfect in all ways, smelling slightly of his sweat and cologne.

"You have no idea how long I've waited to do this," I said, my voice husky with need.

"How long?" he asked, equally needy.

"Since college. You're the first man I've been with in almost seven years." I opened my mouth and took him then. His flesh was warm and very hard, and I leaned forward, sucking gently, taking almost half his shaft into my mouth, one hand leading the way while I cupped his heavy balls with the other. He sighed deeply and stood very still as I slid my mouth up and down his shaft. He tasted salty and smelled wonderful, and I sucked harder as I grew more and more aroused. His breathing became louder and I could feel his body begin to shiver. His cock was now rock hard. I wasn't going to stop.

"I'm going to come," he cried out seconds later and I readied myself. I moved until just the head was in my mouth and stroked my hand along his wet shaft quickly and smoothly. His body tensed and then he cried out and began to shake. His balls contracted in my hand, and I felt the first wave of semen shoot into my mouth. The salty acrid taste was like wine to me, and I drank down every drop as he moaned and came in wave after wave. Finally, with a soft whimper, he moved back, pulling his beautiful cock from my mouth. "That was incredible," he said, sinking to his knees in front of me. My cock was aching now, and the head was coated in dripping precum. He helped me onto my back on the thickly carpeted floor, spread my legs wide, and knelt between them. He took my cock in his hands and began to kiss and lick the tip very gently.

"Your cock is so big and heavy. Will you put it in me later?" he asked, his eyes shining with desire.

"Anything you want," I groaned as he took me deep into his throat and then sucked hard while his fingers found my puckered hole and teased it. I closed my eyes, focused on his touch, and time went into a liquid state. All I heard were my gasps and the soft sucking and licking sounds he made as he sucked my shaft and balls and tongued my sensitive anus. Finally, I felt him slip a warm, slender finger into my ass and a huge wave of heat shot through me. He was sucking my cock with incredible force, his head moving up and down rapidly. I felt my balls tighten and cried out as I shivered and then exploded into his hungry mouth. I heard him gulp and swallow. His mouth never stopped, and his finger slipped in and out of me until, with a final swallow, he stopped and sat back, letting my cock flop back wetly onto my belly.

We were both breathing heavily and coated in sweat. I sat up and saw his penis was once again hard. "Will you make love to me?" I asked. He smiled and nodded. I dragged myself up and got my lubricant from the bedside table. I lay on the bed and handed him the bottle. I placed my hands under my thighs and pulled my legs up high and wide, fully exposing my anus to his hungry eyes. "Just like this," I said, the desire in my voice plain and deep.

He knelt before me and carefully, thoroughly lubed me, working one, then two fingers deep inside me until I moaned in ecstasy. Then he coated his stiff shaft with lube and positioned himself. He took my legs and moved them onto his shoulders and then bent forward and guided his penis to me. The first touch of his warm, slippery head against my tight hole was incredible. "Oh, God, yes. Give it all to me!" I cried out as he slid slowly into my sweating, straining body. His slim shaft fit wonderfully and instead of the pain I felt with the dildo, there was only warmth and the smooth motion of his flesh as it sank deeper and deeper into me until I felt the soft touch of his balls on my ass.

I clenched my muscles around the slender intruder in my body and moaned in sheer pleasure at the warmth that radiated from my anus. He smiled at me, his green eyes glowing, and began to thrust. Each time he slid out of me, I heard the slick wet movement, and each time he slid back in, I felt his balls tickle my ass. The heat there became a fire racing through me, and sweat poured from everywhere. His hands cupped and squeezed my ass, toyed with my nipples, and stroked my cheek as his cock drove in faster and deeper.

I watched his face, gauging his orgasm, and as his eyes closed and his movements became frenzied, I knew he was about to fulfill my greatest desire. With a soft cry he slammed into me, and I felt the first jet spill into my burning body, the touch of his manly essence sending me over the edge. Again and again, he ground into me, his beautiful cock filling me with semen until I felt it drip down the crack of my ass and onto the bed. With a final groan, he stopped moving and eased my legs onto the bed. He stayed on his knees between my legs, his cock shrinking slowly inside me, and our eyes locked. I reached up, he moved forward into my arms, and we kissed.

I held him tight and wrapped my legs around his middle, trying to keep him inside me for a few more seconds before he slipped free with a soft, wet pop. "Thank you," I whispered as I nibbled his earlobe and kissed his wonderful lips. I uncoiled my legs and he rolled off me and onto his back. We lay staring at the slowly rotating ceiling fan for a few minutes as the sweat on our bodies cooled. Then, I felt his hand reach out and grasp my semierect cock and begin to stroke it. "I guess I know what you want," I said, turning to smile at him.

"I want to suck your cock until it's hard, then I want to

climb on top and impale myself on this thing until you blow me right off with your cum," he said with a broad smile. He moved around into a sixty-nine position, and I felt his lips encircle my organ in a wet, warm embrace that had me hard in seconds. I moved my head up and began to lick his tight brown hole, eliciting moans from his otherwise full mouth. He tasted very sweaty and musky, and the smell and feel of his hairy, puckered hole was fantastic. I poked my tongue in deeper and deeper, intoxicated to be so wonderfully intimate with another man after so long. Finally, just when I thought I couldn't handle any more and my cock was vibrating in his skilled mouth, he moved off me.

He picked up the lube, and after he'd smoothed the thick fluid all over my stiff, aching cock, I watched as his fingers applied the clear fluid to his gleaming anus. He was shaking as he positioned himself over my thick shaft, and he eyed me with a flash of fear. "Don't move for a bit. You're so big it may take me a minute or two to get used to you," he said.

"You just tell me what you need," I moaned as his hole brushed my cock.

"I need you inside me, baby," he groaned as he began to slide onto me. His beautiful ass opened slowly as my thick bulbous head slipped inside him. After an inch of my shaft slid in, he held still, his breathing labored, sweat gleaming on his pecs. I reached up and softly tickled his nipples, making them pucker and harden. He moaned and slid farther down, slowly and steadily, until I felt his ass press onto my balls. "God, you feel so good," he said, his voice thick. His ass was fiery hot and tight.

He moved up and down slowly at first, pausing every so often to clench and unclench his inner muscles, bringing a groan from my lips each time. I felt every tiny movement of his inner walls on my shaft, and the pressure and slippery skin pressing around my sensitive head was almost unbearable. "I don't think

I'll last much longer; you're so damn tight," I said, my voice almost a cry.

"Come anytime, I want to feel it so bad," he whispered as he slid up and down faster and faster. The heat was so intense I began to gasp with each thrust, and my cock was now so sensitized it almost hurt. My balls bounced and were pressed each time he slammed down until I cried out and felt my entire body go rigid. My cock felt as though it was going to burst; the muscles down there did a jump and I began to come so hard I could feel nothing but heat, my heartbeat, and my aching, spewing cock. I closed my eyes and saw colors explode, and I screamed and bucked my hips upward to bury myself in that burning, slippery hole. My cum flowed like a river, filling his moving body and sliding out and down my shaft, down my balls, and mixing with his essence as it leaked from my ass.

David bobbed up and down once or twice more before I grabbed his waist to still his movements. "Please, no more, I can't take any more," I moaned, sitting up and hugging him tightly. His arms came around my back and we held each other in that position, me embedded deep inside him, our sweaty bodies pressed together in a liquid embrace. We kissed deeply and then slowly parted to lie back and rest. As if psychically linked, we rose in unison and I led him to the master bath. We took turns cleaning up and then had a wonderful shower together. As he dressed, he smiled at me.

"You know, I really need to fix your modem and get back out there. I think I have to see at least two more people today. But I'd really like to come back," he said, suddenly vulnerable. I was still nude, not at all interested in getting dressed while he was still so close.

"Why don't you come by after your last call? You can check and make sure my systems are all working properly," I said, kissing him. He took hold of my limp cock and gave it a gentle squeeze.

"Mmm, yeah, I can see your systems need a lot of special attention," he said, bending over and kissing my cock lightly.

He quickly hooked up the new modem and called the office to report the changed hardware serial number. He gave me a quick peck on the cheek as he left my office and I sat nude in my chair, staring at the screens, my mind still in my bedroom, our joined, sweating bodies filling my senses, my cock growing quickly. I smiled and switched my mind to practical matters like work. But as I thought about him in the back of my mind for the rest of the day, I knew that I just might have found what I was looking for. Only time would tell, but it was one heck of a start.

FANTASY MAN

Aaron Michaels

Mitchell sat in his tenth-floor office staring at the high-rise going up across the street and thought he was losing his mind.

It wasn't the fact that construction of the new fifteen-story luxury condos meant he'd be saying good-bye to his spectacular view of the mountains beyond the city. He'd come to grips with that as soon as cranes started lifting steel girders into place. No, what was threatening his sanity, not to mention his ability to concentrate on his work long enough to earn a living, was the lanky young man with the hard hat and clipboard currently inspecting progress on the open-air tenth floor of the condo project.

The man looked like he was in his late twenties, although from this distance Mitchell couldn't be sure. Mitchell had seen him before, often enough to recognize the dark hair curling out from beneath his hard hat; the confident, athletic way he walked around a building that, as yet, had no outside walls; and his full, easy smile that transformed what looked like a pleasant enough face into something truly extraordinary. Mitchell couldn't get this man out of his mind.

Mitchell thought about him when he should have been making the numbers in his spreadsheets behave. Obsessed about him when he tried to fall asleep at night, alone and hard and needy. What would the pleasant face beneath the hard hat look like up close and personal? Was his hair silky soft, or would it curl stubbornly around Mitchell's fingers? How about that mouth? What would it wrap willingly around? What color were his eyes? Today they were hidden behind sunglasses. Would they be blue and piercing? No, maybe hazel and mysterious, or warm brown and full of good humor. Within a week after the guy had appeared on-site, Mitchell had bought himself a pair of high-powered binoculars, but they were no substitute for an up close and personal inspection.

The man turned around to inspect a section of wall, and Mitchell let himself stare at the man's ass. It was hard to tell whether the man was lean and muscular beneath his clothes or simply thin. His jeans weren't baggy but they certainly weren't molded to his body either.

"This isn't getting me anywhere," Mitchell muttered. He had a ton of work cluttering the top of his desk, but crunching numbers didn't have quite the same appeal as the view outside his window.

The man with the clipboard bent over. Mitchell groaned. He'd been on his way to a nice afternoon semi just imagining what the man looked like beneath his clothes. Now with an unobstructed if somewhat distant view of the man's ass up in the air, Mitchell's comfortable arousal had swelled into aching hardness.

"Numbers," Mitchell said. Concentrate on the numbers.

Yeah. Like sixty-nine. Or half of sixty-nine, which in Mitchell's current state of mind wasn't thirty-four point five but a curly-haired head bobbing up and down on his cock, swallowing him whole.

Fuck.

Mitchell had his own office, and most importantly, he had a lock on his door. It only took him half a second to make up his mind to flip the lock. Still standing, he leaned his back against the door, took a deep breath, and unzipped himself.

He'd never jerked off at work, not even in the men's room, but then he'd never had such vivid fantasies in the middle of the day before now. He was painfully hard, the head of his cock nearly purple. When he wrapped a fist around himself, he groaned out loud. This wasn't going to take long.

He opened his eyes and stared at the man in the hard hat. The object of Mitchell's fantasies was scribbling something on the clipboard. The worker he was with, a middle-aged man in overalls and a hard hat but carrying no clipboard, must have said something funny, because he laughed hard and slapped the other man on the shoulder.

Mitchell wanted to be that other man. He wanted to see for himself what the man with the easy laugh looked like. Experience what he felt like, tasted like. Hear the noises he made when he came.

Mitchell's hand sped up on his cock. He bit his lower lip to keep himself from moaning. The burn low in his belly was starting to consume him. His balls felt tight, his cock full. He imagined lips and tongue and wonderful wetness and suction surrounding him.

When he came it was with a groan he couldn't suppress. He staggered a little, hips thrust forward tight again his fist, as every muscle in his body went from hard steel to satiated putty. He had to put his other hand out on his desk to keep his balance.

"Damn."

He'd come on a report he'd left on top of his desk. At least it was something he could print out again. Now that he was done, he felt a little sheepish about being unable to control himself. He was a grown man, for fuck's sake. Old enough to have a kid in college, if that had been his inclination, and here he was jacking off in his office like a horny teenager to a fantasy man he'd never meet.

He cleaned himself off with a tissue from the box he kept on his desk. Just as he was finishing, he raised his eyes to look across the empty space between buildings to the tenth floor of the condo.

The object of his fantasies was staring back at him.

Mitchell swallowed hard. No, that couldn't be. No one could actually see in through the window, could they? It was the middle of the day. It wasn't like he was in his office at night with the lights on and his dick in his hand. The man just happened to glance Mitchell's way. Coincidence, that's all.

Mitchell tucked himself away, zipped up, and sat down at his desk. He kept his back resolutely toward the window as he reprinted the report on his own printer. He folded up the report he'd ruined and shoved it in the bottom of his wastebasket. He needed to get back to work. He had numbers to crunch and none of them were sixty-nine.

As he worked, he thought he felt eyes on him, but he told himself it was just his imagination. Fantasies were just fantasies, and unless he wanted to look for a new job, they damn well better stay fantasies. Anything else was just too dangerous.

Two nights later, Mitchell went to Friday night happy hour at a bar across the street from his office with a few of his buddies from work. The bar served a decent choice of beer on tap along with a variety of foods dipped in batter and fried. Not great for the cholesterol count, but Mitchell had decided long ago that the only way to eat zucchini was breaded, fried, and with a healthy helping of marinara sauce.

After his buddies left, Mitchell was finishing up the last zucchini stick and thinking about the curly-headed man with the clipboard. The guy hadn't been around since Mitchell had embarrassed himself coming all over his report, and that was probably a good thing. Mitchell missed the view but he'd gotten a remarkable amount of work done in the last two days. It made him feel better about his momentary lapse into teenage horniness.

He was startled out of his reverie by the waitress, who brought him a fresh plate.

"I didn't order that," Mitchell said. He definitely didn't order the side of ranch dressing.

She grinned at him. "From the gentleman in the last booth."

Mitchell turned to look where she nodded. The booth was partly obscured by a couple who were making selections on the jukebox; the rest of the booth was in shadow. All Mitchell could see was the vague outline of someone slouched in the corner.

The waitress leaned closer. Mitchell saw amusement in her smoky eyes. "You're being hit on, honey. He's pretty cute. I'd take him up on it myself, but I don't think I'm his type."

Huh.

The waitress winked at him and walked away.

The plate of zucchini sticks was certainly a variation on the standard buy-someone-a-drink routine. Maybe the guy in the booth thought food would be harder to refuse than a drink. And why should Mitchell refuse it anyway? It had been a long time since someone had hit on him like this. It wouldn't hurt to be nice.

Mitchell picked up the plate and his beer and wound his way

through the crowd. When he got a good look at the man who'd sent him the zucchini sticks, he nearly spilled his beer.

"Hello," said his fantasy man.

The booth was too dark for Mitchell to get a good look at the man, but even without the hard hat, the brown curls and infectious smile gave him away. There was no mistaking that this was the same man Mitchell had jerked off to in his office two days ago.

"Uh...hi." Mitchell swallowed hard. This had to be random, right? A coincidence? The bar was as close to the condo project as it was to Mitchell's office.

"I hope you're hungry," the man said.

His voice had a hint of an accent and was surprisingly deep. He was sitting sideways in the booth, one leg bent, arm propped up casually on his knee. If he felt at all insecure about sending a stranger a plate of food, he certainly didn't look it.

Mitchell, on the other hand, was glad the bar was dark because he could feel his face heating up. He'd never expected to meet this man for real.

The man didn't say anything else, and Mitchell realized it was his turn to say something. He had to clear his throat before he trusted himself to speak. "Thanks. I...uh..." Well, that was certainly a lame attempt at casual. Even if the man didn't know what Mitchell had done in his office the other day, Mitchell was going to give it away. He tried again. "People don't usually buy me food in a bar."

"Their loss." The man shifted to lean forward. "Would you like to sit down?"

Mitchell put the plate and beer down on the table and slid into the booth opposite his fantasy man.

They exchanged names. The fantasy man was Owen, and he worked as a foreman on the condo project.

"Kind of young for a foreman, aren't you?" Mitchell asked.

"I'm old enough." Owen leaned forward and picked up a zucchini stick, swirled it in the dressing. "And I'm good at what I do." He held the stick out to Mitchell, but when Mitchell reached for it, Owen drew it away from Mitchell's fingers.

Damn. Mitchell's mouth went dry at the thought of his fantasy man feeding him. "I don't usually like ranch," was all he could think of to say.

"You'll like this." Owen touched the end of the stick against Mitchell's lips. "Open wide," he said in a voice that was liquid sex.

Mitchell opened wide.

If this wasn't a prelude to sex, he didn't know what was. He didn't even taste the ranch. Somewhere between sitting down and introductions, his cock had come to life. Now it was pressed so hard against his trousers, he'd embarrass himself if he stood up.

"See?" Owen dipped the stick in more dressing. "I knew you'd like it."

"Let me," Mitchell said. He took the zucchini from Owen and fed it to him. Owen wrapped his lips around Mitchell's fingers and his tongue briefly flicked against the tips. Mitchell felt more than heard the sound of pleasure Owen made.

Mitchell had never been one for food play. He was rapidly changing his mind. He just wished they weren't doing this in the middle of a crowded bar. The dark booth gave them an illusion of privacy, but it was only an illusion.

"This may sound kind of lame," Mitchell said, "but you want to get—"

"—Out of here?" Owen finished. "Thought you'd never ask."

Owen had started to slide out of the booth when Mitchell remembered his predicament. "Uh…you're gonna have to give me a second."

Thankfully Owen didn't laugh.

"I feel kind of silly," Mitchell said when Owen sat back down.

"Don't. I take it as a compliment."

Mitchell swallowed some beer as a distraction. An old Rolling Stones song started on the jukebox, and Mitchell tried to focus on numbers, but the only one that came to mind was sixty-nine. Not a good choice.

"There're still some guys from my work around somewhere," Mitchell said. "I get up with a hard-on, I'll never live it down."

Owen's eyes glittered in the reflected light from the neon over the bar. "I could take my shoe off and help you out with that. They'll never know."

The extent of Mitchell's exhibitionist tendencies had been jacking off in his office behind a locked door. Sex in public? He wasn't into that. "Maybe later."

Owen grinned. "I take it as a good sign you're talking about later."

Mitchell took Owen's response the same way.

They sat in the booth and finished their drinks and the plate of appetizers. By the time they were done, Mitchell's cock had calmed down enough that he could get up and look somewhat like his normal business self.

"So where are we going?" he said as they left the bar.

"I need to check on one more thing at the project before I leave for the night. It'll give me a chance to show it off a little. You mind?"

Mitchell didn't.

They walked to the site in a companionable silence. Up close, Owen's walk was smooth and steady, with a kind of natural athletic grace. His clothes were casual and comfortable looking—khaki trousers and a sand-colored silk tee—and he wore something around his neck on a chain hidden beneath his shirt. For all that they'd looked at each other in the darkness of the bar, Mitchell still didn't think he'd gotten a good enough look at Owen's eyes. All he could tell was that they were dark and seemed to burn with a combination of good humor and sexuality. His face was clean shaven with only a hint of a beard around the point of his chin and on his upper lip. His skin looked smooth, and Mitchell very much wanted to touch it. He just might be able to do that, and soon, if this evening was headed the way he thought it was.

Owen unlocked the padlock on the gate in the fence around the construction site and ushered Mitchell in. He was prepared to wait on the ground, but Owen surprised him by handing him a hard hat. "C'mon up. Unless you don't want to."

"You sure?"

"Absolutely."

Owen showed Mitchell how to adjust the hard hat, then they rode up in the construction elevator. The lower floors were enclosed—the outer walls complete and drywall going up on the internal skeleton of beams and girders. But Owen kept the elevator heading up until they reached a floor that was mostly flooring, exposed studs, and a bit of bare drywall here and there. The exterior walls weren't fully completed.

"Recognize the view?" Owen asked.

It was still light enough out that Mitchell had no trouble figuring out where they were. He could see his office building across the street. Not only his office building, but his office. The plant his assistant had given him on his last birthday was right there on the windowsill.

Fuck.

Owen had seen him.

"How did you...?" Mitchell could barely get the words out,

worried now that Owen had brought him up here just to embarrass him.

"I've been watching you." Owen came up behind him and wrapped his arms around Mitchell's waist. "Not all the time. The sun's not always at a good angle for that, but I figured out what times I could actually see more of your office than just your plant, as long as I kept my sunglasses on to cut down the glare. I've been trying to get up the courage to meet you." One of his hands slid down the front of Mitchell's trousers. "You gave me quite a show the other day. I took it as an open invitation."

Mitchell's heart was thudding in his chest. He'd been on such a roller-coaster ride between horny and scared ever since he saw Owen sitting in that booth, all he could do now was stand there and wait for Owen to make the next move. It didn't take long.

Owen found Mitchell's cock and squeezed, and at the same time he planted a wet kiss on the back of Mitchell's neck. Mitchell moaned at the dual assault.

"You have any idea what watching that did to me?" Owen's voice was back to being liquid sex. "Seeing you come while you were watching me?"

"I didn't know—" The last word came out strangled as Owen rubbed his thumb around the head of Mitchell's cock. Even through his trousers, the feeling was incredible. "Didn't know you could see me. Didn't think anyone could see me."

"Like here?"

Owen reached for the zipper. Mitchell's hand flew to cover Owen's and stop him. "Not here," Mitchell said. "Not where everyone—"

"Can see?" Owen chuckled and pressed himself against Mitchell's ass. The hard ridge of Owen's cock was unmistakable. "And here I thought you were an exhibitionist."

Not usually, but damn, Owen felt good.

Mitchell turned his head. He wanted to taste Owen's mouth, but the hard hat was in the way. Mitchell reached up and knocked his hat off. He dimly heard its *thunk* on the hardwood of the subfloor.

"Careful, don't let the inspector catch you," Owen said right before Mitchell claimed his mouth.

And oh, what a wild kiss it was, full of tongues and teeth and need. Mitchell couldn't get enough. It was the culmination of his lonely fantasies, only with a twist: his fantasy man's hand on his crotch, a hard cock pressed against his ass, a light breeze lifting his hair, all out in the open for the world to see. If anyone was still left in his office building at this time on a Friday night, they could see it all. What would they think of quiet, reserved, number-cruncher Mitchell now? The man with the window office who never even talked about the few times he did date.

Owen started to pump his hips against Mitchell, and it was all too much. Mitchell didn't care what anyone thought. He turned around in Owen's grasp and grabbed for his crotch.

"That's more like it," Owen managed to say in between wet, open-mouthed kisses.

Mitchell squeezed Owen's ample cock through his trousers, then he dove for the zipper. The kiss continued, wet and wild and all consuming. Just about the time Mitchell got his hand on Owen, he realized Owen had managed to open his trousers, too.

Owen yanked Mitchell closer with one hand. The other hand closed around both their cocks, and then Owen thrust up.

Fuck.

Mitchell had to breathe in through his nose slowly to keep himself under any kind of control.

Owen kept pumping the two of them together through his hand. His pupils were dilated, and he wasn't breathing too steadily himself. "This is so fucking hot," he said as he grabbed

Mitchell by the back of his neck and pressed their foreheads together. "What else will you let me do to you? Out here in the open."

A shudder ran through Mitchell. What else? Oh, God...at this point he felt so good, he'd probably agree to anything. "What'd you have in mind?"

Owen spread his hand out to cradle the back of Mitchell's skull. "I want to fuck you," he said. "I have what we need. It'll be safe, I promise you."

Safe? Out here where anyone could watch? But God, Mitchell did want it. He hadn't been fucked in a long time, and nothing like this had ever happened to him.

"We have to...in there somewhere." Mitchell tried to nod his head toward the interior of the building where the setting sun created deep shadows. "Can we...?"

"God, yes." Owen seized his mouth again, and Mitchell let him. He opened wide, closed his eyes, and let Owen take as much as he wanted. Owen started walking him backward. Mitchell kept his eyes closed. For this one wild ride, Owen was in charge, and that only added to the thrill.

Mitchell read the change in the light on the inside of his closed eyelids as they walked farther away from the unfinished edge of the building. He felt the solidness of a wall behind his back, then the cold drywall on his naked ass when Owen shoved his trousers and underwear down around his ankles.

"I'm going to turn you around," Owen said. He kissed Mitchell again, then let both their cocks go.

Mitchell turned toward the bare drywall, shifted forward so his weight was on his arms, spread his legs as far as his trousers would allow. He felt exposed, lonely and on display without Owen's hands on him, but the feeling didn't last for long. He heard Owen fumbling with his own clothes, the rustle and rattle of belt and trousers being pushed down, and then Owen was pressed up against Mitchell's back, as naked from the waist down as Mitchell was. His cock fit into the cleft of Mitchell's ass.

"It's been a while for me." Mitchell made the admission with his eyes closed once again. He wanted to be fucked, but he wanted to be able to sit down afterward.

Owen's fist wrapped around Mitchell's cock, which had wilted a little while Mitchell waited, but it came back to life fast enough once Owen started pumping.

"I'll make it good for you," Owen said.

He was true to his word. He was careful with the first slick penetration of his finger. Owen worked Mitchell's cock and ass until Mitchell's entire groin was on fire. Mitchell had long since forgotten he wasn't in his own bedroom, safely surrounded by four walls, a curtained window, and a closed door. He moaned and grunted and thrust back against Owen's fingers and forward into Owen's hand with no heed for where he was.

All too soon Owen leaned forward to whisper in Mitchell's ear. "You ready?"

Mitchell nodded. Then there was that moment when Owen's hands moved away to deal with the condom, and Mitchell felt all alone again. But this time he had no doubts, only a burning need and an impatience with the necessities fucking a stranger required. Mitchell wanted to hurry Owen, wanted to feel the cock that had been resting on him, in him.

And then the wait was over.

With a grunt and a push, Owen filled him. More than filled him. Mitchell squeezed his eyes shut tight and willed himself to relax. He concentrated on the dusty, chalky smell of the drywall beneath his hands, the smell of Owen's sweat and the beer still on both their breaths. He heard traffic from the street below and wondered if all his buddies had left the bar yet. Would they wonder where he went? Unless they saw him, they'd never believe this. Was he out here like this, with a stranger's cock up his ass, because he wanted someone to see him? Was he fed up with being safe, quiet Mitchell? Had he been a closet exhibitionist all along?

Mitchell chuckled as the pain went away, leaving only the incredible feeling of Owen inside him.

Owen thrust in a little harder. "Should I be worried that you're laughing?" he said.

"God, no." Mitchell shifted so that he could push back to meet Owen's thrusts. "I just suddenly realized how much I'm actually enjoying this. Not just what you've been doing," he added quickly, in case Owen might misinterpret things. "But where we're doing it."

"Mmm." Owen moved a little more, shallow thrusts like he was warming up. "Told you you'd like it. And we're just getting started."

It didn't take long before Owen was pumping hard and fast, ripping grunts and moans from both of them. Mitchell tried fisting his own cock for a while but gave up when it became apparent he'd need both arms to keep himself from being driven face-first into the drywall. He wasn't sure he could come just by being fucked. He needn't have worried. When Owen's thrusts became erratic and Mitchell thought Owen was close to coming, Owen reached around and pulled on Mitchell's cock, and then Mitchell did come, spurting over Owen's hand and the drywall and very nearly losing his balance when his knees threatened to give way.

Owen gave two more hard thrusts, then his body jerked and he gasped, and Mitchell knew he'd come, too.

They didn't say anything as they both stood there recovering.

Owen pulled out, and Mitchell heard the snap of the condom as Owen tied it off. His ass felt sore but he was fairly sure he'd still be able to sit. What he wasn't sure about was what happened now. He wasn't all that experienced with random hookups.

"I don't know about you," Owen said, "but I'm still hungry." He kissed the back of Mitchell's neck. "We've got a working restroom on the third floor. What say we go clean up a little, then we find a proper restaurant for dinner?"

"We?" Mitchell turned around and slumped against the wall. His legs still didn't feel all that steady. "You asking me out on a date?"

Owen finished wiping his hands on a piece of paper towel he'd pulled from a nearby cart. "Well, yeah." He smiled, and amazingly, the smile looked a little on the shy side. "I've been wanting to go out on a date with you for weeks, ever since I first saw you. And more than just to get in your pants. I was hoping you…" He made a vague gesture and glanced away. "Well, that you might want to date me, too." The last bit was said in a rush, like he wasn't sure how Mitchell would respond.

"You want to date me." Even with everything that had just happened, Mitchell was having a hard time wrapping his mind around the fact that he was apparently his fantasy man's fantasy.

Owen looked back at him. His eyes were brown, Mitchell realized. Brown and warm, kind and understanding, and right now, a little on the unsure side.

"Yeah," Owen said.

Mitchell smiled. "Okay."

"Okay?"

"Yes."

Owen broke into a huge grin, just like the ones Mitchell was used to seeing from his office window. "Outstanding."

"You just have to promise me one thing," Mitchell said as he tucked himself away and zipped up his pants.

Owen stopped in the middle of buckling his own belt. "What?"

Mitchell leaned forward to give Owen a quick kiss on the lips. "If we're going to make a habit out of fucking in public, give me a little warning, okay?"

Owen laughed. "Deal." He finished arranging his clothes and retrieved Mitchell's hard hat. "I think I've created a monster," he said as he handed Mitchell the hat.

Created one? No, maybe just let one out of the bottle, like a genie. Personally, Mitchell thought he'd found his own genie, one with warm eyes, a contagious smile, and an amazing cock. And really, what fantasy could be better than that?

HAZARD PAYOFF

Landon Dixon

tipped the paving stone–loaded dolly back and walked it ahead a few feet. Then I hit a rock on the half-completed driveway and the bricks shifted, pulling me and the dolly forward. I struggled to keep the stack upright, running now, clipped the dolly with a steel-toed boot and sent the whole thing flying over, pavers spilling everywhere. Right in back of my foreman where he was kneeling on the driveway.

Once the dust had settled, Blake pushed a couple of pavers away from his backside and got to his feet. I sheepishly grinned at him. He shook his head. "Hazard, try not to live up to your name, huh? For the good of the health of me and the crew."

I nodded, amazed and gratified that the guy hadn't fired me on the spot. I'd only been on the job an hour, and this was already my second dolly wreck.

Actually, not a bad hour for a guy with my safety record. That's why they call me Hazard. I'd lost my previous three summer jobs when I'd: (1) accidentally pulled the ladder out from under a residential window-washing colleague, (2) smacked three guys in the head with a sheet of drywall at a house construction site, and (3) spilled boiling grease all over the brand-new shoes of my boss at a fast-food fry job. Even the placement counselor at the student employment office called me Hazard. But I kept applying, because I needed tuition money for college. And I kept getting hired, because the skyrocketing price of base metals had turned our northern mining town into a boomtown.

Blake crouched back down, once again picking up and placing the pavers into their interlocking pattern, building a driveway to last a lifetime. I began stacking another load onto the dolly from the pallets at the end of the driveway. That was my job: delivering the stones to Blake, who then fit them together in the sandy jigsaw puzzle. Ideally, I would deliver them smoothly, right next to the guy, rather than catapulting them onto his back.

It was hard, hot, muscle-straining and forearm-scraping work. But the job had its good parts: all on Blake.

He was in his midtwenties, muscular all over from lifting and planting and stamping pavers for a living, with short black hair and warm brown eyes. He filled his faded jeans tight and taut, round in all the right places, his asscheeks looking hard as the stones he was setting down. And since it was so hot and the work so heavy, he had his shirt off, his chiseled torso gleaming smooth and pumped in the sunshine. The guy was actually a good half-foot shorter than I was, but then I'm a carrot-topped beanpole.

I ogled my boss's rock-hard, glistening body constantly, my mouth hanging open and eating dust, craving to lick the salty sweat from his muscle-humped chest and rigid nipples. I strangled the handles on the dolly, yearning to finger the soft, perspiration-slick crack of his ass. And what with all my sweating and drooling, I was soon parched with thirst.

"Uh, is there anywhere I can get a drink of water?" I croaked, towering over Blake's broad, muscle-bunched back like a loving shade tree. The rest of the crew had gone on their dinner break, so it was just me and the boss.

He turned his head and squinted up at me, making sure I wasn't holding anything that could fall on him, no doubt. "Yeah, sure. The people who own the house are gone for the weekend, so it's locked up, but there's a hose in the backyard they said we could use." He grinned and added, "Don't flood the basement or anything, okay?"

I grinned back, said, "Okay," then tripped over the heel of his boot and went sprawling onto the front lawn as I tried to move around him.

I managed to make it through the wooden gate that led into the backyard with only a slight tear to my T-shirt from a snagging nail, and spotted the hose hooked up to a faucet at the rear of the house. As I was cranking the handle, getting the water to flow (after lifting my big feet off the hose), I heard some yelling and splashing coming from the house next door. So I walked farther into the yard, past the garage that blocked my view, playing out the hose and sucking sweet, cool water from the spout.

A six-foot-high plank fence surrounded the entire backyard, but that was no eyeball obstacle for a galoot like me. And when I peeked past the garage and over the fence, I choked on the water and just about swallowed the hose.

There was a swimming pool next door with two guys waist deep in the middle of it, in each other's arms, in the midst of a hard, hot, passionate kiss!

I gaped at the men blatantly sucking face. They were really feeding on one another, lips chewing, tongues flailing, arms grappling, locked together so tight not even a sliver of light showed between their suntanned and water-washed bodies.

One guy had blond hair, the other a shaved head. Blondie pulled back from Baldy's ravenous mouth, sealed his lips around the other guy's tongue, and sucked on it, the bald dude groaning his encouragement. I openly watched them going at it in that neighboring dunk tank, as I dropped the waterhose, and wrapped my fingers around my own hose, which had swollen in my jeans. I squeezed and rubbed my cock, eating up the erotic aquatic action next door, the two water sports too wrapped up in each other to notice my jughead floating over the fence.

Baldy reeled his sucked-dry tongue back in, dropped his head down to Blondie's chest, and started to lick the guy's protruding nipples. He swirled his chunky pink tongue all around the slick, tan buds, Blondie tilting his head back and moaning, gripping his lover's cinder-block shoulders.

The dude with the high-polish chrome dome vigorously sucked on Blondie's nipples, bit into them, tugged on them with his shiny white teeth. Like I was tugging on my pulsing prick through my jeans, my body burning with a heat more than sun and work related. This was the kind of manual labor I could really get into.

After working over his tub-buddy's boyish chest for a good, long while, Baldy steamed the guy through the water and up against the side of the pool. He lifted the sleek little blond out of the water with the greatest of ease and plunked him down on the pool's edge. Which is when I gleefully noticed that the guy was totally naked, his hard, all-man cock bobbing like an inflatable beach toy as he splashed down on the rim of the water bin.

Baldy quickly swam in between Blondie's legs, latched on to the guy's lean thighs, and began capturing and swallowing his glistening cockhead. Blondie groaned, sprawling his hands back to hold himself up under the muscle-stud's onslaught, Baldy's head diving down between his quivering legs. My hand froze on my bulging cock, as I witnessed the dick-defying sword-swallowing. Baldy consumed his buddy's entire prick like it was nothing, and everything.

I held my breath, along with my writhing neighbor. Finally, Baldy pulled his head back and gleaming meat oozed out from between his thick lips like a greased snake. When he got to the cap, he bit into it, then inhaled the whole shaft again, his tongue shooting out to lick at Blondie's blond balls.

I started squeezing and rubbing again, singing the bald man's deep-throating praises with the palm of my hand. The shaven muscleman gripped his buddy's legs and bobbed his head up and down, earnestly sucking cock. Blondie rode his lover's cranium with one of his hands, his lithe body quivering with the wicked vacuum power of the awesome blow job.

"You workin' or jerkin'?" a voice exploded in my ear.

I twisted my head around and saw Blake at the open gate. He was looking at me, and my sweaty paw clutching my thread-straining cock. "Uh..." I stammered, my face going even redder than my sunburn.

He walked over to me, then went up onto his tiptoes and peered over the fence, taking in the erotic sights. "Not bad technique. You might actually learn something," he casually commented. "Wanna give it a try, Hazard?"

I stared at the stud, hardly believing my burning ears. He just smiled and placed his warm hand over mine on my throbbing cock. And I just about jumped out of my work boots.

Blake unfastened his belt and unzipped his jeans as I sank to my knees in the grass, ready and willing and eager to worship. He pushed his pants and briefs down, and his cock flopped out into the sunlight, big and getting bigger. I trembled with delight, inhaling the musky, ball-sweated scent of the man, watching his beautiful vein-ribboned tool rise up and up, expand, and point at my face. Here was finally something I could truly handle on the job, the best job in the world.

"Suck it, Hazard," Blake rasped. I went to work.

I seized his thick dong with just my forefinger and thumb, forming a ring that I rode up and down his pink, pulsating length, quick and light and teasing. He grunted, urging me to grab on and fist him. But I O-ringed his cut cock from balls to cap, sailing up and down his bumpy shaft with my circle jerk, neat and clean and tantalizing. I might be all thumbs in the workplace, but in the sexplace I consider myself a bit of a master craftsman.

Blake groaned and grabbed at my hair as I pumped him fast, then slow, then fast again, tickling his tight, shaven nut sac with my other hand. Moans and groans from across the fence mingled and merged with Blake's gasps of lust in the superheated air, until the guy just couldn't take my sexual taunting anymore. He yanked my head into his groin, begging me to suck him.

But I didn't suck him, at first. Instead, I noosed his hood, pressed it into his grated abs, and licked at his meat, up from his tightened balls and along his pulsing shaft in one smooth, wet motion. He clawed at my hair, his legs shaking, as I sensuously painted his pipe with delicate and bold tongue-strokes that left him drenched in saliva and sweat and my fingers sticky with precome.

Then I dropped his cock. It strained in the still, electrified air, sniffing at my lips. I breathed all over it, steaming it raw, driving the man wild. Then I clipped the jumping cap with my teeth, causing Blake to cry out his sweet torture.

I sank my teeth into his meaty cockhead and slowly chewed it into my mouth, until I tasted shaft. At which point I shot my head forward and swallowed the guy right down to the balls. Then I bounced back up again.

"Fuck!" he gasped, stunned. He stared down at me, unsure if what'd just happened had actually happened.

I proved that it had, sealing his cap between my lips and dive-bombing his shaft again, hands-free and balls-deep, over and over. Blake dug his fingernails into my scalp and hung on, growling, his cock filling my mouth, bouncing off the back of my throat and beyond.

Then I took a page out of Baldy's X-rated book, quick-downing my man's cock and holding it. And holding it. Nose pressing into his abdomen, chin pushing into his balls, I locked him down tight and wet and let the superheated, viselike pressure build to outrageous proportions. Fortunately for the both of us, my gag reflex is like the rest of my reflexes—virtually nonexistent.

"Holy shit!" Blake cried, pulling on my ears, banging on my head. His watery brown eyes were frantic, his pressure-packed cock gone from his sight for an excruciating minute and counting.

The tension tightened like a wrench on a bolt, sweat pattering down off Blake's agonized face and onto mine. Humid breath steamed out of my flared nostrils and bathed his stomach, my cheeks and throat bulging with meat.

At last he grunted and shoved me back, before his balls boiled over. His dong burst out of my mouth in a gush of saliva, a slickened spear still tied to my lips by strings of spit.

"Want me to fuck you, Blake?" I asked, breathing hard hardly at all.

The guy nodded in amazement, and respect.

He ended up on his back on the picnic table; stark, stunningly naked; legs up and spread. Very receptive to learning a further thing or two from his work-inept apprentice.

I shoved my jeans and shorts down around my ankles and shuffled in between his legs, letting him get a good look at the fat, squat tool that was going to pound him like the compactor he used to pound the paving stones together in the sand. Then I gripped his ankles and slapped my cock against his cock. He moaned.

His legs were as gorgeously muscled as the rest of him and just as smooth, and I slid my hands down and around his clenched calves, squeezing them. Then I shouldered his legs and ran my hands along his thighs, inner and outer, digging my fingers into his big, bunched quads. His muscles twitched and his cock bounced up and down on his flat belly all on its own, as I felt him up.

"Fuck me!" he implored, playing with his golden nipples and staring up into the sun.

I could see the perverted neighbors over the fence again. Blondie was on all fours on the diving board, like a tawny animal, Baldy at the top of the steps gripping the steel railings and hammering the guy's upraised ass. The board quivered like the pair of them, hanging out like Blondie's tongue as his chute got reamed. I nodded my approval at the workmanship and then teased Blake's asshole with the tip of my prick.

"Yeah, fuck me!" he responded, rolling his nipples, rolling his head back and forth on the smooth-sealed slats in sexual agony.

I squatted down, his legs riding my shoulders, and dug around in my grass-level pants pocket, came up with a condom and a one-session portable packet of lube. A good worker always comes prepared with his own tools. I suited and greased up my dick, nice and slow for Blake's benefit, and mine. Then I oiled his crack, wriggling a couple of fingers two knuckles deep inside the hunk just to hear him squeal, see him squirm. Finally, I steered my shiny cockhead up against his smooth-as-silk asshole again.

But if he'd thought I was going to take it slow and gentle, ease my way into his tight crevice, then my cocksucking hadn't taught him anything about the way I work the body. I punched through his starfish and plunged bowels-deep inside him, buried to the hilt in an instant. He jumped on the table like he'd been electrocuted, shouting obscenities to match our neighbors'.

I gripped the pale soles of his feet and thrust sure and deep, full-cock fucking the stud, out to the cap and all the way in again, over and over. He was supertight and burning hot; smooth-riding; the sight of his prone, cock-rocked body sizzling. The firm smack of my thighs against his shuddering ass filled my ears, the sensual feel of his gripping chute milking my churning cock and stoking my body with heat.

He frantically tugged on his own prick as I crammed his ass strong and steady. I tickled his feet, licked at his puckered soles, sucked on a tender toe or three, all the while pumping my hips, fucking his sweet anus with authority.

A scream sailed over the fence, followed by another. I jerked my head up and saw Blondie shaking out of control on the end of Baldy's ramming cock, jacking ropes of sperm out of his own cock and onto the diving board as Baldy tilted his head back and let out a roar, emptying his balls in the blond bottom's rippling ass.

"You're going to come all over yourself!" I instructed my boss, pumping faster. "Right after I do!"

He groaned and flung his head from side to side, his sun- and cock-blasted body shaking.

I grasped his armored thighs and dug in, force-fucking the gorgeous man, brutally slamming his ass. We smashed together, my cock pistoning his chute, the wet-hot friction unbelievable. I surged with an incendiary heat, balls flapping and boiling; Blake's hand flew up and down his shaft in rhythm to my savage fucking.

I caught fire, and my cock exploded in the stud's sucking hole. I ripped out of Blake's ass, tore off the condom and fisted wildly, spraying white-hot semen onto his jacked-up cock, torquing his action even more. He cried, "Fuck!" and sperm jetted out of his jizz-slick cock, splashing down onto his heaving chest and stomach in great, sticky gobs.

I still have plenty of goof-ups on the job. But it's great finally having a boss who's so forgiving. Among other things.

HERCULES TO THE RESCUE

Gavin Atlas

How was I supposed to work when the Cramers' son was always walking around the house practically naked? The place was supposed to be empty during the repairs, but their boy Dylan had just finished finals at the University of Miami and had told his parents he needed to stay in town to find a job. Never mind that Hurricane Ava had torn half the tiles off the roof and took most of the north wall from the bedroom next to his.

"How the hell am I supposed to talk on the phone with you guys making all that racket?" he yelled while my assistant, Alex, sawed away at the tree branch that had come through the wall. Dylan only wore tiny gym shorts and pumped a small barbell with his left hand, an angry expression trained on the two of us.

I looked at him calmly. "That looks like a cordless phone, buddy," I said. "It would be easier for you to take your call downstairs than it would be for us to move the tree."

"You guys were supposed to be finished already," he said, "and you've hardly started."

"And if you keep kicking us out for your pool parties, your parents will be back before we're done, and we'll have to let them know the cause of all the delays, won't we?"

He seemed to consider this and then walked out in a huff. I took a long look at his tight, round ass before going back to the branch. The real issue was not his parties so much as the fact that the whole neighborhood needed work done after the hurricane. The people who were supposed to remove the tree never bothered to show up. So Dylan wasn't the main problem, but still, I didn't appreciate his ordering us around or his snide smirks when I answered my cell phone, "Hercules to the rescue!" When he pays my bills, he can criticize.

It was hard to concentrate on the huge tree branch in front of me when all I could think about was Dylan's body. He definitely worked out a lot—his ripped arms and thick thighs showed it. His stomach was flat, but his obliques weren't defined, which was perfect. I'd rather have a guy look like a human than some bodybuilding machine. He was tan and smooth, and his piercing dark eyes made him appear confident and not the least bit innocent.

In fact, from the way he talked on the phone, he had a lot of sex. Dylan hadn't gone back downstairs, and I could hear bits and pieces of his conversation.

"Chuck, you know I'd let you fuck me, but I need at least one person to be my friend instead of my top," he said. "And I told you, I'm only into daddies."

Well, that was interesting information.

"Uh, no, I think not," he snapped. "I meant rich daddies, not construction workers. I mean he's hot and built like a tank, but I'm just not into the blue collar thing. My dad's boss is coming over to play around. We've been planning this for a while."

There was a pause and then he said something I couldn't hear.

Then I heard him say loudly, "Of course I'm doing it for the connections. If I did as bad as I think I did this semester, I need a job fast." Another pause. "I don't know. He's okay, but he's not what I would call good looking. No matter how much time I spend in the gym, I never get the hot daddies. But it'll get me employed and, just as important, it gets my ass fucked." I heard him hang up and then I heard the shower running.

"Hey, are you going to stand there, or are you going to help me carry this?" Alex asked, referring to the large branch. We thought about tossing it out the hole in the wall, but we didn't want to risk damaging the patio out back. We'd carry it all the way out the front door.

"So it sounds like the son is one of your kind," Alex said with a leer as we made our way down the stairs. "Why is that always the way? Not once have we run into a horny college girl."

"Like you'd have the balls to do anything about it if we did," I said.

"And you do? You're going to nail this kid?"

"Did you hear that 'blue collar' shit? He's a snot."

"Just as well," Alex said. "It'd be risky diddling a rich lawyer's boy."

"He's an adult." I figured he was around twenty-one. From what I'd heard him tell his friends, it sounded like his parents thought he was going to graduate, but he wasn't.

As we climbed back up the stairs, Dylan emerged from his room wearing only a towel. His muscled torso looked wonderful spotted with water droplets and his wet, black hair fell haphazardly into his eyes.

"Hey, I have a job interview. You guys need to clear out... *now*," Dylan ordered.

Alex rolled his eyes.

"Look, buddy," I said. "We could lose other contracts if we

keep putting up with your bullshit. Do you know how many people need repairs? What are your parents going to think if we decide to skip out on this job because their son kept us from doing our work?"

He hesitated. Another thing I knew from Dylan's constant blabbing on the phone to this Chuck person was that he feared his father's wrath.

"Fine," he said. "But you need to disappear for a while."

I had an idea.

"Alex, there's not much more you can do with the wall until they get the tree. Why don't you go home? I'm going to see what kind of repairs need to be done to the ventilation. Sound good, kid? I'll be in the attic. You won't even know I'm there."

"Whatever. Fine." He turned back to his room, his hair flicking water on my face and shirt.

Alex gave me a dubious look, but I didn't care. Hercules Construction was my company, and I could do what I wanted.

Twenty minutes later I heard this boss guy climbing the stairs. It seemed like he'd let himself in and knew his way around the house.

I happened to be situated right at the air vent above Dylan's bedroom and had a clear view of most of it. Dylan was dressed like the perfect little prep—neatly ironed striped shirt and a navy tie combined with dark dress pants that hugged his rear. The boss entered with such a forceful manner that Dylan backed up a little.

"Hi, Cliff," Dylan stammered.

"I told you to call me 'Mr. Tyler,'" the older man said, immediately grabbing Dylan's bulge and rump. "And I thought I told you to be naked with your legs in the air."

"Yes, Mr. Tyler." Dylan rapidly stripped.

"Leave just the tie and keep the lights on. I like watching my cock go in and out of you."

"Anything," said Dylan. "I'll do anything you want if you give me a job."

In less than two minutes, this Mr. Tyler had Dylan on his back and had begun lubing up his hole. The boss had a small dick, but Dylan must have been very tight because his face turned red with effort when Tyler pushed in. *God, if I got my dick in Dylan, I'd split him in two.*

The boss rammed in and out furiously. Dylan groaned. His eyes were closed, and he did his best to push his hips up to meet every thrust.

"If you want to get a job with me, you'll be giving me this ass all summer long, boy," barked the boss.

"Yes, Mr. Tyler," Dylan said, gasping.

I felt ashamed at being hard. How could the boss do this? No kissing, no caressing. Just taking his pleasure in Dylan's ass.

The boss came in practically no time, shouting twice and collapsing on top of Dylan. The exec looked haggard and disheveled.

"Good enough," he said, rolling off the bed and immediately beginning to dress.

That's it? Dylan didn't even get to come.

"So when can I start work, Mr. Tyler?" Dylan asked, keeping his legs in the air obediently, his very pretty hole still on display.

"I don't know yet, boy. We don't have much available right now. I'll bring by a colleague from another company to play. Tomorrow, same time."

"Another new guy?" Dylan said. He seemed to frown but quickly recovered. "Is he rich? That'll be hot. Do you think he'll hire me?"

"Maybe if your ass is good enough."

Dylan lowered his legs and looked a little pissed. The boss left, and Dylan picked up the phone.

"He didn't offer me a job," Dylan complained. "This has been fun, but if I'm not getting anything out of it, then I want a daddy who's better sex." There was a pause and then he said, "I told you, I'm only into rich guys, but I don't know. Never say never. Maybe if I keep being obnoxious to him, he'll take it out on my ass." He started stroking himself. "He has total access to the house. It would be really hot if he would walk in while I'm sleeping and just start fucking me. That'd be incredible." There was a pause while his friend said something. "He's probably not even gay, but I'm gonna jerk off thinking about him," he said and hung up. Hmm, it seemed like a lot of guys had total access to this house, but maybe he meant me?

He put his legs back in the air and fingered himself with one hand while pulling on his fully hard dick with the other. "No," he whispered to himself, "You can't have my hole…" He worked himself up a bit. "Okay! Okay! I give in! I'll do my best to take your dick, Demetri."

Uh, *holy shit*. Did he actually notice the name on my shirt?

I watched his body grind against the sheets, and he muttered "Construction dick" as copious spurts of come shot onto his taut stomach. I couldn't stop myself from grinning.

I watched him clean himself off with a towel. Then he curled up on his side, still wearing his tie—probably now spattered with jizz.

The next morning my cell phone rang while I was climbing the stairs, and I heard giggling coming from Dylan's room when I said "Hercules to the rescue." It was Dylan's father calling from the Bahamas. I explained that even though the county still hadn't taken down the tree, we should be able to replace some of the missing two-by-fours and repair the damaged roof joist. But until the tree was safely out of the way, we couldn't put up insulation or new siding. I mentioned that I might need to do some work in the attic without going into details.

"Is Dylan giving you any trouble?" asked Mr. Cramer.

I decided to lie. "No problem at all."

Dylan slept on and off for half the day. If he wasn't snoozing, he was on the phone. He stumbled into our work area nude around noon, half-sloshed. "Can you keep it the fuck down!?" he yelled. "I'm trying to sleep. What are you doing here so early? And why the hell are you chipping away at the wall? You're supposed to be fixing the hole, not making it wider."

I gave him a steady look. "Well, see, buddy, dry wall comes in square sheets. So, yes, to make it fit we do need to make your hole wider."

Alex stifled a snicker as Dylan turned beet red.

"What the fuck ever," Dylan griped and huffed out. I don't think he was clearheaded enough to know he was showing off his bare ass. Crazy kid.

Around midafternoon I heard Alex say, "Your boy is up to no good," as he hammered at the gash. "He's getting seriously wasted on Daddy's booze."

I peered out the hole in the wall and saw Dylan floating around the pool on an inflatable lounge chair, wearing sunglasses and the skimpiest of bikinis. He drifted around with a bottle of some kind of clear liquid. I noticed he kept rubbing his eyes and grimacing like he was crying.

"Geez, what's wrong with him today?" I said.

"I can tell you," Alex said. "While you were on the phone, I heard him call someone and whine about a letter saying his college is kicking him out for good. Now he's sure his dad's gonna kick him out, too."

"His dad would do that?" I said, wincing. That made me sad. "Keep an eye on him, Alex. We shouldn't let him swim."

Alex leered at me. "Oh, so we care about him now?"

"Just do it," I said, mock-threatening him with a nail gun.

Not twenty minutes later we heard a loud splash followed by a huge, anguished gasp. I was already flying down the stairs before Dylan screamed for help the first time. When I reached the pool, he was completely submerged, but still flailing wildly. I didn't have time to kick off my boots. I just dove in and grabbed him. He was disoriented and reflexively struggling, so I had to use all my strength to yank his head above water. Again, he gave an enormous gasp, desperately sucking in air. I held him tight around the chest as he shook and coughed.

"I know how to swim," he muttered as he spat out water.

"Yeah, sure," I said. "But prove it to me later." I dragged him out of the pool and hoisted him up in my arms.

"Whee," he mumbled between coughs, his head lolling.

I carried him up to his room and dropped him gently on his bed. "Try to get some rest," I said.

"Wait, where are you going?" Dylan said, his eyes barely open. His chest still heaved from his near-accident.

"To get you some juice or something. You probably should have some fluids so you don't get dehydrated from all that alcohol."

"Wait…" he said, rubbing his head absently. "Why do you call your company Hercules Construction?"

"Hercules is my first name," I said. "People give me grief if I use it, so I just go by my middle name, Demetri."

"I like Hercules," he said. He stripped off his bikini. "I can't sleep in a wet bathing suit," he said in explanation. God, he looked incredible nude.

"I wish you were gay," he said, his voice creaky with exhaustion and liquor.

"Oh, really? I happen to know you only like rich guys."

"Are there rich guys in construction?"

"I can think of one guy who drives a Porsche and vacations in Aruba twice a year." I turned to leave.

"Demetri?"

"What now?"

"Thank you."

I had Alex get me a change of clothes. Then I said he could take the truck back. I'd get a cab again because I wanted to make sure Dylan was all right. I didn't want to make any noise, so I didn't hammer up any two-by-fours. An hour later, I heard a couple of car doors slam. I went out to the hall and saw a big black Lincoln parked outside and Mr. Tyler coming up the walk with some other suit.

I scrambled up to the attic and crept over to the vent in time to see the execs barge into Dylan's bedroom, waking him up.

"Oh, hey," Dylan said.

"At least you're nude this time," said Mr. Tyler.

"Damn, he's a hot one," said the other man.

"Dylan, this is Mr. Wells. He'll be fucking your ass today, too."

"Let me take a quick shower," Dylan said, and he left the room.

"Are you really going to hire him?" Mr. Wells asked in a low voice.

"God, no," said Tyler with a scowl. "None of us will. It's a terrible idea for all kinds of reasons. Besides, I have an inside contact at his university. He flunked out."

"That's not going to fly at my corporation," Wells said, unbuckling his pants.

"Exactly. There's no point. He's just a piece of ass to fuck."

Wells chuckled.

"And fuck and fuck and fuck," Tyler continued as Wells laughed some more.

Dylan came back, scrambling to the bed, dripping wet and eager to please.

"So you want a job, eh," Wells said, grabbing Dylan by the ass.

"Absolutely." Dylan grinned and arched his back, offering himself. "What kind of company would I be working for?"

"Investments," Wells purred as he fingered Dylan's hole. "You have a degree?"

"Uh, no," said Dylan, lowering his head sheepishly.

"Then your ass better be incredible," said Wells, pushing Dylan on all fours.

"Trust me, it is," said Tyler, pushing his dick toward Dylan's lips.

I watched as the men penetrated Dylan from either end. When I saw what an enthusiastic cocksucker he was, my dick got so hard it hurt. Wells' penis wasn't much bigger than Tyler's, but Dylan moaned and grunted with each thrust into his ass. It looked like Wells was pushing in and out for all he was worth considering how winded he was. After a minute he came, shouting "I'm fucking your ass! I'm fucking your ass good!" Then Tyler flipped Dylan onto his back to take his turn in Dylan's hole. He yanked Dylan to the edge of the bed, and began plunging in feverishly. Wells straddled Dylan's face and dangled his balls in the boy's mouth.

"Mine. All mine," said Tyler, panting. "Mine to fuck as much as I want."

"Ours," said Wells. Dylan moaned at this and started jerking his dick harder.

Tyler apparently heightened his pleasure when he heard his own voice. "That's right. If you want a job with either one of us, you've got to be our fuck boy!" Then Tyler started shouting for God and Jesus as he came forcefully inside Dylan's ass.

"Ours," he said grinning, shaking hands with Wells while still deep inside Dylan's rump.

I suppose ass-wipe executives with pencil-dicks must always come and go quickly without a thought for their bottom's orgasm. After they left, Dylan remained on his back, looking dejected. He jerked off for a few minutes and then quit to pick up the phone.

"Chuck, I overheard my dad's boss say that he's not going to hire me, and he's telling all his friends that they shouldn't either; they should just fuck me... Yes, I'm hurt. And there's no way my dad is not going to kick me out. I'm sure of it." Dylan began playing with himself again. "Something else happened, Chuck. I was kind of drunk, and I think the construction worker saved me from drowning in the pool... Yeah, I should apologize. He probably thinks I'm an asshole. I can't believe he'd rescue me after I was so rude to him... No, I would have told you if he fucked me. He can't be gay. I stripped and practically offered up my hole to him. I can't stop thinking about him slipping in while I'm asleep and nailing me. He has a key and that's been my fantasy all week...Hey, I'm still feeling out of it. I'm going to crash and then pack my stuff. I'll probably get kicked out the day my folks get back. Bye."

He hung up forcefully. "Gee, thanks for offering me a place to stay, Chuck!" he yelled. He exhaled and started stroking himself again.

He beat off absently, but I could tell he was thinking about having nowhere to live, which did nothing to keep him aroused. He soon fell asleep.

I had a cramp in my leg from sitting still for so long, but I stayed put and thought. He wasn't such a bad kid. And he seemed to want me a lot. God knows I wanted him. I sighed.

Okay then, Hercules to the rescue.

I sneaked into his room, just like his fantasy, and started to strip. But I just couldn't wake him by rudely sticking my dick in his ass. I had to kiss him some first.

He had barely stirred by the time my mouth was on his.

"Wha—?"

"It's me," I said. "Is this what you wanted?" I reached between his legs and gently massaged his pucker with one hand and caressed his face with the other.

"Holy shit!" Dylan shouted. He was so startled he jumped. Then he settled back against the pillow. "Holy shit," he said again softly, spreading his legs. "You're—you're going to fuck me?"

"I happen to know that's your fantasy," I said.

"Holy…holy—" He couldn't complete the interjection because I kissed him again. His lips were soft and inviting. His skin's fragrance was a sweet mix of sweat and talcum.

He reached down between my legs and grasped my heavy cock. "Geez, you're huge! And so thick! Oh, damn, I can't wait for you to be inside me." He lifted his legs impatiently.

"Let me kiss you some more, baby," I said, although I felt more than ready to be buried in him. I just didn't want to be crude like the pricks from earlier.

"Please," he begged. He reached over to his bedside table and grabbed lubricant and condoms. He quickly lubed up his hole while I stretched a rubber over my shaft.

"I love your dick already," Dylan purred, and then he winced as I tried to push in.

"Damn, you're very tight for someone who gets fucked as much as you do."

"I know," he said. "I have a really small hole. I'll be tight no matter how much you fuck me."

I raised an eyebrow. "You think that will happen a lot?"

Instead of answering, he leaned his head back, closed his eyes and took some deep breaths. He began stroking himself. Soon his ring relaxed, and my dick began to slide inside him.

"Unnnnh," he cried as my cock hit his prostate for the first time. He was so warm and tight I could practically feel the throb of his pulse. This was sheer heaven.

He rolled back farther, surrendering his ass to my deepest penetration. I thrust in and out slowly. I stopped to kiss his chest now and then, but I luxuriated in every stroke. I must have fucked him for twenty-five minutes, and he obediently took everything I gave him. I knew this was probably one of the best asses I'd ever have. Very tight, but willing and experienced in pleasing a penis.

"Oh, God, your dick is perfect," he whispered, moaning. "I wish you'd enslave my ass forever."

"Then I will," I said with a growl. His eyes grew wide, and his body began to shake with orgasm. He shot spurts of come over his head and onto the wall behind him. Coming made his ass muscles even tighter around my dick, and with a loud grunt I let loose a huge load deep inside him.

"That's just round one," I said to him as I ruffled his beautiful hair. Both of us panted heavily. I squeezed his arm muscle. "You're a very strong young man, and I understand you need a job. Want to learn construction?"

He gave me a gleaming smile, but shook his head. "If I got to spend more time with you, I'd love to, but I'm not sure I should. My dad would kill me."

"It sounds like he's going to kill you anyway."

"Yeah, and I do need a job, like, yesterday…all right, I want to work for you. I want to be even more buff." He flexed his left arm for me.

"Are you done letting bastard executives have your ass? Especially ones that don't even make you come?"

"Yeah, they're history," Dylan said. He lifted his head off the pillow and kissed my cheek.

"If Daddy really kicks you out, you can stay with me for a few days," I said, kissing him back. *Maybe a lot longer*, I added silently to myself.

"Really? Awesome," he said. "I promise I won't be obnoxious anymore."

"You won't be. Otherwise I won't take you to Aruba at the end of the summer."

"Aruba. Damn, that would be sweet," he said.

"And until then," I said, reaching for another condom, "whenever we're not working I plan to be fucking you constantly."

"Absolutely, Hercules," he said with a sweet smile. "Absolutely, whenever you want."

LEAVING MY MARK

Jeff Funk

lower my binoculars and reach for the bottle of lube. I shake the damn thing—shit, almost out. I give it a squeeze and the last few drops splatter into my left hand. I grease my cock and go back to peeping out the window at the construction workers next door. I'm particularly fascinated with the one I've been calling the Dark Lord. He's clearly the man in charge. Tallest, cockiest, the one giving orders. Little buddies come to him with their questions. "It's a hot day, man. Don't you need to take off your shirt like the others?" I say. My cat gives an inquisitive gremlin mew, as if to say, "Are you talking to me?" My mouth runs nonstop when I peek at men. The obscenities flow, I tell you. I'm sitting on the edge of my bed on a white comforter. The curtains are parted slightly with a spider plant providing camouflage.

Living out in the country, I don't get the chance to spy on men very often. It is a rare treat indeed. When my dad died he left my brother and me a nice chunk of land a few miles north of town. There's nothing but fields, woods, and ponds in these parts. I built my house a few years ago. My brother decided that he'd had enough of city life so he's building a home next to mine. I came out to him a little over five years ago. He was way cooler than I expected him to be. If anything, he seemed relieved, as if I'd handed him the final piece to the puzzle. We joke around, shoot the shit. My sister-in-law is always fascinated with my latest dirt. I figure it's going to be nice with them living next door, like a family compound.

Now, I watch the construction workers step aside as the concrete truck makes a slow backward trek toward them. My forefinger dials a tighter focus so I can better observe the glistening sweat on Shorty's washboard stomach. I lick my lips, since I'm a salivating pervert. My cock pulses in my hand, hot and throbbing. I stroke my pud some more, the wet sounds filling the room along with my cat's purring. The workers spent the afternoon yesterday setting up plywood so they could pour the foundation today. They climb boards like monkeys, cross planks like tightrope walkers. No wonder their bodies are like gymnasts'.

Just then, the Dark Lord shouts something to the guy in the earthmover, who, oblivious to the Lord's commandment, backs up and—

Oops!

—down goes the Port-o-John.

"Now that's gonna be a helluva shitty mess," I say to Boris. She meows a response. Boris is a female cat, by the way. I named her before I found out her sex and by then the name had already stuck.

I hear the guys on the work site shout and groan. Their masculine ululations send chills capering down my spine. Is there anything more manly than men at work? That camaraderie. Muscles that come from hard labor. Deep voices. Sweat. Dusty boots and dirty clothes. White teeth that shine through grimy faces...

I'm about to crack a nut when I see the Dark Lord walking toward my house.

"Oh, fuck me," I say. I spring from the bed and search for my clothes. Where the hell? Oh, yeah, I stepped out of them an article at a time on the way to my afternoon show. Goddamn it. Cock flopping side to side, I dash to my dresser and grab a T-shirt and pull on a pair of jeans. My turgid prick doesn't want to fit into my pants, so I pack it to the side and zip carefully. I glance at the mirror above my dresser. I look guilty.

The doorbell rings.

I take deep breaths as I walk. I melt ever so slightly at the sight of the Dark Lord through the paned glass.

I open the door. "Yes?"

"Mr. Hamilton?"

"Call me Jake," I say.

He nods. "I'm Scott." We shake. His grip is strong; he has big hands and seems to enjoy holding mine. His brown eyes are piercing. "Your brother said that if we ever needed anything we could come over here—"

Good ole David, I think.

"—and it just so happens that Randy knocked over the shitter."

"Ah, so that's what I heard," I say, pretending to be oblivious to this knowledge.

"Yeah, and it's gonna be a day before I can get another Port-o-John to the site. So I was wondering... I hate to put you out, but would you mind if the boys used your john? Just for today."

"That's no problem at all."

"You sure?"

"Absolutely."

"Mind if I use it right now?"

"Go right ahead," I say. I tell him it's just down the hall, first door on the right. I watch his long legs as he walks. His smell wafts pleasantly in his wake. I spot my underwear on the floor in the hallway. Then it dawns on me: I left my butt plug on the counter and there are smut magazines in the basket next to the john. Oh, God. Will he be freaked out or act like he didn't notice? Then I reason, it's my house and I'm extending a courtesy to him. Can I help it if I wasn't expecting company?

He's in there for a long goddamn while. When he comes out, he seems unfazed. "Thanks, Jake," is all he says. He walks back out the door then turns and gives me a solemn nod.

Curious.

He goes back to the work site and has a brief word with his men. I go back to sitting on the bed, watching them. I notice that every so often, Scott looks my way. The first time he does it, I duck. Can he see me? Then the thought comes again, this is my damn house. If he sees me peeping on them then he'll just have to deal with it. Or maybe he knows I'm watching and likes it.

At the end of the day, the workers pack their trucks. A couple guys exchange whoops and hollers followed by laughter. One by one, they fire up their pickups, music blaring, and drive away, leaving a massive cloud of dust.

All but Scott.

He walks from the work site through my lawn and up to my front door. This time instead of ringing the doorbell, he knocks.

I answer the door. "Hey, Scott. Get a lot done today?"

"Yeah, it's coming along real nice."

"Need to use the restroom?"

He shakes his head. He looks at me with those gorgeous

brown eyes, which now shine with a lusty glaze. He stands close
to me with his arms hanging loosely at his sides, as if he wants me
to hold his hand. He stinks good from his hard day of work.

I point to his black T-shirt, which is covered in dust and wet
with sweat. "You like Nine Inch Nails? They fuckin' rock."

"Right on. Seen 'em many times." He nods slowly while
forcing a breath through his nostrils. His shoulders fall as if his
marionette strings have been cut away from a strict puppeteer.

"I'm really into armpits," I say matter-of-factly. "Would you
mind if I licked yours?"

"I just got off work. They're probably..."

"That's okay." I pull him close to me. My hands rove under
his T-shirt.

"They're hairy...you know. I don't know if you—"

"I love hairy armpits."

I lift his shirt and see flesh stretched tightly over muscle. Male
beauty. My mouth finds a nipple. I flick it with my tongue then
bury my face in his pits, licking through the wetness of the dark
fur. I inhale deeply. "Fuck," I say, "that's nice."

"Man, you're giving me goose bumps."

I look down and see that his entire torso is pebbly. I lightly
glide my palm down the rocky terrain. On my upward journey,
I turn my hand into a rake, the hair flowing between my fingers,
from his treasure trail to the thick curls on his chest.

"Don't leave any marks," he says. "My girlfriend would shit
if she found out."

"I won't."

"Thanks." He chuckles nervously.

I pull his T-shirt up and over his head, tossing it to the floor,
then step back to fully take in the sight. "You're, like, *beautiful*.
You know that?" My voice is down to a whisper, the soft and
awkward language of lust.

He laughs like a shy guy not used to receiving compliments from men. "You, too," he says.

I reach for his jeans and unfasten them. He's wearing blue plaid boxers and I can see the promise of a thick shaft through the gaping fly. I push his jeans and underwear all the way down to his work boots. His penis has a helluva curve to it. It points skyward and looks like a true pole of glory from my kneeling vantage point, a cock worthy of worship. It is the darkest part of his body. Thick and cut with a big knob and an equally substantial pisshole. His nuts are smaller than mine, but that could be because they're pulled up close to his body. He sports a full black bush but his scrotum is shaved. I press my lips against his inner thigh and kiss my way to the ball that hangs the lowest. I touch the tip of my tongue to it before pulling it into my mouth. This elicits a gasp from Scott. *What's the matter,* I think, *doesn't your girlfriend give these the attention they deserve?* I make sure the other does not feel neglected, and as I do he caresses my cheek with one of his strong hands.

He's so tall that I have to come up off my knees to take his dick into my mouth. I'm careful not to rake him with my teeth. No hickeys, no scratches. I'm merely borrowing his body. But I'll take what I can get. I suck slowly, savoring every inch.

His head drops back. Through closed eyes, he says, "Man, you're, like, *way* good at that."

His words encourage my ministrations, making me want to lavish pleasure upon him all the more. The aroma of his manly meat makes me swoon. It's as if I've lost all sense of my surroundings, like I'm *elsewhere*—experiencing a slice of Heaven? The thought of religion right now seems obscene, but also quite right. I realize I'm groping his ass, big handfuls of luscious butt. He doesn't seem to mind that my fingers are probing the sensitive entry of his pucker.

He groans loudly. Then: "Stop, stop."

"What's wrong?"

"You're gonna make me come."

"I know."

"Jake, I can't. My girlfriend. I gotta save it for her."

I look down and see his cock throbbing. God, that's gorgeous. "I'll stop for a while. I want another taste though."

He kisses me and then seems almost surprised. "I've only experimented a little with guys. I've never gone this far before." He regards me with eyes slightly squinted and gestures toward my crotch. "Let me…" He kneels in front of me. His lips are ragged with little flecks of dry skin, signs of a lip-biter, but they're red and plump. His fingers fumble nervously as he undoes my belt, causing me to tremble with anticipation. He pulls my jeans down. I'm so horned up I'm already leaking. His arms are tan, his hands are dirty, and I'm riveted by the contrast of his darkness against my white skin.

Beautiful.

He takes my dick into his hungry mouth and as he does it comes to me that the last time he gave oral sex it was with the flesh of a woman. How forbidden that a straight man—a construction worker, no less—is sucking my cock. He is skilled with his tongue. I resist the urge to rock my hips. I let him take me at his pace. Don't want to choke the straight boy. He really goes to town on my pole.

"Scott," I say through hoarse breath when I can feel that I'm on the brink of flooding his mouth, "you'd better stop." I grab on to myself to calm the impending surge and successfully delay its arrival. If he's not going to come, I won't either.

"How was I?" he says with a proud smile.

"You were great," I say. "Here, lie down."

He does and I remove his boots and socks. He has nice feet.

I'm a sucker for a man with pretty toes. Boris comes over to say hello to Scott. "Hi kitty," he says, scratching her behind an ear.

"Boris, this is no place for a lady." I pick her up and put her in the living room.

"Boris is a *she?*"

"Tranny cats need love, too."

He laughs. "Listen, I can't stay long."

"Ah, I figured."

"But I wanna do this again. That is, if you don't mind."

"You can come over any time you want," I say, wishing I didn't have to share him. I'll have to remind myself not to fall for him. It's just sex. Don't get attached.

We lie naked together kissing and caressing for a few stolen minutes before I put his dirty work clothes back on him and send him on his way. A warm breeze blows through my red pubes while I stand nude at the door, waving to him as his pickup makes its way down the country road. He honks his horn.

I go back inside and try not to picture him going home to his girlfriend. No doubt he showers when he gets home, which is convenient for him. Otherwise she could possibly smell the distinct aroma of saliva on his cock. Will he look himself over in the mirror to make sure I didn't scratch him? What does his girlfriend look like? What will they do tonight? Will they make love? All these thoughts run through my mind in an instant, but the worst thing I worry about is that he'll get a case of the "guilties" and not want to see me again.

But that is not the case. We see each other every day after he's finished working. Each afternoon, I wait patiently for the others to leave and for Scott to come walking through the grass to my front door. We ravish one another the instant we're alone. The powerful way he looks at me often leads me into false hopes that one day we'll be together. But then I remember that he likes his life as it is. I used to think that there was no such thing as a bisexual man; I always believed they were gay and couldn't face up to it. But maybe there is a certain *somewhere in between*. I think of Walt Whitman's life and his "comrades" and the love letters he wrote to men. He probably loved someone like Scott, too.

Scott says that he'll only be at my brother's site till the end of the week, then he will be on to the next gig. The night he tells me, I wonder if this means good-bye. But when the weekend comes, I receive a surprise phone call.

"My girlfriend's out of town. She went to see her mother. So...I kinda wondered, could I come see you?"

"Yes," I say. "Come right now. I need you."

After I hang up, I scold myself for that last line. *Jake, when are you going to learn?* I look at the clock. He'll be here in fifteen minutes. I'm giddy with the possibility that we'll be able to shower together, a first. We can take as much time as we need to do what has to be done. I'll, of course, be careful with his body. But it is my hope that with my actions and my love, I'll find a way to leave my mark.

RANDY ROOFERS

Bearmuffin

It was spring break and I was staying at my parents' townhouse in South Florida. Over the weekend, I'd been busy fucking and sucking some of the hottest collegiate studs in town but today I decided to take it easy and just lie naked by the pool. Mom and Dad had taken our golden retriever to the vet so I had the place all to myself.

I could hear the sound of hammering coming from next door. One of those famous Florida storms had hit town the other night. Luckily, we emerged unscathed but our neighbor wasn't so lucky, so he was having his roof fixed. I tried to see who was working up there but except for an occasional glimpse of golden thigh or brawny bicep the mystery roofers were hidden by the leafy branches of the trees separating our properties.

Ordinarily, my lust would have been piqued. But right now I wanted to work on my tan. Maybe later I'd strike up a conversation with them and see where that would lead. I spread a generous amount of oil all over my muscles, put on my shades, and

dozed off on the chaise lounge. Some time later, I was awakened
by a loud splash. I opened my eyes to see a big hammer sinking
to the bottom of the pool.

Moments later, I heard pounding on the redwood patio door.
When I opened the door I saw a gorgeous six-foot-two blond
hunk with a dazzling smile on his handsome face. "Howdy," he
said, extending his hand. "The name's Hank." Hank's T-shirt
was tucked behind his wide leather belt. I saw that his bronzed
muscles were covered in sizzling sweat. Meaty golden brown
nipples capped Hank's firm pecs.

"Sorry about that," Hank said casting a glance at the hammer lying on the bottom of the pool.

But I could have cared less. My eyes were glued to
Hank's body. I loved the way his denim cutoffs exposed his
heart-stopping tree-trunk thighs. And I was equally excited
to see the thick straps of his jock as it ran over his firm blond-
haired butt that peeped lewdly from a big tear in the back of
his jeans.

A wild, devilish grin broke out on Hank's sensuous lips. His
hands groped his bulging crotch. His sexy blue eyes immediately locked on to mine as he reached out to shake my hand. I
returned the firm, hearty handshake. I felt my heart skip a beat
and a sudden twitch jolt my groin. It was instant lust.

Hank stepped closer to me. He licked his lips as he took in
every inch of my hard muscled body. I could resist anything but
temptation so I immediately ran my tongue over Hank's pecs.
Hank locked his hands behind my neck. When I saw the golden
tufts of hairs glistening inside Hank's armpits, I began to lick off
the salty sweat. I felt my cock twitch and throb, intoxicated by
Hank's raw, pungent aroma.

I slowly licked my way down over Hank's wonderfully
furrowed abs. I dug the tip of my tongue into each sweaty,

fabulously muscled groove. Then I reached Hank's crotch, where I intended to bury my face.

Hank quickly popped off the buttons of his denim cutoffs and pulled them down over his magnificent legs. I dropped to my knees and began slurping at Hank's jockstrap pouch. As I sucked, I grabbed two meaty handfuls of Hank's gorgeous ass. Then I worked a finger inside Hank's crack. Hank moaned so much that I was encouraged to dig even farther with my forefinger. This really inflamed Hank's lust, so much so that he uttered a harsh, guttural "A-h-h-h f-u-c-c-k!" So I figured now was the time for some good old-fashioned butt eating.

"Turn around, dude, so I can eat your ass," I said to Hank. Yeah! I wanted more than anything else in the world to press my face into Hank's hot sweaty butt. When Hank turned around, I started licking down the crack of his ass and lingered to taste the raw sweat at the spot between his ass and balls. Hank was moaning and groaning. He bent over and pushed his butt against my bobbing face. I eagerly wiggled my tongue between Hank's buttocks.

Suddenly, Hank blurted out, "That fucker. Look at him. He's watching us!"

I pulled off Hank's meaty buttocks and glanced up toward the neighboring roof. There was the other roofer with his beefy legs spread apart. His cutoffs were pulled down over his thighs. His big, thick cock was pulsing wildly in his fist. A wicked smile creased his handsome face. With his free hand he waved hello.

I laughed and waved back. I turned to Hank. "Tell your friend to come join us," I said.

He shook his head. He reached out and grabbed my left nipple and squeezed it. "I want you all to myself." He turned around again and playfully shoved me down. Now I was lying on my back, faceup. Hank squatted over my smiling face. "Now eat my fuckin' ass," he rasped. Without a moment's hesitation I drove my hot tongue into Hank's butthole and started to fist my cock. Fuck, there was nothing better in the world than eating a hot man's sweaty, ripe butthole.

Hank must have loved the rough sensation of my expert tongue fluttering on his asshole because he moaned and groaned with pleasure as he fisted his cock until it got good and hard. Then he spun around and jammed it right into my mouth. I sucked hard and long on Hank's spasming prick. I loved the way his thick cock-veins swelled and thickened inside my mouth. Then he grabbed my neck as he shoved his cock all the way down my sputtering throat. "Take my fuckin' load, stud," he screamed as he shot hot gobs of cum all over my face.

It was right at that moment that the other roofer walked in through the patio door. When he saw the thick streams of cum dribbling down my face, he laughed.

"Fuck, Hank! Did ya save some for me, buddy?"

Hank looked at Mike and grinned. "You fucker. You were watching us!"

"Fuckin' A!" Mike said.

"Gotta get back to work," Hank said, pulling on his cutoffs. He gave my nipples one last playful tug before he left.

I was a bit disappointed because the prospect of a three-way had excited me ever since I saw Mike on the roof watching us as he masturbated. Maybe later I'd talk Hank into it.

I gazed at Mike, who was grinning wolfishly at me and squeezing his bulging crotch at the same time. Mike was just as tall as Hank. But where Hank was smooth and golden, Mike was dark. He had deep-set black eyes and furry eyebrows that blended together over the bridge of his thick nose. I found Mike's square-jawed good looks ferociously exciting. Mike shucked off his grimy T-shirt and cutoffs. His thick cock bolted upright and was throbbing angrily in the air. I was thrilled to see that Mike's entire body was covered with a thick pelt of fur that fanned all over his thick pecs and ran down to his furrowed abs.

But where Hank was playful and laid back, Mike was rough, down and dirty. I could tell by the way Mike was glaring down at me that he was a man who liked to take charge.

I was amazed by Mike's superbly muscled body. Thick curly hairs ran across his huge pecs and traveled down over his washboard abs until they swarmed around the thick root of his uncut cock and massive hanging balls.

I was equally wide-eyed at the sight of the thick, uncut dick bobbing in front of me. Mike raised an arm and exposed the slimy tufts of hair swirling inside his armpit. "Lick my pits, stud!" he barked.

I immediately obeyed. I nuzzled my face into the thick hairs that swirled inside Mike's hot, musky armpits. I wrapped my fist around my spasming cock. I began masturbating while I lapped at the smelly pit hairs. Mike watched me masturbate. Yeah! No doubt about it. I was really getting off on licking Mike's raunchy armpits.

Mike groaned. "You love my smell, don't you?"

I looked up and said, "Yes, sir! I do!"

"Then keep licking," Mike grunted.

I obeyed, but the sight of Mike's manly pecs was just too tempting. I stopped masturbating and focused my attention on Mike's luscious body. Soon, I was running my tongue all over Mike's hairy pumped-up pecs. I took one of Mike's thick nipples and drew it in between my lips.

"Fuck, yeah!" Mike grunted. "Suck my tits, stud!"

Mike grabbed my head, holding me steady while I chewed on his protruding nipples. Then he guided my head down along his hairy, sweaty abs. He made me stoop lower so I could kiss and lick the washboard ripples of his muscular belly until he finally shoved my face down to his groin.

Mike thrust his cock and balls against my bobbing face, filling my nose with the strong stench of his manly, sweaty body. My probing tongue slurped noisily at his smelly crotch. I mashed my face into his stinky pubes and worked my tongue up and around his big thighs. I licked the sweat off of his big hairy balls. And I could tell that Mike loved having his balls sucked on because he made big deep bearlike growling sounds of supreme macho satisfaction.

Then Mike cupped his hands behind my head. His cock quivered violently. The doorknob-like tip of Mike's precum-oozing cock hovered just an inch away from my trembling lips. My eyes glittered when I saw the piss slit yawn wide open. A huge drop of precum slowly trickled out. Eagerly, I stuck my tongue out. I teasingly brushed my tongue-tip against Mike's oozing piss slit and let a salty precum drop ooze onto it.

"Lick it," Mike said. "Yeah! Stick out that tongue. You're gonna get a good taste of my fat dick 'cause I'm gonna shove it up your fucking hole!"

My pucker twitched impatiently at the prospect of Mike's monster cock flying up my asshole. I opened as wide as I could to allow his sweaty prick to slide into my panting mouth. Now my face was buried in his groin. My nose and lips were lost in the thick, musky nest of Mike's smelly pubes. When he hunched forward, his big sweaty balls slapped against my chin.

Hot foaming spit drooled out of the corners of my mouth. I sucked in my cheeks and slurped like mad on Mike's bull-cock. All the while, my cock was spasming wildly between my thighs. Hot, lusty tingles coursed all over my muscles when I tasted the thick drops of precum oozing from his piss hole.

I ran my hands up and down Mike's hairy thighs. I grinned

lasciviously as I slipped my fingers in between the crack of Mike's sweaty buttocks. And when I wiggled my forefinger inside Mike's hot and sweaty bunghole and churned it around, Mike went berserk.

"Awww, fuck!" he cried. Mike tossed his head from side to side. His muscles trembled wildly. His eyes glowered as he rammed his cock all the way down my cocksucking throat. "C'mon, stud," he yelled. "Eat that cock. I'm gonna fuck your face but good!"

My throat was sore from all that cocksucking. I was gagging and choking on Mike's huge cock. But I loved every minute of it.

I sucked so hard on Mike's cock that for a moment I thought he'd shoot his heavy load down my throat. But at last he slapped my butt and made me turn around. "Bend over!" he barked at me. *Good,* I thought. Now I was going to get fucked just like he'd promised.

Mike grabbed my firm buttcheeks and wrenched them wide open. Now my puckered hole was exposed to view. "Fuck," he grunted. "Your hole looks like two horny lips waiting to suck my big, fat dick!"

Mike leaned forward, gripped me tightly around the waist, and slammed right into me. I cried out with pain. My hole was tight and at first resisted his anal assault, and he pulled out again. Mike ran his rough hands over my buttocks, massaging them. "Such a fuckin' hot ass, stud. Such a nice hot ass," he said. The massage relaxed me so I took a deep breath. Mike tried to insert his hot cock up my hole again. Maybe it was the massage or maybe it was the suntan oil dripping down my back and coating my asshole. Whatever the case, I managed to relax my hole so this time Mike's big cock popped right through my sphincter.

I gritted my teeth as I felt Mike's thick cock work its horny way up my hole. And I gasped when I felt Mike's fat cockhead nudge against my prostate. Mike grunted hard and grabbed my shoulders as he plowed even farther up my hole. My cock was rock hard by now and I started to fist it wildly.

Mike continued to piston his cock in and out of my sore butt. I gasped in wonder at the incredible sensation of Mike pulling his cock out to just beneath his cockhead and then slam-dunking it in again until his big fat hairy balls were smashing against the root of my cock.

Mike continued to powerfuck me until finally he gasped, "Fuck! I gotta come. Fuckin' now, stud!"

I felt Mike's rough hands grab my waist. Mike screamed as he lunged one last time into my butt. My tight hole clenched around the root of Mike's spasming cock as huge jets of sperm squirted out of him and hurtled up my asshole.

"Unngh, unngh," I groaned. "Gonna shoot my wad, dude. Gonna fuckin' shoot my wad!" Then a heavy fuck spasm shook my entire body. My hot, teeming cock erupted, squirting cum all over the floor.

Suddenly, Hank poked his head through the trees. "Hey, Mike!" he said. "Get your horny ass over here. We got work to do!"

With a lusty grin, Mike slapped me on the butt. "Hey, stud," the swarthy roofer said. "Just want you to know something. Hank told me the minute he saw you he just had to fuck you. So I threw that hammer into the pool on purpose. He was so fuckin' horny, I just told him: go for it, stud. Go get him."

I grinned right back at him. "Thanks, Mike," I said.

Mike dove into the pool and retrieved the hammer. He looked so gorgeous as the water dripped off his muscles. He didn't even bother to dry off. But I figured the hot Florida sun would take care of that. He pulled on his cutoffs and sprinted out the door.

Now I was alone. But Hank and Mike's manly smells still

wafted lazily in the air. I looked on the ground and smiled. There was Hank's jockstrap. I was more than happy to see he'd left it behind. I picked up the grimy, soiled jock and pressed it to my nose. The odor embedded in the pouch rushed up my nose, and I felt my cock rise and stiffen.

I started to whack off again as I thought about Hank and Mike. *Maybe we'll have another storm that'll blow the fuckin' roof right off the house. Yeah, anything to bring those two hot studs back here.* I grinned as yet another hot load came gushing out of my hard cock.

GLORY DAYS

Laura Bacchi

Aren't you getting too old for this shit?"

I knew that voice. My hammer stopped in mid-swing, and I turned to see Mack's huge frame filling the doorway. He held a sagging box in his arms.

"Long time no see," I mumbled and got back to work pounding in a tack strip before moving on to the next one. Yeah, it had been a long time, ten years at least. I waited for him to leave, but he stood there watching me—I could see him from the corner of my vision as I moved to the next wall.

"You lost?" I asked. But I didn't turn completely around. Seeing him the first time had been enough of a shock to my system.

"Nope. Just admiring the view." He lowered his voice. "I always liked you on all fours, Kenny."

I pretended to ignore his little commentary, but my cock was listening. It perked up its ears and made a beeline for the waistband of my jeans. I swung the hammer, this time on my thumb.

He laughed and came into the room. I waited for his boot on my ass or some other reminder of the old days, but he walked past me to enter the monstrosity of a walk-in closet to the right.

This was supposed to be an easy job—just help a buddy with a remodel, install some carpet, that kind of thing. Knowing that Mack would be working so close made this anything but easy. My cock, now fully erect, throbbed in agony. I grabbed another strip and aimed. Hell, I'd even mash my thumb again if it'd keep my mind off Mack and his thick, hairy arms and the way his brown eyes were always looking for trouble.

I heard him drop his big box then whistle long and low. "Damn... A family of four could live in this closet."

No argument there. The master bath alone was bigger than my apartment. He started checking things out, his heavy boots clomping through the closet and into the adjoining bathroom.

"They did good work in here," he said.

Finally some conversation I could respond to. I got up and met him at the bathroom door on my side of the suite. "Yeah, Robert did the tile. His wife did the mural."

He nodded his head in appreciation, then went back to the closet by way of the bathroom's side door and shut it. I started to leave, but a noise caught my attention. It was his finger tapping on the door. In the mirror, one of his eyes stared back at me through the crack. He eased the door open wider and stuck his head through.

"Remind you of anything?"

His eyes were looking down now. I followed his gaze to where the antique doorknob would go once it arrived. I shook my head.

"You sure?" he asked.

Of course I remember, asshole. Like I could forget that night he did a little switcheroo in a bookstore called Glory Days downtown. I'd been hot for him for months. He knew it. We hooked up one night and I offered him my ass on the other side of the wall. Too bad he'd snuck two friends into his booth. They all had a go at me before I figured out what the hell was taking so long, the starting and the stopping, him laughing at the end. It was the start of a rocky eight-month relationship, if you could call it that. More like my sorry ass waiting for him to phone so we could meet, him fucking me hard in some alley across town then leaving me there while I caught my breath and tried to find the clothes he'd ripped off in his rush to be inside me.

I couldn't move. Mostly because the racing of my heart told me I missed that. Missed him.

When I finally forced myself to leave, he slipped the handle of a screwdriver through the hole and wiggled it around. "You get bored," he said, "you just put your finger through one of these holes, hear?"

"I'm not some stupid eighteen-year-old anymore."

"You still look eighteen."

"Fuck you, Mack."

"Any time, Kenny."

I went back to work. He unloaded his box, shuffled around and played with his measuring tape on the other side of the door. Then he started nailing something. The odor of cedar wafted through all the doorknob holes and gave me a headache. When he left that afternoon, I found some painter's tape and a newspaper downstairs and used them to cover all the holes. I didn't want to smell the cedar, and I didn't want to catch sight of him.

I'd wasted enough time that day peeking every chance I got.

When he arrived the next morning, he didn't say a word—he simply chuckled at my makeshift attempt to block the smell and the view. As he carried another massive box through my work area and into the closet, I watched his shadow and wondered if those muscles were still firm or if he'd gone soft like me. I shook my head. Mack and soft were two words that didn't go together. *Back to work*, I told myself, mainly because I was hard again.

I cut strips of padding to size and began installing them. It was good padding—my knees were thankful as I stapled my way from one end of the room to the other then started on the next strip. I had a good rhythm going and was about to trim the excess around the perimeter when I heard the sound of paper being cut. I faced the closet's double doors. A silver blade had stabbed through one of my newspaper circles and was slipping around the interior of the hole in a slow, perfect arc.

The circle drifted to the floor. He bent down and eyeballed me through the hole. I gave him my back. He returned to nailing that obnoxious cedar, and I did a good job of ignoring him until I picked up on a different sound...the rhythmic movement of him pressing against the door. I couldn't help but turn around.

"Jesus, Mack!" His cock, thicker than I remembered, had poked through the hole. I could see his fingers on the other side jacking hard at the base and a bubble of juice shining at the slit.

I got up and moved my toolbox and lunch from the direct line of fire, then frantically spread out yesterday's remaining newspaper to catch his jizz—the padding I'd put down would soak it up like a sponge.

"Hey, Kenny..."

I made the mistake of looking up when I heard him call me in that husky voice of his. In that instant, he angled his prick up and let loose a pulse of white. I scrambled away to keep from getting hit in the face. My jeans weren't so lucky.

"You're a bastard, Mack. Robert's gonna hear about this—"

"No, he's not. You're not gonna tell him. Hell, you're probably hard as shit right about now."

I shut my mouth because it was the truth. After washing his cum from my leg in the bathroom, I finished the underlay while his cheery whistling made my damning silence all the more humiliating.

No, Mack hadn't gone soft at all.

The next morning, I got to the site early. Since the carpet was ready to roll I wanted to get it in place and be ready for whatever crap Mack had in store for me. I'd knee-kicked about half the room before he arrived.

"Pretty carpet," he said.

I looked up. He was grinning.

And it's going to stay that way, I wanted to tell him. I'd brought a boom box today to tune out his whistling, so I reached over and turned it up louder. No sense in waiting for the whistles. His deep baritone laugh gave the bass a run for its money. Once he shut the closet doors, I turned down the volume—I didn't want to miss the telltale thumps of warning before he shot his load.

They started up before lunchtime.

I got up and casually walked to my toolbox. The plastic drop cloth inside opened up in a jiffy and after positioning it below both holes in the double doors—I didn't want to leave anything to chance—I went back to my work and waited for him to pull out once he realized I'd screwed up his plans. The steady bumps of his meaty fingers against the wood kept their pace for a few more minutes, then stopped.

"You can come on the tarp. Hell, I'll leave it out all week if you want."

Mack pulled out. But he starting moving around—a body that big couldn't keep silent no matter how hard it tried. He went into the bathroom. I pictured him cupping his thick cock until he shot into the toilet or wherever part of the room he chose to splatter. At least the tiles would clean up easy, and chances were I'd be the one doing the cleanup. My hand grabbed my own prick. As I stroked it outside of my jeans, I thought about that dick in my ass like it had been all those years ago.

I checked my watch. He'd grab lunch soon, and I'd go in the bathroom and jerk off—

"I prefer the carpet, Kenny."

Shit! I spun around to find him at the side bathroom door, yanking away while standing over the pristine carpet. He aimed straight for the middle of the room, his prick ready to blow any second now. I'd never crawled so fucking fast in my life. I could probably clean it up, but it was the principle of the thing…I lunged for where I thought the load would land and took it right in the face.

"You sonofabitch!"

I charged him, but he pulled the door closed and held it shut. I was no match for him, but I shoved into it anyway, then banged my head against it in frustration. The bastard grabbed my T-shirt through the hole and tugged.

"What do you want from me, man?" I asked between gritted teeth. "You wanna fuck, is that it?"

He pulled my shirt harder, until my hard-on slammed into the wood. But he didn't answer.

"Thing is, Mack, I can't tell if you wanna fuck my body or my mind. I don't play games anymore." His words from the other day came back to me. "I'm too old for that shit. And you are too."

He pushed the door open again, my shirt still in his fist on the other side of the hole. A muscle in his cheek began to tic. He looked at the cum on my face, then scraped it off with a finger and held it up to my lips.

I shook my head, half out of fear, because no matter how safe I'd been in the past—since giving up on him—I wasn't so sure I could refuse. And I hated myself for even thinking about opening up to taste it. To suck every drop from his hairy knuckle.

Thank God he didn't press me and wiped it on his jeans instead. Then he let go of me and gave the door a small push. It wasn't mean or angry, just unexpected, and it sent me sprawling backward. I stumbled to regain my footing but failed and crashed into the plush pile below. He stepped toward me, his zipper still down, his cock still throbbing and ready for more. It was only natural for me to part my tangled legs for him. He dropped to his knees. I didn't move, not my eyes, not my lungs— I lay there frozen and waiting.

He squeezed my thigh and let all his weight down on one palm. When he moved his hand higher, toward my balls and cock, I knew it would hurt. At least a little. But he eased up a bit and gently cupped the erection that was burning the flesh inside my briefs like a fucking brand. He popped the snap and undid my fly. I worked my jeans down and he lay down on me. I couldn't breathe, couldn't think. All I could do was want.

"Where the hell did you go?" he asked. "I looked for you for months."

"I..." I didn't know what to say. His revelation hit me in the gut first. Then it reached up and grabbed my heart and held it in a vise. "I had no idea you'd even care," I finally choked out.

He opened his mouth to reply when someone started up the stairs. Mack rolled off me, taking his heat with him, and disappeared into the bathroom. I had enough sense to zip up and get to my feet.

"Rob ordered pizza for us," some new guy yelled. "Beer, too.

Come on down." He headed back downstairs, but the moment was lost.

Mack reappeared, all zipped up but still hard. "You want pizza?" he asked.

No, I didn't. I didn't want anything but him on me. In me. And the look on his face told me he knew this. I shook my head.

"Me either. Come on."

"Where are we going?"

He didn't answer. The stairs groaned under his weight as he half-walked, half-ran downstairs. I followed him out to his Ford pickup. It was as massive as he was. When I climbed inside, I sucked in the scent of the interior, of him after a hot day on the job. He hit the gas and put his hand on my thigh, his fingertips pushing down to the bone. When I closed my eyes to the sweet pain, he must've been watching. Must've thought it hurt too much. He loosened his grip.

"It's okay," I told him, but he didn't go deep again. So I leaned over. Put my mouth on his neck. I licked him and grabbed the bulge at his crotch. The heel of my palm pressed into the outline of his cockhead.

"Jesus, Kenny."

He eased off the road and drove up a dirt path. At the top of the hill, in a clearing, was another big-ass house newly framed. I figured we'd fuck in the truck, but he got out. I had to walk twice as fast to keep up.

"Nice. You work here, too?" I asked.

"No. This is my place. You like it?"

"It's huge."

"I know it is, but do you like it?"

"What's not to like? Lots of trees. Two stories and, what, about three thousand square feet?"

He nodded and pointed to the makeshift cinderblock steps to

the entrance. I climbed up into what would be the foyer, Mack beside me now, his strong hand pulling me this way and that to give me a tour.

"And this is the master bedroom."

We stood in the middle of the room, our bodies close but not touching while I pictured a big waterbed on the far wall and a small army of guys like me on it, doing whatever he asked.

He touched my arm, and the vision evaporated. "See my tub?" he asked.

How could I miss it? I guess a body like his needed one that large. It hadn't been put into the bathroom wall yet. We walked over to it and he scooped out some stray curls of wood and sawdust. Then he started to unbutton his plaid flannel shirt.

"Get in," he said.

"In the tub?"

"Yeah."

"There's no water."

My heart kicked against my ribs. I was stalling, and he knew it. He rolled his eyes at me, smiled, and reached for his fly. I unlaced my boots but didn't take anything else off. When I stepped into the tub, it rocked until I sat down then rocked again as he joined me, completely naked. My shirt didn't last long. Neither did my other clothes. His fingers found my nipples and balls, and his mouth met mine. I pulled back. He'd never kissed me before. God knows I'd wanted him to.

He caught my face between his giant hands and kissed me again. This time I didn't back away even if I could have, he tasted so fucking right. I sucked his tongue and let his beard burn my skin. I needed to grab hold of something—his shoulders, the rim of porcelain behind me—anything to anchor me and keep me still while he scraped into my hips with ragged fingernails or bit on my lip.

My sweaty back slid against the cool surface and Mack let me go. Even kneeling, he towered over me, his cock throbbing, dripping, ready to explode. His knee dragged over my chest to pin my arms to my sides.

"You want this, Kenny?"

He was asking? Mack wasn't the asking type, so the least I could do was answer.

"Yeah, but…"

I didn't have to spell it out for him and when his arm went over the tub in search of the jeans he'd discarded, I held my breath, not quite believing how much he'd changed. But to watch him tear the foil and roll the rubber down the length of his thick shaft made me start breathing again. He was beautiful, so fucking beautiful. Some of his dark chest hair had faded to gray. I reached up to run my fingers through it.

He stopped rolling the condom. "You okay?"

I didn't answer. I wouldn't be okay until I got him in my mouth or my ass or maybe just cock against cock. So I grabbed him by the base and sucked in inch after inch. He eased my head back down to the hard porcelain, fucking my mouth raw then numb, the tub creaking against the subfloor with each thrust.

Then he pulled out. His arm went back over the side, and he turned around to face my dick. Soon my smaller cock was swimming in latex. He made it work though, and he did the unthinkable—he sucked me. I lifted my hips to give him everything I had. That earned me a squeeze on the balls.

"Don't be greedy." His chuckle echoed in our hiding place.

How could I not be? He'd never done that for me before. A quick tug as he fucked me from behind? Sure. But nothing like this. His tongue swirled around my head, and I nearly shot my wad like I was eighteen again.

His lips began pumping up and down and when I let out a

moan, he backed off and licked my sac until I stopped panting. Then he pulled my legs apart and fingered my hole. I returned the favor while his sweat rained down on me, slicking my body, cooling me off. His mouth swallowed more of my shaft, and I burrowed my finger deeper into his ass. When the tip of him touched the back of my throat the next time, I stopped moving, no more craning my neck back and forth as I lost myself while he worked my prick with a tight fist and tighter lips. A few strokes more and I was there, a place I'd never imagined being—in Mack's hot mouth, my head swimming, my bones like water.

He gripped me hard and came off of me in one agonizing long suck. I flooded the loose condom and felt each spurt run back down to soak my balls. He cradled my fading stiffness until I recovered, then I went after him, pushing his cock in and out of my mouth with brutal speed. His ass contracted around my finger. My free hand caught his balls and he began to pound into me, fucking my face again. I didn't have to move my finger—he did all the work, forcing me in and out of that snug part of him my cock would probably never know. Then again, with all of his other changes, maybe one day I would.

A spasm shot through him. He pumped harder, his balls coming down on my nose so fast that I was panting as hard as he was just to keep breathing. He yelled when he came. I remembered the sound well, knew how loudly it echoed off bathhouse walls and other places we used to meet. He seemed more powerful then, nothing like the man who now dropped his full weight on me to rest his head on my hip.

"You miss the old days?" I asked. "I mean, this wasn't at all what I'd expected."

He got back on all fours and hung his head down to meet my eyes. He looked offended.

"Not that I was disappointed or anything," I added quickly, with a smile.

He smiled back at me, looking a little sadder. A little wiser. "You mean our glory days?"

"Yeah. If you want to call them that." What I wanted to know was did he miss the rough stuff and me being younger, more boy than man. Did he miss the parties and the wild, care-free sex? Those times were long gone. At least for me.

"Sometimes."

He turned around to face me, our limp cocks bumping under layers of latex. The tub was big enough for him to lie down in all the way and he pulled me to him, chest to chest.

"Things change. People change." As he said the words, he seemed to be searching my face for any sign of disappointment.

He wouldn't find a single trace, not today. Not with him beside me.

SOOTY

T. Hitman

The truck pulled up the last leg of the long, winding drive. It was big and white, masculine. A man's sort of truck. The silhouette of a soot-blackened chimney sweep was tattooed across the driver's side door. Tire treads chewed gravel, pine needles, and clumps of dirt on that final turn toward the house. Then the roar of its engine cut out; in the void, the ever-present sigh of the wind and the occasional croaking groan of an elder's trunk in the nearby woods resumed.

The man behind the wheel was a shadow, like the chimney sweep logo on the truck. He wore a baseball cap, bill aimed forward. Sunglasses created twin ovals of liquid silver in the shadow of the cab. He scrambled for a clipboard on the passenger side seat. Then the door opened, dispelling most of my questions. He was a short man dressed in a white T-shirt with a logo identical to the one on the truck's door, faded blue jeans, and soot-covered work boots. He closed the door. Temporary thunder shattered the calm. A man gets used to the quiet of remote places when he's been part of the landscape long enough. I had. My heart pulsed as he stared at the lodge, unaware that he, too, was being studied.

Eyes peering through the part in the blueberry curtains, I sized him up. Yeah, short. Not more than five-five, five-six. But cute. Really, truly damn cute! Short dark hair in an athletic cut beneath his ball cap. A bit of scruff from not shaving that day. The last trace of a tan from all his trips up to people's roofs. Little guy, with big muscles puffing on arms covered in patterns of dark hair. As he stretched and shifted the clipboard from one hand to the other, I caught a hint of dampness under an armpit. All the moisture drained from my mouth.

He approached the house. I straightened the curtains, hand-stenciled with a pattern of blueberries and leaves, and crossed to the door.

"Mister Ellis?" he said, a smile twisting his mouth. Flash of clean white teeth inside that playful smile.

"Mister Ellis is my dad. Call me Aaron." I opened the door, extending a hand to bid him welcome. As soon as he was inside the sunporch stretching half the length of the lodge, he made a similar gesture. We shook hands. Nice to meet you. Welcome to the town of Lonesome Oaks, so remote it doesn't appear on most maps. There was deceptive strength in that small, sexy hand. Electric pinpricks tingled up my arm and threatened to unleash a shiver down my spine.

"Wyatt," he said, his voice one of those masculine, playful growls that a guy who loves other guys could easily get used to hearing on a regular basis.

First thought: how that voice must sound in the bedroom, when breaking commandments and grunting alternate takes on Heaven.

Suck my hairy fuckin' cock! Yeah, like that. Now lick the

sweat off my nuts! Can't wait to bend you over. Fuck you in the cunt, fucker!

Second observation: those hands. Releasing the one he offered, I noticed soot on fingertips, beneath nails, and permanently etched into the flesh of his palm. Smaller than mine, but twice as powerful. Awesome hands, matching the rest of him.

"Nice to meet you, Wyatt."

His closeness washed the scent of soap, deodorant, and clean sweat around me. Beneath it was a smell that conjured happy memories of childhood winters. The first snow, woodstoves and fireplaces filling the cold air with a smoky bite.

Wyatt scanned his surroundings: the great room, extending past the open-concept kitchen; one accent wall painted a rich pomegranate red, another, eggplant-purple, with soft, soothing gray connecting everything together. Beautiful antique furniture. Shelves loaded with books. Writing desk, laptop computer open and humming atop it beside legal pad, uncapped pens. The screen on the computer, blank. A few lines scratched longhand across the legal pad—flat, lifeless prose destined for the paper-recycling bin on the sunporch. Some of my book covers blown up to poster size and framed on one wall, relics of a lost era. Even so, *home.*

"Great little house," Wyatt sighed.

"You should have seen it when I moved in."

"A mess?"

"That's being kind. I rescued the lodge from the wrecking ball. My realtor told me somebody wanted to knock it down and put up a McMansion. Can you imagine doing that to a house like this?"

I pointed out the wide pine floorboards, built-ins, exposed beams, and tile work. The fieldstone fireplace with airtight woodstove awaiting his care brought the tour to its conclusion.

"You've done a great job with the place."

"I'm not done yet. Still need to replace a floor, gut a bathroom, and get the chimney swept and repaired so I don't freeze my ass off come winter."

"Well, that's why I'm here."

More bullshitting about: wood heat, other houses in the area, New England winters, and the baseball playoffs. My eyes wandered over Wyatt's musculature. The T-shirt tucked into his belted blue jeans showcased taut stomach (probably hairy, too, if his arms were any indication). Decent legs. Feet, looking bigger than their actual size because of sooty work boots. The magnet of his package kept drawing my glances: nice, full relief of dick and balls packed in denim.

"Let me get cracking. It's supposed to cool down significantly over the weekend, as I heard it."

"Yeah," I babbled.

"Start out on the roof—"

"Sure. Just come back in when you're ready. No need to knock."

He nodded, tipped me a wandering glance from face to feet, then exited the house.

Sometimes, on rare occasions, a chemical spark goes off between two people upon their first meeting that is undeniable. It erupts thanks to scent receptors, and leaves you with that feeling of having your nuts squeezed by rough, fumbling fingers in lieu of words. It had for me. And, if that glance over the shoulder Wyatt shot me on his way out the door was to be trusted, the same was true for him.

Back at the blueberry curtains over the kitchen sink, I peered out the window. Wyatt removed the long aluminum ladder hanging on hooks above the bed of his truck. He unfolded it. Secured it in place. Scaled up to the lodge's roof, a long-handled chimney brush going up with him. As he ascended and I watched, the stain on his armpits looked damper, bigger. His crotch, so clearly displayed in the sunlight, passed between the ladder's rungs. Big feet next. A flash of sanitary white sock at the tops of both sooty work boots triggered a sensory rush of images in my head: clean cotton, toes damp with buttery sweat, a hint of pine sap caught like amber in the treads beneath the sole. My carnal foot-thoughts pushed my dick out of its coma into an erection so steely, it ached. I adjusted myself and saw stars.

Wyatt was shorter than me (not my usual type); blue collar (definitely my usual type); and mostly, probably straight, with just a hint of curiosity. The kind of guy who drank beer, peed in the woods (and over the edges of roofs on occasion, no doubt), hollered at the widescreen during baseball and football games, and secretly wandered through a wide range of fetishes and private perversions while masturbating. One of those jack-off concessions was probably allowing a dick-hungry writer at a remote lodge in the woods (me) the honor of humming on his erection. The chemical spark steadily consumed the rest of my body in the seconds that followed. On the sofa, out of focus, phantom versions of us moaned and fucked.

The clunk of booted feet on the roof played counterpoint to the drumming solo of my galloping heart. I fondled my hard-on, teased a finger against the sensitive flesh of my asshole. How long had it been since I'd joined the world of the living, except to shop for groceries or home-improvement supplies?

You're losing it, Aaron. You been living out here alone way too long.

The scrape of Wyatt's brush in the chimney slithered through the air, and even that to me sounded sexual, gloriously deviant. I was actually thinking about jerking myself to what promised to be a hell of a climax, if my length was any indication, when the clatter of falling metal jarred me out of my fantasy. A not-so-subtle reminder that both the house—and I—were far from complete in our restoration.

Cock half-hard, standing at the window, I saw: Piney, sniffable/lickable booted feet hasten down the ladder. Blue jeans and crotch followed next. White T-shirt lifted out of pants to show a magnificent stretch of tanned six-pack, treasure trail of coarse black hair bisecting it straight down the middle. Wyatt's sunglasses now rode the bill of his baseball cap as he hurried back into the house.

"I've got some bad news."

My inner-Aaron was used to such cries of doom. When you buy an old house and try to fix her up as a method of healing your own shit, bad news comes in bulk supply.

"There should have been a crown over your flue, shaped like this." Wyatt steepled his sooty hands together, forming a round dome. "The genius that put that *T*-joint up there left off the cement, which shields the flue from rain and snow. Which has been pouring down your chimney long enough to rot all that metal into rust. I shoved my—"

(...*dick up your sweet, tight ass, fucker!*)

"—brush down there and everything fuckin' came apart."

"Yeah, so I heard. Let me just say—"

(...*you won't be saying nothing, not with my cock stuffing your mouth shut and my sweaty nuts bouncing off your chin!*)

"—that nothing surprises me. I've already painted the place front to back, fixed and replaced doors, floors, plumbing, electrical. When I first moved in, I discovered that genius who owned the house before me had taken all the switch plates with him when he left. All the outlets were bare, too."

"No shit." Wyatt folded his arms. "Did you get a home inspection before you bought the place?"

"Naw, like I said, sold as is. The previous owner figured it would be a knock-down. Just because it was older, neglected, needed to be fixed...that's no reason to demolish the place, just to put up something newer, bigger, and better looking. Those houses are cookie-cutter cheap, and made of unnatural building materials."

"I thought you were talking about people there for a moment, not houses," Wyatt said.

"That, too."

Wyatt nodded, that snarl of a smile returning to his face. "Good news is it can be fixed."

It was a comfortable, sunny day, the last trace of an Indian summer edging toward a long New England winter. But in the lodge, the temperature was rising, despite the absence of a log fire.

"You need eighteen inches of stone board on your floor to bring it up to code."

"How many?" My eyes were on Wyatt's crotch when I asked this.

"Eighteen."

"That's a lot."

He snorted a laugh. His pen ceased scratching on his clipboard. He unashamedly adjusted his package. I tore my eyes off Wyatt's crotch and choked down a dry swallow. Yes, the heat was definitely rising. That whole chemical reaction thing we seemed to have going was like the flame of a lit match to pure oxygen. Only it felt stronger, nuclear, the Big Bang that started all life in the universe.

"It's not that big," he said, cutting through my fugue.

"Huh?"

"My dick," he said, his voice drawing out, distorting into a

feral growl. "You've been staring at it long enough, so you gotta
know it's pretty average."

A jolt of ice cut through the heat. Had I just heard him correctly?

Wyatt tugged on his zipper. Crisp white cotton appeared
among the denim, what I first mistook for simple tight-white
briefs. The clipboard vanished from his hands in a puff of dark
magic, there one instant, gone the next. Thus freed, he worked
his pants down to his knees. I saw he was wearing boxer briefs:
black elastic waistband, the cotton hugging concrete butt muscles in the back, expanded in front with meaty heaviness, leg
bands clamped around solid, hairy flesh.

"Fuck," I moaned, lowering to one knee on the aforemen-
tioned wide pine floorboards, not the most comfortable position,
but perfect for our present needs. "You handsome fucker..."

I pulled Wyatt's pants down to the tops of his sooty boots.
Showing the same ease with which he'd disposed of his clipboard, he unlaced them and kicked them off. I caught sight of a
big toe poking playfully through a hole in one white sock before
pressing my face into the warmth of his underwear. I inhaled the
musty smell of a real man's crotch and almost ejaculated without even touching my dick.

The intoxicating scent of balls; hard, sweaty cock; and lush
patch spoke to me. High on Wyatt's smell, I went on automatic.
One hand fondled the prominent bulge tenting his shorts. The
other stroked a length of hairy leg from calf to thigh. Wyatt
moaned. A sooty hand on the back of my skull held me in place.

"That's right, dude," he urged in that addictive voice, now
even more musical in its lust. "Suck on my dick. Yeah, I fuckin'
need this..."

You *need this?* my inner-Aaron chuckled. For a blinding instant, all the travails that had led me to this place made it past

the lodge's protective outer walls and were in the room with us. The stresses that had devoured my creativity, leaving me unable to write. A lover's betrayal. A death in the family. Breakdown. All of it swirling into one giant personal Perfect Storm. This was the most contact I'd had with another human being since coming here, walling myself up inside my little lodge deep in the woods.

Wyatt's underwear dropped to his sweat socks. His cock snapped up at attention. I inhaled the sweaty odor of his balls and smiled, leaned forward, sucked the straining head of his erection between my lips. The peehole was gummy with a trickle of clear, salty liquid. He was average, as he claimed, but thick, circumcised. A long blue vein snaked across the starboard side of his shaft. Like his voice, a man-loving man could easily get used to enjoying Wyatt's cock, balls, and lush dark thatch of hair on a regular basis.

One hand bracing on his leg for support, I closed my eyes and sucked Wyatt's cock down to the curls, inhaling the raw, wonderful odor of his balls between gulps. His erection flexed on my tongue, and for an instant I swore I could feel the pulse of circulation inside it, the blood and excitement surging through, spurred on by rapid heartbeats and lust for me. His cock was full of life, and having it in my mouth made me feel alive as well.

Reluctantly, I released it, but only to lick at his balls. My tongue explored the sensitive, smelly patch of skin behind his scrotum, and to my shock—and joy—Wyatt walked forward one giant step, over my face, permitting me access to the most private, secret part of him hidden back there. I swabbed my tongue over his asshole. The slightly metallic, primal taste my palate has never been able to get enough of consumed me. I stabbed higher, deeper.

Wyatt moaned in response, the sooty fingers of one hand raking my scalp. "Hot fucker! Damn, you're good…"

I grunted a breathless swear up into his hairy knot in agreement.

"...the *best!*"

He yanked his asshole off my lips and resumed plundering my mouth. A glop of precome dribbled down my chin. He leaked rivers, nectar of the gods. I sucked his dick, ogled his nuts, massaged a hairy calf with the hand that should have been trying to free my own dick from solitary confinement.

As if reading my thoughts, Wyatt grabbed hold of my shirt collar and shoved me onto the sofa. He tugged at my pants. A seam tore. Soon, the only stitches of clothing between the two of us were socks and Wyatt's baseball cap. A gust of cool air teased my naked butt. Fingers pried cheeks open, and the next breeze across my flesh was hot, rabid.

"*Oh, fuck,*" I grunted. He wasn't planning to—

But Wyatt did.

His tongue explored my hole with even more hunger than I'd shown his. He didn't touch my dick; he didn't have to. Then his weight upon my back, the pressure-filled thrusts, each equal parts pain and pleasure, forced my erection into the sofa cushion. Bent over the arm in much the same position as I'd imagined us in not long before, I felt the drag and slap of his swollen balls against my backside, was mystified by their cadence; his warm breath, now puffing at my ear; the prickle of his unshaved face on my neck. That voice! So easy on the ears, the brain. The brain, biggest sex organ of them all...

"I said it's not that big."

I blinked myself out of the trance. Wyatt stood holding the clipboard and pen. T-shirt covering his chest. Denim over dick. Work boots on feet.

"Huh?" I asked, dazed.

"The job. It's a day's work. But it's not going to be cheap to replace that flue, get some proper cement up there on your chimney, and bring you up to code. You're looking at twelve hundred bucks. And this is a tight time of the year for me. End of summer, with it getting cold out. Every sweep and mason in this part of the world is booked solid through Christmas."

I barely heard Wyatt's words. The effect of the powerful daydream, which had pushed my cock out of its stupor and into the biggest erection I could remember having since puberty, trumped any bad news about this latest in an endless succession of repair jobs. My creativity, incorrectly believed extinct, had reasserted itself. Like the lodge rescued from the wrecking ball, it was coming alive again, and Wyatt was my muse.

He must have mistaken the look on my face for horror when, in fact, it was total awe. "Tell you what," he continued. "I was planning to take the weekend off. Chill out. Drink some beer. Watch the baseball playoffs. You like baseball?"

"I like baseball."

"I could knock out replacing the flue, get the necessaries installed to bring you up to code. Then we could hang out here, have a few, watch the game. Whatever."

"You'd do that?"

Wyatt's eyes circled the room, found their way back to me. "This is a great house. I could get used to spending some time here."

"You're always welcome to hang out."

"I'd like that," Wyatt said, the snarl of that sexy smile playing crookedly at one corner of his mouth. "Friends can be few and far between up here in this neck of the woods, if you know what I mean."

I nodded.

"Be back first thing tomorrow."

On his way toward the door, Wyatt tucked the clipboard under an armpit and clapped his free hand against my butt in what would have been a typical safe and friendly gesture between guys had his fingers not lingered a second longer than what could be viewed as innocent, and his eyes not checked me out with a lust-filled glance.

And this time, I didn't imagine it.

THE
LANDSCAPE
GUY

David Holly

For the past four hours, I had been peeking out the kitchen window at the landscape guy who was bossing a group of flunkies. The flunkies were using shovels and machines to dig holes in my parents' yard. About every forty-five minutes, trucks arrived loaded with full-grown trees and massive bushes, and while the flunkies righted the foliage in the holes, the landscape guy consulted blueprints and shouted. Of course, I could have told that the landscape guy was the boss even if he hadn't been the only one doing no actual physical labor. The flunkies were wearing dirty yellow hard hats and the landscape guy was wearing a flashy clean white one.

The landscape guy not only acted differently from his crew, but he looked different. The workers had big stomachs that made their jeans ride down in the back so that they were constantly exposing the cracks of their fat hairy butts. Since the landscape guy's chest and ass were bigger than his waist, his clothes fit. Did they ever fit—I was drooling into the sink over the way his clothes fit. His T-shirt and jeans were tight, particularly the jeans, which were real cookie cutters that showed off a nice set of manly curves and an even more enticing package in the front. I would not have minded seeing the landscape guy's butt crack, and as for the rest—yeah!

Though my attention was riveted on his lower body, particularly his cock and balls, I still gave some consideration to his powerful chest, brawny arms, and mighty shoulders. He had a handsome tanned face, and thick chestnut hair with blond streaks. As he pointed toward spots in the yard that set his men to digging, his rounded butt muscles tightened. I imagined that powerful ass driving his thick shaft right into me and nearly creamed my shorts.

I looked at the kitchen clock hopefully. I'd last carried lemonade to the workers forty-five minutes earlier. The garbage bin was nearly overflowing with squeezed lemons from my three previous trips outside to refresh the workers. I just had to wait another fifteen minutes.

I managed to wait ten. By then I had another batch of lemons squeezed and I had filled tumblers with ice and red cherries. I poured in the lemonade and added a garnish of orange slices and mint. Before going outside with the tray, I again checked my appearance in the hall mirror. I still looked like a fresh-faced college sophomore, though there was a touch of self-indulgence beginning in the corners of my eyes. I no longer looked the dewy virgin of my teens, but perhaps that was to the good (so long as I didn't age any more). My hot red tennis shorts fit my ass just so, and my white Adidas shirt enhanced my torso.

"Tighten your zippers," shouted one of the yellow hats as I crossed the half-excavated yard carrying their tumblers on a bamboo tray. "Here he comes again."

I couldn't see the landscape guy's face, but his workers

thought the joke hilarious. My hands shook, and I dropped the tray into the fresh-turned earth. Turning, I raced back into the house and upstairs, where I threw myself facedown on my bed and wept bitterly.

I had not been sprawled there long before I heard a soft noise from the hall. I lifted my face from my tear-damp pillow and saw the landscape guy framed in my doorway.

"I'm sorry about my guys, Rich," he said. "I wish they hadn't hurt your feelings, but you gotta understand that being gay is a big joke with them."

The landscape guy knew my name! Of course, my parents would have told him when they hired him just before departing on a two-month cruise and leaving me at home to suffer through all the remodeling. But he had remembered.

"You know I'm gay?" I asked.

His face reddened. "Shit, sorry."

What was he apologizing for? I wondered. "What aren't you telling me?" I asked.

Amazingly, he entered my room and sat down on my bed. "You know how guys talk," he said.

"Sure," I agreed, having no idea what he was on about.

"It's kind of a story going around," the landscape guy admitted. "About how you've gotten all the workmen to...uh...well, you know."

"Huh?"

The landscape guy drew a deep breath. "That you got them to fuck you—in the ass. The drywall hanger. The contractor. The plumber. The electrician. The roofer. The painter. Even that weird cabinetmaker."

"Not all at once," I protested. "Not even all in the same week."

"Holy shit. You mean it's true?"

"Uh, yeah," I said. "I did have sex with those guys. I'm surprised that they bragged about it."

"Maybe they didn't," the landscape guy said with an enigmatic smile. "Maybe I was just seeing how you'd respond."

"What?" I asked hopefully. Did he mean what I was hoping he meant?

He was. Though it turned out not exactly in the way I thought. His next words were music to my ears.

"I like a little ass action myself," the landscape guy said, reaching out and touching me for the first time.

Promptly my cock stiffened in my shorts. I rolled onto my side and touched the landscape guy's cock through his tight jeans. "You can fuck me," I said. "I'd like that. I have condoms and lubricant in that drawer right next to you."

The landscape guy opened the drawer and pulled out the suggested items including a couple of my best butt plugs and anal vibrators. "Nice toys," he said. "But you don't get it, Rich. I might fuck your ass if I feel like it. But first you gotta fuck mine."

That was a situation I'd never considered. I'd always been the bottom. Always. Nobody had ever asked me to play the top. "Are you sure?"

"I'm sure, college boy. You're gonna piss with the big dogs this time. I 'spect you to cornhole me like a boss sticking it to a day laborer."

So saying, the landscape guy started to undress. He removed his white hard hat and pulled his T-shirt over his head. His muscles rippled under his light downy chest hair. "My name's Bob, by the way. We oughta get names straight between us before we commence to fucking."

I was too thunderstruck to respond. At least I couldn't speak, though my cock was responding superbly. Bob the landscape guy had politely removed his work boots before coming upstairs, so only heavy white socks covered his feet. He pulled those off before standing to unfasten his jeans. I rubbed my cock through my tennis shorts as I watched Bob push down his jeans. A pair of almost pristine Jockey briefs hove into view, briefs so distended that they pulled boldly into his rear.

"Just look at that crack," Bob suggested, turning so I could see his ass. "In a few minutes you're gonna have your fuckin' dick right up there."

In my excitement, I nearly tore my shirt getting it over my head. Then I rolled back and pushed down my shorts and underpants together. It hadn't been this way with the other workmen my parents had hired. I had to come on to them, seducing them by degrees until they were so horny they couldn't resist fucking me. Bob was working off a totally different script.

"Whoa, that's a nice pecker you got there, Rich," Bob said. I hadn't realized it before, but my dick was a tad larger than Bob's. Not that there was anything wrong with Bob's. It was standing tall and looked plenty thick and even tasty.

"Here, now, college boy," Bob protested. "That weren't what I had in mind." His protest was rather feeble, however, and he did not try to push me off his prick. He let me kiss the head of it, lick down the shaft, and even suck on it a bit. Finally, though, he decided that I had sucked enough.

"You can't sidetrack me from my aim," he said, gently raising my head from his cock. He threw himself facedown on my bed and drew up his left leg. "Why don't you just slip some of that lube into my ass. Maybe use one of them plugs on me a bit."

His asshole was a brownish bud winking at me. I dolloped some lubricant onto it with my finger, and then I lubed my smallest butt plug. I didn't know how much experience Bob had, and I certainly did not want to cause him pain. My own first fuck had been slow and gentle, so pleasant that I wanted that same experience time after time. Of course, I'd had so much penetration since then that I could have accommodated King Kong, had the big monkey been gay.

I eased the plug into Bob's anal sphincter, which opened readily. Bob sighed as I pushed it into him and slowly fucked his asshole with it. "That's nice, but I can take a bigger one," he said.

"Okay, but I want you to slip one into my ass too, so I can hold it in while I work on you," I suggested.

"You stick it into your own ass while I watch," Bob countered. "I want to see you pop it into your ass."

Nodding in compliance, I selected an anal vibrator, lubed it well, rolled onto my back, pulled my legs up, and positioned the thing against my asshole. It was already vibrating merrily with a loud humming throb. Bob's eyes were bright with glee as he watched it disappear into my asshole. I closed my eyes in bliss as I pushed it in, and I nearly shot a load as my asshole opened around the vibrating mass and the throbbing lip reached my prostate.

"Oh, fuck me," I moaned.

"You still gotta fuck me first," Bob demanded.

The vibrations were urging me toward greater acts of lust, so I picked up another vibrator, one equal in size to the one I was holding up my rear, turned it up full power, and pushed it into Bob's ass. He howled with joy.

"Oh, fuck, yeah," Bob moaned. "Fuck me with that thing, college boy."

Bob really knew how to take it, so I fucked him hard with the vibrator, sometimes massaging him deep, and other times shallow. Then I would find his prostate and hold the toy in place until he was close to coming. My own cock was leaking a thin stream, and I knew that if I was ever going to have the experience of fucking a man's ass, the time had arrived. I lubed my dick and slid an extrastrength condom onto it.

Holding the vibrator in my own ass with one hand, I used my other to remove the one in Bob's ass and then position my cock against his butthole. The landscape guy was open and ready for me. "Shove your cock into me, college boy," he wailed in the extremity of his lust. "Fuck me 'til I can't walk."

His asshole was hot and rough. Even through the condom, I could feel the friction as I pushed with my own ass. The vibrator up my ass was trying to come out as I drove my hips downward. I tried to hold it in with one hand as I bored into Bob's ass. Then I was in him all the way, feeling as I never had before and lusting to come inside of him just as all those other men had come in me. I raised my ass and humped downward. Up and down I rose until I lost hold of the vibrator and it flew out of my ass with a popping sound. At that point, I wasn't about to go looking for it. I continued humping while Bob continued to moan, demanding that I fuck him hard and fast.

"Fuck me like I'm a girl," he howled, which was a bit of a turn-off, but I ignored the sentiment and continued humping him.

"Take it like a man," I quoted. "When you're butt-fucked, you'll take it and like it."

"I fuckin' like it," he howled. "Give it to me harder, college boy. Fuck me 'til I come."

I didn't know about making the landscape guy come, but my exertions were about to make me come. I could hardly believe it—I who had always played the bottom, who had been the one with the cock in his ass while the other guy howled with pleasure, not that some of them hadn't brought me around—I was just about to shoot my load into a guy's ass, an absolute first. The deep tingles had already started in the head of my cock. Bob's moans were virtually unheard. He could have cried out for mercy then and I would have ignored him. I was committed to orgasm and ejaculation. I humped him harder, thrusting wildly in his ass as he moaned and howled with joy, and the rapturous tingles traveled up my cock and through my pelvis. My asshole was throbbing, my nipples were crinkling, my eyelids were fluttering, and my lips were curling back into a snarl.

Then the powerful muscles at the base of my cock contracted and I shot my first splat of hot semen into the condom buried deep in the landscape guy. I fucked him harder and faster as I shot my load and the strong spasms shook me. Waves of pleasure washed over me, their undercurrents pulling my whole body into giving up its bounty. Storms seemed to be blasting my brain, for I could not think. I was thunder, lightning, hailstorms, tornadoes of passion as I blasted my hot spunk into Bob's ass.

Then I sprawled beside him, the rubber pulled from my dick and deposited in the wastebasket. My breath came in gasps and my heart thundered as if after a hard workout in the gym.

"That was a great fuck," I managed.

"Most gratifying," the landscape guy echoed.

As my breathing eased, I propped up on one arm and let my hand glide over the mounds of his most gratifying ass.

"Tell me something, Bob," I urged.

"What would you like to know, Rich?"

"Well," I stalled, wondering how to broach the subject delicately. "It regards your grammar and diction."

"Ah, that," he said, rolling over and grinning at me. "You noted some inconsistencies?"

"More than a few. When you first spoke to me, you spoke fairly normally. Then you degenerated into a hick. You know, calling me 'college boy' and using words like 'cornhole.' Now you're talking like a college professor."

"I was speaking crudely earlier to enhance your experience. Let the wealthy blue blood bang the ignorant hard hat."

"Wearing the hard hat doesn't make you ignorant."

"Of course not. I have a bachelor's in ornamental horticulture and a master's in landscape architecture from Ohio State University. And, yes, I did teach some courses there while I was working on my graduate degree."

Somehow, he had been just a bit more exciting when I thought him ignorant. Noticing my slight disappointment, Bob suddenly pulled me close and kissed my mouth. His hot tongue slid into my mouth and warred with mine. I could feel his hands on my shoulders, before they traced gently down my back until he reached my ass. He went on kissing me while both hands fondled my buttocks.

"Oh, I want you inside of me," I moaned when I could get a breath. "I want you to take me. Fuck me."

"Just like you fucked me?" he asked.

"You won't need to use a vibrator. Just your big cock will serve." I didn't want to waste time on preliminaries; though the vibrator was always fun, I could play with it when I was alone. I wanted real man-flesh inside of me.

"Why don't you prop your back against the headboard," I urged. "I'd like to sit on your dick."

Bob complied, so I anointed his cock with lubricant. Though I had touched many cocks in my lifetime, his gave me a thrill like the buzz I received when I handled my first. I almost hated to wrap it, but I tore open another extrastrength condom and unrolled it onto Bob's cock.

My asshole was already lubed from the vibrator, so I smeared a light coat on the outside of Bob's condom. Bob leaked a bit of precome into the condom while I stroked it with my hand.

"Are you going to sit with your back to me, or will you face me?" Bob asked.

"First with my back to you," I said. "After a minute, you can slide

your ass down the bed a bit and I'll sit on your dick facing you."
Bob held me as I lowered my ass onto his cock. His mighty
upper body strength came in handy, for he could hold me up
while I positioned my asshole on the head of his cock. When
I had the right spot, he let gravity lower me onto him, and I
pushed hard with my anal sphincter to open it up and let him in.
Again I felt that wonderful fullness of a hard cock in my ass.

"You're taking it all the way, Rich," Bob assured me. I rocked
forward and back, gently fucking his dick with my ass. My asshole was hot and wide open, stretched around his thick shaft.

"Oh, that's good," Bob moaned. "I could shoot my load this
way in no time."

"You want to?" I asked.

"No, I'd still prefer you facing me. I want to look into your
eyes when I come in your ass."

"I'd like that," I said. "Help me raise off of it."

In a twinkling, we had repositioned. Balancing with both
hands gripping Bob's shoulders, I slowly lowered myself toward
his cock while he guided my ass. I felt his cockhead against my
hot hole; then it was sliding inside again as I rode it down until
my buttocks were sitting solid on his loins. His eyes were shining with delight, and through the full delightful fuck, my eyes
never left his.

As I rocked to and fro on his cock, I watched Bob's nostrils
flare and his face flush with exertion. Pulling me forward so that
only the tip of his cock was still inside my asshole, he brought
his lips to mine and slid his tongue between them. I sucked his
tongue while I rocked lightly on the head of his cock.

I felt rather than heard the keening sound rising in Bob's
throat at the same instant he began thrusting his cock upward
with greater urgency. I let his tongue slip from my mouth as I
slid back down his cock. Rising and falling on it, I tightened my

asshole on the upstrokes and relaxed on the down.

"Oh, this is it, Rich," Bob wailed. "Oh, yes, I'm gonna come in your ass. Oh, yeah. Here it goes, Rich. Here it goes."

I rocked upon his cock wildly as he tried to thrust upward. I could see the wild light of orgasm in his eyes, and indeed, I was nearly ejaculating again myself. My cock was so hard and swollen that I could not resist grabbing it. Just the slight touch of my fingers on the head of my cock set me off. My second orgasm bit deeper than my first. My first had been a storm, and this was a room filled with violets. Still, I ejaculated freely, my semen splattering onto Bob's muscular chest while he filled the condom in my ass.

After that fantastic fuck, Bob and I had to take a hot, lingering shower. When I had toweled him off, he dressed and looked out the window.

"I better get back down below," he said reluctantly. "Those guys are slacking off. I have to watch them every instant."

"I wonder what they think you've been doing?" I asked.

"Who cares what they think?" Bob said. "That was great, Rich." So saying, he pulled me close and kissed me hard. Then without another word, he was down the stairs, and after a quick stop to pull on his shoes, he was out the door and hollering at his crew.

"Quit loafin'," he yelled. "Them bushes ain't gonna plant theirselves." Watching out my window, I could only laugh.

During that summer, I seduced most of the workmen my parents had hired to remodel the house and the grounds. Roofers, wallpaper hangers, painters, stonemasons, and chimney sweeps found relief for their itchy cocks in my eager ass, enough that I cannot remember them all, if I ever knew their names. However, one I will never forget. For the rest of my days, I will remember the afternoon I diddled with Bob, the landscape guy.

DANIEL IN THE LYONS DEN

Neil Plakcy

Though my degree was in business, the only job I could get after graduation was as an assistant project manager on a new shopping center construction site. I felt like an idiot, walking around the site in a total fog. What did I know about site plans, transformers, sewage inlets? But I did know how to use Microsoft Project for scheduling, and that's why they hired me.

I spent most of the day in a tiny office in a trailer, sitting in front of a computer plugging in variables. The form work couldn't begin until the site was graded. The concrete pour couldn't begin until the first set of forms was finished. The details were enough to make my head spin.

Occasionally I had to go out on-site and talk to the contractors, to find out how long the grading would take, and how the projections for rain might affect the schedule. The worst guy to talk to was the site foreman, Joe Lyons. He was a tall, sinewy guy, close to forty, with a raspy cigarette voice and a potty mouth that would make a sailor blush.

His most common greeting was "Fuck you," to which, I learned, the correct response was "You'll never go back to dogs." I couldn't say anything like that; Joe Lyons had me quaking in my Timberlands and my dick tenting my khakis. He was just the kind of guy I went for: a tough, sexy daddy with muscles and attitude.

It was always tough to mumble out my question and then, with a shaking hand, scribble down his response. Then I'd hurry back to my office, desperate to beat off in the john. But the trailer was rickety and the walls paper thin, and if you spent too long on the toilet somebody was always banging on the door accusing you of beating your meat.

It didn't help matters that in the middle of July, most of the guys on-site were shirtless, many of them wearing shorts so tight they were molded to their sculpted asses. There was more testosterone and muscle mass on the site than you'd find in any city gym, and the guys were always teasing each other about pieces of ass, dick size, and stamina.

The contractors knocked off at three-thirty, though the superintendents, like Joe Lyons, were often around for a few hours longer. One Friday afternoon, with thunderheads looming over the site, my boss stuck his head in my office and said, "I want to know what's going to happen to our form build-out schedule on Monday if we get a downpour this weekend."

"I'll get right on it," I said. Forms are wooden molds that hold the concrete in place until it sets. We'd had a crew of laborers out all week, digging trenches and hammering the forms together. We were supposed to begin pouring concrete on the exterior walls of the west wing of the mall on Monday morning, with the form workers keeping ahead of the concrete.

If the forms got washed out over the weekend, it would throw the whole schedule off, leading to a cascading effect on all the other trades. It could be a serious setback.

I found Joe Lyons just stepping out of the RV he had parked at the edge of the site. Most of the contractors and foremen were local, but Joe moved around from city to city and site to site, living in an RV that he hooked up to site utilities. "I need to ask you about the pour schedule for Monday," I said, barely getting the words out.

"Already two steps in front of you, peckerhead," he said. "I'm going out to inspect the forms right now, see how I think they'll hold up if we get a gully washer. You can tag along."

The ground was already wet from a morning thundershower, and my boots kept getting stuck in the mud as I followed him across the site. Maybe it was just that I was paying more attention to the snug fit of his jeans over his tight ass than where I was stepping. I loved the way the two mounds of his ass moved when he walked, the confident swing of his shoulders.

We came to the start of the form work, and he said, "What the fuck, over." Lots of the guys spoke in this kind of quasi radio language, even when face-to-face, and it always threw me. Plus, the testosterone Joe Lyons generated just standing there was enough to make me tongue-tied.

I looked down at the trench and saw that there were varying distances between the edge of the trench and the start of the form work. In some cases, the trench was just wide enough for the forms. In others, there were six or eight inches between the side of the form and the edge of the trench.

"Is it supposed to be like that?" I asked. I fumbled over describing what I saw.

Joe Lyons gave me an appraising look, the corner of his mouth turning up in what might have been a smile. "There might be some hope for you yet, peckerhead."

He squatted down and motioned for me to do the same. He explained what would happen to the forms and the trenches if it rained, and how long the damage would set back the schedule.

Joe Lyons was so near I could smell the tobacco on his breath and a faint trace of his cologne. Leaning over me to point something out, his face was so close I could have kissed him.

And gotten my ass kicked, I was sure. Joe Lyons exuded a sexy machismo, and I knew from the ribbing he got around the site that he was quite a cocksman. The ladies were allegedly lined up for a piece of his sausage.

And speaking of that, I looked down at his thighs and saw his meat outlined against the taut fabric of his jeans. It had to be eight inches long, thick as a salami. It made me even more nervous to squat there next to him, and I lost my balance, almost tumbling into the ditch in front of us.

He reached out and grabbed my arm, and I fell back against him. For a moment, he held his arm around my shoulder, and I nearly melted under the strength of his grip. "You all right, peckerhead?" he asked.

"You bet," I said, standing up. The best part was that I understood everything he'd said. I was amazed. I guess I wasn't so dumb after all. If somebody just explained something to me, I could get it.

I wrote down everything I needed and hurried back to the trailer to work on my schedules. I was so caught up that I didn't notice the rest of the trailer emptying out. It was Friday afternoon, and they were all ready to party at the local bar, the Cranberry Bog. Nobody'd stopped to invite me, and it wasn't until I looked up after a deep clap of thunder that I realized I was alone.

When I finished, I saved my work and closed down my computer. Just as I stood, the trailer's metal roof began rattling with a noisy downpour. Looking out through the front window, I saw the rain sheeting down and knew I'd be soaked through before I made it to my car.

Staring out at the rain, I noticed Joe Lyons come running across the site. He'd obviously been caught out at the far edge of the property, looking at something. Even at a distance, I could see how the rain had soaked through his shirt and jeans, molding them to his body. He might have been slim, but he was a hell of a muscular guy. Watching him lope along was like seeing poetry in motion, and my dick stiffened up in a heartbeat.

Then I saw him go down. The edge of a big drainage ditch at one end of the site, adjacent to his trailer, gave way under his feet. He slipped and slid down into the gully.

Without even thinking, I dashed out the door of the trailer and headed toward Joe. My light cotton shirt and khakis were soaked in a minute but I didn't notice.

I'd done some junior lifesaving in high school, and I could pull a drowning swimmer out of a pool and administer CPR. So when I saw Joe Lyons lying facedown in the muddy ditch, I jumped in beside him and lifted his head out of the water. He wasn't breathing, so I pinched his nostrils shut and started mouth-to-mouth resuscitation.

The rain poured down around us, plastering my hair to my forehead and my thin shirt to my back. But I shut it all out to focus on Joe. In a minute, he was coughing up water. I was kneeling on the ground, holding his upper body in my arms, when he looked up at me. "What the fuck, over?" he croaked.

This time I knew what to say. "You fell into the ditch, numb nuts," I said. "I had to rescue your scrawny ass."

He started laughing, which turned into a choking cough. "I might need some more of that mouth-to-mouth," he sputtered.

I was only too happy to oblige. Only what I was really doing was kissing him—and he was kissing me back. He wrapped his arms around my back and pressed himself against me, as the rain poured down on us. Most of him was covered in mud, and that rubbed off on me.

Finally he looked up at the sky. "We'd better get the hell out of here before this whole ditch collapses on us," he said. He stood up, still shaky on his feet, and tried to climb out. He was having trouble until I put my hands on his sweet, tight ass and pushed.

Up he went. I scrambled up beside him. "Shit all to hell," he said. "We look like a pair of dirty, drowned rats. You'd better come into my trailer and get cleaned up."

He got no argument from me. I followed him across the site, peeling off my shirt as I saw him do. When we reached the door of his RV, he said, "No way either of us are going in my house like this," and he reached down to untie his boots. In a moment they were off, his white socks, stained brown with mud, right after. Then he shucked down his jeans, and I could see that his white briefs were soaked through.

"Come on, what are you waiting for?" he said, as he stripped the briefs off.

While I stripped down, he stood out in the rain, buck naked, letting the water cascade around him and wash away every bit of dirt. His dick was stiff and his nipples erect as the rain beat down on him. He even bent over, opening up his asshole and letting the water stream in.

Oh, man, to be that water!

We were alone on the big empty construction site, the steel skeleton of the east wing looming over us. The trenches containing the forms were filled with water, and thunder crackled in the distance. But it was nothing compared to the sexual tension coming off Joe Lyons.

He stood up and bundled his filthy clothes with mine as I let the water rinse me clean. Then he opened the door of the RV and stepped inside. "Come on, peckerhead," he said. "I ain't got all night."

I stepped right in behind him and closed the door. He stalked ahead to a small washing machine and dropped the clothes inside. Then he threw me a towel, and began to dry himself off. When I finished, I wrapped the towel around my waist. He didn't, though; he dropped his in the washer.

As if we were naked in front of each other all the time, he took his time, measuring soap, setting dials. Then he turned to me. "You can't stay wrapped up in that wet towel," he said. "You'll catch pneumonia. Hand it over."

I tossed it to him. He dropped it in the washer, closed the lid, and turned it on. Then he walked over to me.

"You're shivering," he said. "Shit all to hell. I'd better warm you up."

He wrapped his arms around me again, the way he'd done in the ditch, and pressed his lips to mine. I couldn't get close enough to him; I tried to wrap my leg around behind his butt and press him into me.

He led me to the bed at the back of the RV, then pushed me down on it. In a moment he was on top of me, all his sinewy muscle pressing against me, skin to skin. Our dicks rubbed together as he slid his body up and down over mine, keeping his eyes locked on mine. We built up heat that way, our two damp bodies moving against each other, until my skin felt like it was burning in a hundred places.

Then he sat back on his haunches, leaving his stiff dick facing me. I leaned down and took him in my mouth. He tasted clean and fresh, like rainwater with a touch of salt. He rubbed his fingers through my wet hair and said, "What the fuck, over."

I responded the best way I knew how, by sucking him until I felt his body start to stiffen; then I pulled back. "I want you to fuck me," I said, twisting around and presenting him with my butt.

"Damn, that is one sweet ass," he said. He reached into a drawer next to the bed and pulled out a bottle of lube and a rubber. I heard the packet tearing, and then felt something cold and wet squirt up my ass. Quickly it warmed up as he entered me with a finger, then two.

I could barely catch my breath. I felt myself panting, heard myself whimper, "Fuck me, please."

"You'll never go back to dogs," he said, and plunged his thick hard cock into me. There was a moment of pain, and then the most intense pleasure, as I felt his body connecting with mine, his groin slamming against my ass, his hot breath on my back.

He couldn't hold out for long, and suddenly, he was howling, like a wolf in heat, as he made one last push up my chute. "Damn, you are one hot little peckerhead," he said, pulling out. His calloused hands reached down to my shoulders and flipped me over, so I was facing him again.

His dick was still leaking cum as he leaned down and kissed me again. Then he said, "Let's see what kind of pecker you've got, peckerhead," and he took my dick in his mouth and started sucking.

I came almost immediately, and he swallowed every drop. Then he flopped down next to me, snaking one long muscular leg over mine. The rain was still pounding the roof of the RV. "Ain't no way we're going out in this weather," he said.

"I can stay right here," I said, snuggling up against him. "Though I could use a beer."

He laughed. "Demanding little peckerhead, ain't you?"

"Hell, you haven't seen demanding," I said. "I'm just giving you time to catch your breath and wet your whistle, then I'll be demanding that dick again."

"I can see we're gonna be working together a lot, peckerhead," he said.

FOOT BRIDGE

Landon Dixon

'm the boss of a road repair crew for a private construction outfit. We do a lot of work for the state of South Dakota, watering and oiling down dirt roads, spreading asphalt and pouring concrete on highways, and shoring up vehicle and pedestrian overpasses. The work's hard and usually hot, but the pay's good and the fringe benefits are often more than even I bargained for.

Come early summer we get the greenhorns fresh out of high school or on break from college to spell off the regular guys on vacation. It's my job to break these new guys in; in some cases, make 'em or break 'em. Like Rafael, from this summer just past.

"What would you like me to do, Mr. Hunter?" he asked, once we'd spilled out of the crew cab and into a blazing dawn out on Highway 14.

"First off, I'd like you to call me Dave," I said.

The guy looked like he was built more for office work than highway work. He was maybe five-eight, slim, with skinny arms and legs that were wrapped up in a plaid cotton work shirt and green nylon work pants, despite the ninety-plus heat. His black hair was cut short, his eyes were brown and intelligent, and he had an almost delicate-featured face.

"You'll be shoveling and spreading asphalt. It's gonna be hot and it's gonna stink," I told him, pulling no punches. It was the worst job available, but that's where I start all the new men, and women.

He nodded downright eagerly, and we started unloading the truck. Then we sat around on our asses, scarfing down the coffee and donuts we'd bought in Montgomery, waiting for the machine operators to show up. When they finally did, we got down to the serious work of resurfacing an overpass that carried vehicle and foot traffic over the highway.

Twelve sweat-soaked, lung-burning hours later, we broke for the day. We piled back into the truck and headed for town. Rafael and the other four guys in my crew zonked out as soon as they hit the bench seats, and stayed that way for the twenty-mile drive in. I was plenty tired myself, but I wasn't going to let the guys see it. I may be pushing way past fifty, my crew cut as gray as it's out of style, but I can still lay down a hard week's work on the road with the best of them. As Nana used to say, "That one, he built like a brick shithouse, and just as dependable."

When we eventually rolled into the Come 'N' Stay Motel, the woman tenting the muumuu behind the counter informed us that we were all sharing rooms instead of getting singles. The new girl back at the office had screwed up our normal sleeping arrangements. I quickly claimed Rafael as my bunk mate. He'd been the lightest snorer on the ride back to town.

I tossed my gear onto one of the queen-sized beds and said, "Gonna grab a quick shower. Then we can go and get some chow."

"Sure," Rafael responded, setting down his own bag.

I turned the jets on full blast, relaxed under the hot spray, and let the water soak into my sore muscles. After ten minutes or so, I reluctantly stepped out of the tub, toweled off, and padded back into the room to throw on a clean shirt and a clean pair of pants. And that's when I got a couple of surprises.

One, Rafael hadn't cranked on the air-conditioning, and the room was stiflingly hot, humid with steam. And two, the young guy was stretched out on his bed in just his underwear, watching TV, his bronze legs gleaming smooth and taut, his golden-brown feet crossed and wickedly arched.

I had to stop and catch my breath. What does it for me, what's done it for me ever since I was a Boy Scout in hot pants, is a well-turned pair of legs with a pair of shapely peds attached. I've been worshipping male lower limbs and feet for fifty years and counting, got the footprints on my dick to prove it.

"All done in the bathroom, Mr.—Dave?" Rafael asked.

"Huh?" My eyes were running up and down the guy's toned, caramel legs, following the curved contours of his feet, bouncing over his slender, wriggling toes.

"Can I use the bathroom now?" he said, his eyes leaving my face, shifting lower. And that's when I noticed that my cock, which had been dangling between my legs with the nonchalance of casual roommate nudity, had suddenly stiffened up, as it took closer note of things. "Huh? Oh, yeah, sure," I mumbled.

He slid off the bed. I followed his flashing legs past me and into the bathroom, watching the muscles ripple sensuously on the shiny limbs. He popped his head out the door, looked me directly in the cock, and said, "We'll get something…to eat after I'm done, right, Dave?"

"Riiight," I breathed. The door closed again. My cock was a hardened slab of meat, rising up and sniffing the steamy air. I

met it with a warm, accommodating palm. The sound of running water and young man laughter filled my reddened ears, as
I vigorously fisted.

I inhaled soup, salad, steak, and baked potato.

"Jeez, you're sure hungry tonight, boss," Fat Manny commented, mopping up the remains of his own thirty-two ouncer.

"Yeah, hungry," I mouthed, staring at Rafael across the table.

"We're gonna try out that new bar on the corner. You
comin'?"

"Nah, I don't think so. I'm gonna take a dip in the pool, hit
the sack early. How 'bout you, Rafael?"

"A swim sounds great," he responded, poking at his inch-
thick wedge of semiraw beef.

Manny snorted, said, "You kids behave yourself," as he
pushed the table away from his gut and heaved to his feet. He
and the other guys trundled off down the empty street toward
the neon oasis, while Rafael and I legged it back to the motel.

The Come 'N' Stay had a scenic view of the interstate on one
side, the bald prairie on the back side. But it did boast an in-
ground swimming pool and Jacuzzi tucked away in a corner of
the three separate buildings that made up the place. And when I
watched Rafael stroll out of the bathroom in his bathing suit—a
red Speedo that bulged in all the right places—his legs stretching
out long and lean, his small, tender feet tiptoeing through the
carpet, I vowed to heat up that pool and soak tub way past their
normal temps.

Rafael's body was smooth as a sheet of copper, slender but
wiry, his nipples dark like his eyes. I trailed after his bouncing
bottom, his swishing legs, as they and he made their way out of
the motel and into the green water of the medium-sized swimming pool.

It was just before ten, the temperature still hovering in the low nineties, but we had the pool all to ourselves (after I'd shooed away a couple of kids who should've been in bed by then). We swam four or five laps, me right on Rafael's tail, following in the wake of his kicking, pale-padded feet, his churning, glistening legs. Then we paused to catch our breath in the deep end, and I splashed water in Rafael's face.

"Hey!" he yelped. He grabbed on to the silver ladder at the edge of the pool and lay out on his back, kicked water in my face.

My mouth was hanging so far open, watching those playful peds kick out at me, those golden legs flex on the surface of the froth, that I almost drowned. I spat chlorinated water and grabbed hold of one of his mischievous feet, then the other. He thrashed his legs around, but no way was I letting go.

His feet were warm and wet, incredibly smooth and soft, exquisitely curved. They were almost dainty in their elegance, and I gripped and squeezed them, thumbed their bottoms, my cock and resolve hardening. Rafael stopped struggling and stared at me with his liquid-brown eyes, floating on the surface of the suddenly stilled water. The "deep end" was less than six feet deep, so I was standing with the water just up to my shoulders, which made it easy for me to lift the guy's left foot and sole-lick him from rounded heel to outstretched toes.

"Jesus," he breathed.

He didn't try to pull away, though. I hard-licked the hourglass bottom of his other foot, my big, calloused hands now gently cradling his slender, tendon-cleaved ankles, putting his feet up on a pedestal where they belonged, where they could be righteously worshipped by a fetisher like myself. I dragged my velvet-sandpaper tongue over the contoured sole of his left foot again, and his legs started trembling, his foot-bottoms crinkling, telling me I was getting through to the guy, bridging the generation gap one glorious foot at a time.

"D-don't stop," he whimpered, confirming my thoughts.

I shoved my thick tongue in between his big toe and the first piggy in line, slithered it around. I went down the plump-topped row on his left foot, tonguing in between his toes. His legs really started shaking then, the water rippling with my erotic footwork.

"Jesus, that feels good!" he gasped.

"Tastes good, too," I muttered, popping his cute little pinky toe into my mouth and sucking on it.

I went back up the row, sucking on his toes this time, one by wiggling one. His foot-digits were neat and trim, oh-so-succulent, and when I took his big toe into my mouth and tugged on it, he moaned with pleasure. And almost as breathtaking as the sight of the guy's sensuously molded feet and legs was the sight of his swelling cock. The snake in his soaked-through Speedo was shifting around on the water's surface, expanding dangerously with desire.

I consumed Rafael's right foot, lapping at his sensitive foot-bottom, writhing my tongue in amongst his delicate toes, sucking and nibbling on them. His cock strained the thin material of his skimpy swimsuit, his entire body trembling now as I fed on his feet.

I couldn't get enough of the guy's pretty peds, my hunger for manly feet and legs a thing that could never be fully satisfied. I lapped at the curved tops of his feet, pressing his peds together, my own cock tenting the loose, wet fabric of my trunks.

I opened his legs up again, and this time I nipped at his ankles, bit into the bunched muscles of his calves. Then I shoved his left leg up higher into the air, dunking him in the water. I swabbed the soft, vulnerable back of his knee with my tongue, my hands shaking now with excitement. He tasted wonderful, his legs and feet a goddamn delicacy. He had to conk me on the head with his leg to get himself upright and breathing again.

I attacked his other leg, but he was ready for my oral assault this time, urgently rubbing his cock as I sank my teeth into his calf. The sight of what I'd done to him and his cock drove me crazy, and I waded in between his legs, my big mouth open and hungry for meat. I shouldered his thighs and grabbed on to his waist and captured his balls in my mouth.

"Jesus!" he yelled again.

I was like the shark in *Jaws*, swallowing the guy whole as the boat went down, tugging on Rafael's sac through the damp material of his bathing suit, juggling his balls around with my tongue. His head went under the water, popped up again. He anxiously scanned the horizon, the motel windows, for curious onlookers. But I didn't give a damn. I was a relentless man-eating machine. The whole town could've come out and watched the spectacle, for all I cared.

I sucked on Rafael's pouch, my throat working. He closed his eyes and moaned, abandoning himself to my loving mouth. A different kind of warmth, not air or water related, was washing over him now. I pulled him down a bit, unmouthed his balls, and dragged my tongue up the rigid outline of his cock.

He bit his lip and clung to the metal ladder, as I licked his shaft over and over. I soon got sick of the taste of spandex, however. I yanked his Speedo down; let his dick pop out and catch some air, some direct tongue. His cock was clean-cut and golden brown, veined and throbbing. I teased its tensed surface with the tip of my tongue, and Rafael groaned and did a pelvic thrust into my face, slamming his hard cock against my soft lips. I tongued his naked shaft, slow and sure, from fur-matted balls to mushroom head.

"Yes! Yes!" he urged, knuckles white on the railing, eyes wild.

God, but it felt good! Inhaling the musky scent of that young man, his muscled thighs resting hot and light on my big shoulders, his tightened sac and swollen cock within easy reach of my mouth, the warm air and water swirling all around us. It was enough to make a guy poetic, if he was so inclined. Me, I bluntly lapped at his shaft, then swallowed his hood.

"Fuck!" he wailed.

My lips sealed around his cap, I wagged my tongue back and forth, scouring the sensitive spot where shaft meets head. Then I took in more of his cock, bending it back like a lucky guy pulling the lever on a slot machine. Rafael arched his slick body to meet my demanding mouth, and I quickly swallowed his meat down to the balls.

I kept him there at that impossible angle, staring at him, his cock filling my mouth and throat and choking me, my face half-submerged in the water. He shook like he meant it—like he was close to blowing his load. Or maybe his muscles were just wearing thin. Either way, I pulled back a bit, let some of his shaft glide out from between my lips. I stopped its progress with my teeth, biting into his cock halfway down. I started sucking him off, bobbing my head up and down on his dick, polishing his hardness with my lips and tongue.

"I'm—I'm going to cum, Dave!" he warned.

Cum to poppa! was all I thought. I kept right on sucking, blowing that guy with a technique perfected over five decades, vacuuming him down to the fur line and then suctioning back up his shaft again, over and over.

His body bowed rigid as his dick, and then he shuddered, groaned. His cock jerked in my mouth, and I was flooded with warm, salty spunk. I kept my lips locked on his spasming cock, milking him, while his thighs squeezed my neck like a vise. The young man spurted his joy repeatedly, forcing me to swallow fast and often. I drank in his essence without wasting a drop, proudly watching as he thrashed around in the water, blown away by my cocksucking.

He lost his death grip on the ladder and almost went under for good when he'd finally finished emptying his balls in my throat. I dragged him to the surface. I wasn't done with him yet.

"I wanna foot-fuck you," I whispered in his ear.

He nodded vaguely, gasping for air.

I helped him out of the pool, admiring how stiff his bobbing cock still remained. Then I eased him into the hot, swirling waters of the Jacuzzi. I stripped off my own trunks, let my own cock catch some air. It was hard as a divining rod, twitching like it smelled water—and feet.

I dropped into the tub and stood up to my waist in the bubbling chop facing my slumped lover. I fisted my submerged member, getting it good and fully jacked for action, my grizzled chest heaving with excitement and anticipation.

"You—you don't want to fuck me in the ass?" Rafael gulped, sitting up higher.

"Sure I do," I replied, grinning and fisting, fisting and grinning. "Later. Right now I want those pretty feet of yours."

He nodded wearily and extended his legs underwater. I grabbed his ankles, clapped his soles on either side of my raging cock. He went under, came up spluttering, clinging to the sides of the Jacuzzi. He was very, very flexible, like I'd thought he'd be, and his foot-bottoms gripped my cock in the best bowlegged fashion.

I started pumping my hips, fucking the guy's feet. My dick glided easily back and forth between his soft soles, the smooth, heated sensation sending a shiver up my spine, a lightning bolt through my groin. I pumped faster and faster, stirring up the agitated water even more with the brute force of my foot-lust.

Rafael stared at me, struggling to remain topside, as I ruth-lessly fucked his peds, his legs shuddering with the impact of my thrusting body. I gripped his toes and pistoned my cock in between his soles, the tension, the tingling in my balls, building and building with every furious cock-stroke.

Then I abruptly pulled him up out of the water, spilling him back onto the indoor-outdoor carpeting. I scrambled up onto the shelf where he'd been sitting, then fucked away again. My cock went numb, flying in between his feet, my muscles locking up to the snapping point. I tilted my head back and churned like a madman, bellowing, "Fuck, yeah!" at the moon and the stars, consumed by the dizzying sensation of total release.

I blasted white-hot cum onto Rafael's chest and stomach and cock, pumping out rope after rope of sticky, sizzling sperm, the wicked foot-friction sending me sailing till I was drained as an end-of-season swimming pool.

The next day I put Rafael on a new job—sitting in a chair under an umbrella holding up a SLOW sign. I wanted the young guy off his gorgeous feet during the day, 'cause I was going to be on them every night.

CONSTRUCTIONAL VOODOO

Logan Zachary

My eyes followed the drop of sweat as it rolled down the hairy chest that stood in front of me. The tight blue jeans absorbed it quickly in the summer's heat. The huge bulge strained against the zipper and seemed to swell. I forced my gaze up into the eyes of the man at my front door.

"As you can see, we're digging up the street in front of your house." The man stepped to the side so I could see the road. His red shirt hung open all the way down to his furry belly button.

An innie.

"You may want to store some water, in case we need to flush the hydrants."

I forced my eyes back up to his face.

He turned, and our eyes finally met.

Deep blue. I wanted to dive in.

No words were forming in my mind or my mouth. All I could manage was a nod.

"Just thought I'd let you know." The man took out a white

handkerchief and wiped the sweat from his brow. He turned and tried to stick it into his back pocket as he walked down the porch stairs. The handkerchief missed, slipped out of his pocket, and landed on the top step.

He entered the street and slid his goggles, yellow safety vest, and earplugs into place. The buzz of the jackhammer sent shock waves through my house and into me.

I walked out onto the porch and retrieved the sweat-soaked handkerchief. Instantly, I brought it to my nose and inhaled. A deep, sweet, musky man scent assaulted my nostrils. I breathed in deeply again and closed the door.

I headed back to my drawing board, where a blank sheet of paper waited for me. *The Pirates in My Pants* was stuck. I wasn't making any progress on the story line. The comic strip for the new magazine was in dry dock.

A row of figures sat near my drawing board. I reached up and removed one, the construction worker doll, and set him on the drafting table. "We're digging up the street in front of your house." My voice took on a deep gravelly quality.

"Here's your handkerchief," I said, as I offered the wet cloth to the doll, since I hadn't run after the real deal.

"'Why thanks,' you would say, and you'd come in for a cold beer and a hot shower," I said to the doll. "If only it was that simple." I wrapped the handkerchief around the figure. The doll throbbed in my hand, and it seemed to breathe in. The sweat soaked into its clothes as I set it down to watch me work, or as was the case, not work.

The pirates refused to cooperate, as I looked out the window into the street. My construction worker drilled the concrete slab and cracked it into pieces. The doll's red shirt started to bleed into the white handkerchief; the dye must be running from all the sweat. I removed the wet cloth and the yellow safety vest and tossed them aside.

The thunderous jackhammer stopped. The man set it aside, removed his yellow vest, tossed it into my front yard, and returned to work.

I glanced from the doll's vest and back to the man's vest. They matched each other in place and position.

Strange.

I tapped the pencil against my teeth, as the pirate king...as the pirate king...as the pirate king did what? Sat on his fat ass until I could figure out what to make him do next? I didn't know.

I picked up the construction worker doll on my table. His hard hat tipped back off his head and rolled across my paper.

The man in the street stopped the jackhammer as his hard hat flew off the back of his head and rolled over the concrete.

I picked up the hat and replaced it on his head.

The man in the street bent over, showed a nice white slice of butt crack, and placed his hard hat back on his head.

I brought the doll to my nose and inhaled. Manly sweat. It felt warm to my touch, despite the air-conditioning. My finger played across his shirt, and it was even more damp than before. No way could that handkerchief have soaked the figure this much.

Or could it?

On the blank piece of paper I drew my house. I walked the doll to the front door and looked out the window.

The construction worker stopped his jackhammer and walked to my front door.

I made the doll's hand knock on the picture of my door.

Knock-knock, sounded on my front door.

Should I answer it?

Picking up the pencil, I quickly drew the street and walked the doll back into the road.

The man left my porch and walked back to his jackhammer. He shook his head and returned to work.

This was too freaky. I raced to the kitchen and came back with a bottle of water. I twisted the cap off and watched the man work. The jackhammer drilled into the concrete and broke off another big chunk as the cold water slid down my throat.

I recapped the bottle and set it down next to the doll. I eyed it as an idea formed in my mind. Setting the bottle on its side, I rested it next to the doll. With my other hand, I raised my pencil and stabbed the bottle. Water sprayed across the paper and the doll.

Outside, the man yelled.

Looking out the window, I watched a spray of water soak the man and the street. He pulled back from the jackhammer, dripping wet.

Quickly, I walked the doll back to the picture of my house.

The man ran to my door and pounded on it.

I grabbed a towel from the laundry basket sitting on my couch and headed to the front door.

As the door opened, the dripping man looked at me. "Can I use your phone?" He seemed surprised to see the towel in my hand but accepted it. He wiped his face and patted his soaked shirt.

"Come in," was all I could manage.

The man looked down at the entryway floor, and tentatively stepped onto the tile. "I don't want to leave a puddle."

"It's only tile. It'll dry." I walked over to the hall table and picked up the phone.

"I need to call the city to shut the water off." We looked out the front window. The water had stopped. He waved the phone away.

Moving over to the drafting table, I set the phone down and

saw the water bottle was empty. Quickly, I removed the doll's shirt. I held my breath and slowly turned around. The man stood in my entryway...shirtless. My knees threatened to buckle. I licked my lips as I spun around to flip the doll's work boots off. Taking a deep breath, I held it and closed my eyes before I turned to look at him.

His bare feet stood on the tile.

I swallowed hard, staring at his pants.

Should I?

Could I?

Would it work?

I walked back to the door and stopped dead in my tracks.

"Do you mind?" the man asked me as he unbuckled his belt. He unzipped his jeans and quickly removed them. He wrapped the towel around his narrow waist, but not before his white, wet briefs, revealed what was underneath.

Glancing over my shoulder, I saw the doll's pants were balled up in an exact pile.

"I don't know what happened," the wet man confessed. "According to the survey, there's no way that the water line ran there."

"I'm sure it wasn't your fault." I knew it was all mine. "Look, it stopped already. How bad could it have been?"

The man peered out the window again and saw the water had indeed stopped. He looked confused.

"I need to finish something," I pointed to my drawing board, "and then maybe I can explain."

The man just nodded as his hand held the towel wrapped around his hips, tighter.

My hand quickly drew a shower stall with water spraying from the nozzle. With my other hand, I moved the doll into the square.

"Do you mind if I use your shower?" The man motioned up the stairs.

My mouth went dry and all I could do was nod. I tried to lick my lips, but there wasn't any moisture in my tongue.

The man's bare feet padded across the tiled entry and headed up the stairs. The towel loosened as he walked. It slipped down in the back and his wet underwear waistband appeared. At the first step, the towel dropped lower, and the sheer white fabric appeared as a second skin. It hugged his butt and pulled deep into his crease.

I followed him up the stairs, drinking him in as his ass swayed with each step.

The towel fell to the floor once he entered the bathroom. He peeled off his underwear and stepped into the shower stall.

I gasped at the beauty of the sight. His body looked as if it were sculpted from stone but made of flesh. Even my skills as an artist wouldn't have been able to conjure up this...

And then he turned to face me, and I gasped.

"Wanna join me?" he asked.

Water shot out of the nozzle head and flowed over his body. His pelt of hair slicked down and glistened on his body. His pecs rippled as he soaped them. The fur fanned over his chest and narrowed as it approached his navel. From his belly button down, the hair triangled and thickened. A massive cock swelled and rose from the thick bush of pubic hair. As he lathered up his groin, the uncut head bounced and began to rise, thickening and lengthening as white foam combed through the dark hair and cascaded down his long legs.

My hands unbuttoned and unzipped my jeans and gravity took over. I ripped my shirt off over my head and discarded it on the towel.

His heavy balls swung back and forth between his legs as

water and foam flowed over them. They seemed to beckon me to join him.

My underwear slid down my legs as my hand reached through the open shower door for his scrotum. My fingers grasped and juggled the orbs between my fingers. They felt to be the size of golf balls, low hanging and furry.

He moaned and stepped back. "Let me make some room for you."

My hand worked the flesh, and the soap and water mixed into a thick creamy lather. The clumps of foam dropped at our feet.

My smooth skin contrasted against his sun-bronzed flesh. His pelvis stood out from his tanned chest and legs in a white square. "You need to get out more; look how pale you are." He ran his finger across my chest.

Moving closer, his erection brushed my torso. My cock sprang to life, rising up from my body and slipping underneath his. Our engorged parts ran into each other, and waves of pleasure flowed over me and into him, back and forth between us, just as the warm water and foam washed over us.

Water plastered my hair to my scalp as my cock slid up his torso and his penis ran alongside mine. Our balls brushed each other, coarse hair against coarse hair. We ground our pelvises into each other, humping body to body. Waves of pleasure flowed as warm as the water.

"Now you're getting the idea." His hands started to work the soap over my body, stimulating each nerve fiber. They worked their way across my chest, down along my sides as he pulled me close. His cock dug into my belly button, seeking entry.

His hands soaped and massaged their way to my ass. His fingers kneaded the mounds of firm flesh and ran along the groove. His thick fingers played in my crease, gently exploring. He looked into my eyes. "Can I?"

"You may," I said, and my moans encouraged him. One finger stretched and found the sensitive spot. My knees threatened to buckle, but his finger circled my asshole, and I felt as if I balanced on his tip. The soap and water lubed the opening.

"Are you sure?" he asked. His finger pressed forward for entry, as I pressed back against him. My ass welcomed his intrusion. "Yes," I said and took a deep breath, as he drove it home. My balls wanted to empty their load, but I resisted, holding the eruption back.

His rough finger and enlarged joints tortured my sensitive skin. The tender opening begged for more. I impaled myself on his finger.

He brought his mouth down on mine. "Kiss me," he said. His lips inhaled mine into his mouth. His tongue dueled with mine as he threatened to swallow me whole. His tongue was in my mouth, his penis in my navel, and his finger deep inside my shivering ass. My body screamed for more.

The assault stopped momentarily, as he spun me around. My face slammed into the tile as I felt him step up behind me and pin me to the wall. "Spread them," he said as his thick organ slapped against my skin, and his hands pulled my hips to him. His feet kicked my legs apart. I could feel myself opening to him, welcoming him.

Steam swirled around us, soap and sweat and sex filled my nostrils. I inhaled deeply and braced myself.

His cock slapped on my lower back and slid down my crack. It filled the furrow and plowed along the length of the crease. His balls bounced off my ass with each pass. His pelvis retracted and plunged forward. The sheathed head targeted the bull's-eye, sought entry, and slipped up and over.

I drove back against him, willing him to come inside of me, fill me, rip me open.

"Are you ready?" his husky voice asked.

My body shivered with anticipation. "Yes," was all I could breathe out of my mouth.

His fingers dug into my hips and pulled them back onto his cock. His hands spread my cheeks, exposing the target. He rolled his hips and set his cock against the opening. He teased it, rubbing circles and pressing in the center for entrance. As the tip slipped in, he pulled back.

"Beg for it," he whispered, tonguing my ear. The hair on his chest caressed my back.

I pushed back against him, but he resisted entry, teasing and taunting my hole. Finally I hissed, "Please."

The next moment, I felt heaven. With one quick thrust, he was inside me to the hilt. His balls banged into mine as his pubic hair tickled my asscheeks, but it was his engorged cock that took my breath away. As fast as he was in, he was out.

"Don't—" was all I got out before he was inside me again. His thrust pinned me to the wall. His hands pulled me onto his cock, which he slowly slid in and out. The thick head would strain against my opening, threatening to pop out, but at the last second it would plunge back in, to depths I'd never known before.

His strokes were smooth and timed. He rocked my body back and forth, as if to the rhythm of some primitive tribe. My body responded. I helped his strong arms pull me back; my ass sucked him in deeper with each thrust.

The speed increased as the force intensified. Like a well-oiled machine, he pistoned into me. I struggled to breathe. The humidity made me feel like I was drowning, and each thrust drove the little oxygen out of my lungs. Before I could inhale, he drove into me again.

His strong hands released my hips. He pulled out of me and

spun me around. Face-to-face, he picked me up and placed me back on his cock. "More?" he asked.

I wrapped my legs around him and hung on as he drilled into me. His massive forearms held me up as I rode his penis. His right hand released my torso, and he reached between my legs. "This guy needs some action, too." His fingers wrapped around my dick and started to stroke, matching each thrust with his hand. My balls rubbed up and down his furry six-pack as the water cascaded over us.

I threw my head back as his rhythm increased, as did my pleasure. His mouth found mine as our tongues tasted desire and lust. His five o'clock shadow scratched my cheek as he continued to use me. A tension was rising with each thrust, urging me forward, closer, harder, faster.

I welcomed him, and he smiled and quickened his pace.

A low rumble started in his chest and worked its way lower. It flowed from him and into me. The vibration started as a buzz, but intensified to encompass the room. His groans matched my moans as he slid in and out, taking me higher.

His body tensed as he pulled out of me one last time and then slammed back in. I could feel the orgasm start from his balls and explode out of his cock and into me. My prostate absorbed the load. Its heat melted my insides and forced them to shoot out across his hairy chest as I came. Another warm wave filled me, as the next jet exploded from my cock. My body convulsed as wave after wave of pleasure escaped.

We sank down to the floor of the stall and let the water wash over us.

I watched as he donned his clothes in the entryway. "I'm not sure what came over me," he said, as he zipped his fly with his back turned to me.

"Must have been the heat," I offered.

He paused for a moment. "Sunstroke?" He nodded to himself, "Yeah, sunstroke." He turned to me and smiled. "Crazy from the heat."

"Well, if you need any more water, come and knock on the door."

"Isn't that what caused this whole thing in the first place?" He set his hard hat on his head and walked to the door. "Thanks," was all he said, and he was gone.

I walked back to my drawing. The construction worker doll stood clothed on the easel. A huge smile covered his face.

I smiled in spite of myself. Had what just happened, really happened?

Oh, well. The pirates weren't cooperating, and my editor wasn't going to be happy, so the best thing to do was email him right now. I turned on the laptop and logged online.

An email caught my attention, so I followed the link to eBay. After a few clicks, the Mario Lopez, Tom Selleck, and Mark Wahlberg action figures were sitting in my shopping cart.

And with a big, happy grin, I clicked on BUY NOW.

CLIMBING UP THE WALL

Barry Lowe

The noise woke me: loud voices and laughter, the irritating deep-throated opinions of a talk-back radio host. That's the problem with living in the inner city: Sounds. Everywhere. All the time. Personal silent space narrows considerably. No wonder so many people take up yoga. And it's why I slept in the back bedroom of the dilapidated inner-city terrace I rented. My bedroom backed onto a laneway, once a lane for the easy collection and removal of euphemistically named "night soil."

It had simply ended up a repository for garbage and renovation detritus, probably because all of us in the nine-house block were renters, not buyers, and so we had no vampire-like hunger for a few extra square centimeters of backyard. I was a night shift worker so I slept during the day. That's what necessitated my move to the smaller bedroom—away from the light, away from the necessary noise of everyday living.

I opened one eye and peered at the clock until it came into focus. I groaned. I had been asleep for only ninety minutes and it didn't sound as if the noise was going to abate. In fact, it was so close, it sounded as if it were coming from inside my head. I got out of bed to pad across the floor and close the window. It would be stuffy and humid but I had to sleep. I scratched my balls as I tried to remain half asleep. No one could see me as the bedroom window merely looked out on the lane and the painted back brick wall of the house opposite that blocked the sun out until the late afternoon. That enabled me to leave the window open and the blind up and still kip in comparative gloom. It was particularly helpful in the sticky heat of summer.

My brain was as out of focus as my eyes, and I didn't pinpoint the voices until I was near the window. Then it struck me. The voices were coming from above and below. Someone was in my backyard and someone was on the roof. Burglars! I'd been broken into twice already in the short time I'd lived here but this was the most brazen attempt ever. And they weren't being quiet about it.

As if to confirm my suspicions the ladder propped over my window moved. What ladder? I don't have a ladder. But someone did. And that someone was climbing up or down in preparation for breaking in via my very inviting open second-floor window. I had to give them an A for audacity. Most thieves just jimmied the rotting woodwork on the ground-floor window and scampered in and out like larcenous cockroaches.

These guys were better organized. And therefore dangerous.

A boot appeared on the rung closest to the top of the window. The intruder was coming down. I could have run for the window to slam it closed but if these intruders were as brazen as they seemed, they'd have no hesitation in smashing the glass and then I'd end up not only assaulted and battered and bereft of personal electrical goods, but also left with a glazier's bill for a new window.

My hand closed round the handle of an ancient cricket bat

that I occasionally used to prop up tables and beat to death
inner-city vermin. I waited. The boot became a naked leg ema-
nating from a thick woolen sock curled over at the top, followed
then by tanned and almost hairless calves, and then equally
tanned thighs...

My cock gave a twitch that brought me back to the reality of
my situation. I lifted the bat. The cutoff jeans seemed to adhere
to a bubble butt that looked as delicious as two half melons, and
the full package of his cock and balls. For now, at least, I knew
it was a male intruder. The stomach muscles were firm, the belly
button an innie, and the pecs were...well, the pecs were...well,
if I were the sporting type, I could have skied down them. I'm a
chest man.

They say that when you are about to die your life slows and
seconds seem like minutes. That was happening to me now as I
awaited my fate. The arms appeared to be strong and muscular
as the body skittered farther down the ladder. Strong enough to
wrench my neck sideways, obliterating my life in an easy snap,
unless I got in first. I raised the bat with as much bravado as I
could muster. The head...that same head I was about to batter
into oblivion was... Oh, fuck! I couldn't tell whether the shallow
breaths I was taking and the adrenaline beating of my heart was
fear now or lust. His eyes were blue. He was beefy, blond and
beautiful. Not handsome. Beautiful as you would describe an an-
gel or some other ethereal being who was too good to be true.

He was half turned, calling to someone below as I raised the
bat. However, my dick was telling me that there were better
ways of getting revenge. He was too beautiful to smack in the
head and I was about to whack his knees when he turned and
saw me.

He stopped. He blinked. He called down: "The guy's home
after all."

To me, he said, "G'day, mate," in such a warm and friendly manner I almost forgot my intense dislike for the clichéd greeting. "Nice bat and set of balls."

I realized I was totally naked, and erect, and that he was nodding in the direction of my tackle when he made the observation. I dropped the cricket bat and grabbed for my briefs from the end of the bed. I had trouble pulling them over my erection and it poked over the top of the elastic waistband making it look even more obscene than my nakedness had been.

"Don't you just hate piss pricks?" he said.

His mate called up impatiently from below.

"Hold your horses. He wants to discuss indoor cricket."

There was a snort of derision from the backyard.

"Sorry to disturb you, mate," he said. "Hard night?"

I explained that I was a night worker and…what the hell was I doing discussing my sleep patterns with a fucking burglar? Albeit a ravishing burglar.

"Didn't you get the landlord's note?" he asked.

"The…?" Then it hit me. A month ago a note had been slipped under my door telling me the landlord was finally going to fix the problem roof and guttering that leaked like a sieve every time it rained, smearing a moldy stain across a corner of the bedroom ceiling.

"Oh, shit." I wasn't going to die after all. The split-second thought of the relationship between danger and my erectile performance I filed for analysis at another time. Interesting. But later.

"You wanna come in?" I asked

"I don't think there's enough room in there for you, me, and that!" he said nodding in the direction of my blood-engorged cock.

I smiled. "I'll throw some clothes on and let you in the back door."

He okayed the idea and scrambled down as agilely as...well, a cat burglar.

A few minutes later I was unlocking the glass back door and letting him and his mate in. I had the coffee on and thought a little hospitality was the least I could do as a peace offering. They dumped their tools near the door, asking if they could store them in the house to save bringing them back every day. I didn't dare ask how long they'd be on the job in case I gave away my enthusiasm for a slow completion date.

Stig introduced himself with a handclasp that sent sparks of longing through my whole body. He had been raised in Australia by his mum but his dad was Swedish.

His surly mate was Egon, a darkly attractive German who grunted rather than phrased recognizable answers to any of my questions. They told me of the upheaval that my life was to undergo in the next few weeks, right down to my having to move to the front bedroom while they cut out part of the ceiling and replastered it.

Damn. The inconvenience was a pisser. But...well, there was always an upside to every situation if you just looked at it the right way. They finished their coffee, and I told them I'd leave the back door open so they could use the kitchen and bathroom anytime they wanted.

"Most people don't even like us to come inside the house," Egon whined.

"Yeah, mate, that's mighty good of you," Stig enthused. "We'll do a bang-up job for you and get outta your hair real quick."

"Oh, no need to hurry," I stammered.

Egon and Stig had that easy camaraderie that is so obvious among builders worldwide. Stig grabbed a handful of crotch through his shorts and muttered playfully, "Eat me, cocksucker!"

to his boss. Stig looked at me after a swift facial admonition from Egon and muttered, "Sorry, mate."

"That's okay, just builders' talk, I know."

Stig bent over in front of me (deliberately?) to pick up his tool belt and his T-shirt rode up so I could catch a glimpse of that exquisite sweaty butt crack topped with a fuzz of blond foliage. I got hard instantly. Egon noticed me staring. He didn't look impressed. Jealous, perhaps?

Telling them to call me before they left so I could lock away their gear, I reluctantly went back to bed. This time, though, I closed the window and pulled the curtains, leaving them open just enough so that I could watch glimpses of Stig as he shimmied up and down the ladder. They kept their noise to a minimum, but I still couldn't sleep. I kept watching the chink in the curtains hoping for another glimpse of Stig's perfect skin, so perfect it looked as if the color had been mixed on the most exquisite palette and sprayed on with an artist's airbrush. No amount of instructing my body to sleep was going to get it to obey with that in the vicinity.

I pulled down the sheet and began to massage my cock, which was already half hard. It was demanding attention and would not let me have any peace until I helped it out. I stroked it as I thought of Stig and his luscious mouth closing around my knob, his tongue flicking at the slit.... I slowly bent the naked builder over the edge of my bed and pulled his ass crack apart, aiming my hard-on at the moist, inviting hole. I plunged and he grunted.... But every fantasy conjured up in my mind had Egon in the background. Watching. Glaring possessively.

I eventually shot my load into the sheet while I fantasized about anything other than Stig, my mind racing through various fantasy scenarios just one step ahead of Egon. And Egon was there, too, in my dreams. Threatening.

The following week was agony. Stig's presence was enough to send me dizzy with the thwarted possibilities while Egon stood guard over his workmate. Egon did thaw a little and showed me photos of his wife and daughter. They made a beautiful family. He was a little older than Stig, perhaps thirty or so, with tufts of dark hair on his chest. He was less beefy than Stig and less gregarious but I noticed a definite change in the tone of his grunts. Stig, it seemed, had no photos of family or even girlfriends as they came and went as frequently as he came and went. Or so Egon would have me believe. Stig merely confirmed the stories with a blush that looked like it had been applied by a celestial makeup artist.

At the beginning of the second week, Stig arrived on his own. I usually waited up for them with a freshly brewed pot of coffee. They liked that and sat and nattered for about fifteen minutes before staring work. I would then head off to bed and my attempt at a Stig-induced wet dream.

"Where's Egon?" I asked, hoping this would be my opportunity to make some sort of play for Stig or least drop a few spangles so he knew that I thought he was attractive.

"Louisa is sick. He had to take her to the doctor," he said as he slurped the coffee, cream and two sugars. I'd bought donuts on my way home from work that morning, and now I told him to help himself.

"Ta, mate," he said as he took one and dunked it in his coffee.

"That's very American," I commented as he put it to his mouth.

"What is?" he said.

"Dunking donuts."

"It's okay, isn't it?" he asked with some slight concern lest he be breaking some gastronomic rule about donuts.

I laughed. "Of course it is. You just don't see many Aussies doing it." He looked a bit bewildered and went to dunk again but hesitated. "Go on," I said.

He laughed and did as he was told. Oh, that he would do everything that easily.

"His daughter okay?" I asked Stig.

"Just a virus, he thinks. He'll be here soon."

Stig finished up and took the ladder out into the backyard.

"You need a hand?" I yelled.

"Nah, mate. She'll be right."

I made my way upstairs and got into bed. If Stig was around much longer I was definitely going to become sexually dysfunctional. I would have to encourage them to finish up as soon as they could. That way Stig would be gone and I'd get my life back. There was a thundering crash and a loud shout. I bolted out of bed and down the stairs. I wasn't naked this time as I'd learned to wear my briefs to bed while the builders were around.

I laughed out loud. The extension ladder had come apart, Stig had fallen onto my favorite ornamental chili plant, and it was now beyond salvation. He looked so hurt and embarrassed, sheepishly wiping the back of his shorts clean of soil, I couldn't have bawled him out.

"You okay?"

"Sure," he said. "Just a little spill." But when he attempted to get the ladder he hobbled and almost fell.

I rushed to help him. It was the first time I had touched that skin, smooth as icing on a cake.

"Maybe I had better sit down for a minute," he said. He'd been badly shaken and looked quite pale.

I helped him inside and before he sat down I noticed specks of blood on his shorts.

"I think you may have cut yourself. You're bleeding."

"Where?" he asked.

"Your butt."

He tried to look but couldn't see.

"Let me have a look," I offered. "Here, bend over the end of the couch. He did as he was told and I slid his shorts down a little. Yes, those melonlike cheeks had been scraped, and very small spots of blood dotted his rump. And some of the hardier twigs of the chili bush had protested their demise by jabbing into his flesh.

"Um, I may have to pull your shorts down farther," I suggested, just managing to keep my voice under control.

"That's okay; it hurts like hell back there."

His shorts came off, and I whistled at the beginnings of a purple bruise. I touched it gently. "That hurt?"

"Hurts like fuck," he winced.

I tried to cheer him up. "Want me to kiss it and make it better?"

"If you think it will help," he guffawed.

It was now or never.

I leaned over and pressed my lips to the bruise. I could tell it hurt him but I kept my lips there.

"Better?" I said.

"Not yet. A little to the left."

I moved toward his ass crack and kissed again.

"Nice," he whispered. "But maybe over a little more."

I didn't hesitate. I gently pried apart his asscheeks and put my lips to his fragrant hole.

"Yes, right there," he moaned.

I licked gently and sucked voraciously at his blond, tanned ass. This boy obviously went to nude beaches because the tan went all the way. I maneuvered my tongue into his hole and lapped at the doorway to his guts. I wanted to lube him good before I pounced. Nothing was going to stop me from planting my cock inside him. I spat into his inviting hole and then on my cock before I stood up and leaned over him.

"Will this make you feel better?" I asked.

"Better than better," he croaked through a mixture of desire and pain.

He grunted as my cock pushed aside the flesh of his sphincter, whether from pain or pleasure I wasn't sure. I tried to avoid contact with the bruise on his ass, which meant I could not push in my full length. Frustrating, but I had more of my cock in Stig than I had thought I ever would.

"Slam it right in to your balls," he demanded.

"I don't want to hurt you," I said truthfully.

"Fuck that. This is the best hurt I ever had. It was worth every bit of pain."

I pushed gently into him until his warm sock of an asshole slid smoothly around my cock.

"What do you mean?" I asked as I picked up the pace.

"You know how hard it is to throw yourself off a ladder when you're as safety conscious as me?"

He turned his head as best he could to look at my reaction. "How else was I gonna get you to look at my ass?"

"I look at your ass every single day you're here," I said. "I can't take my fucking eyes off it. All you had to do was ask."

He grunted his appreciation with every thrust.

"I don't know how to," he said. "It's easier with girls."

I pulled out.

"Hey, don't stop," he pleaded.

I led him upstairs to the bedroom. I wanted to watch this beautiful creature while I fucked him. I lay him on his back and told him to hold his legs back behind his head, exposing his beautiful pink swollen tunnel. I knelt down and kissed it again. Then I kneeled over him and pushed until he'd swallowed me right up to my balls. I wanted to push them inside him, too. I leaned toward him and held his head steady as I pried open his lips with my tongue. He knew guys fucked one another but he didn't know they kissed, he told me later. I licked his lips and sucked gently on his tongue. He returned the favor, and our mouths opened wide as if attempting to suck out each other's souls. When we came up for air he wiped his mouth with a quiet "Wow."

I stroked his cock as I picked up the pace, and he arched his ass toward me. He was moving to meet my strokes, squeezing his ass round me, trying to absorb me totally. I gasped as his ass spasmed and he shot a load all over his chest. I pulled out and comingled my cum with his, howling as my squirts hit his chest. I collapsed on him and made swirling cum paintings on his stomach with my fingers.

Now comes the awkward part, I thought. But Stig wasn't finished. He ignored his discomfort and leaned down to put his mouth over my cock. I flinched as those wet lips closed around my rod.

"What's wrong?" he asked. "Am I doing it wrong?"

I laughed and moved my body so my mouth was over his still leaking prick—and engulfed it.

"Holy fuck," he shouted, and his whole body bucked. "I want to taste you," he said shyly.

"I want to taste you all over," I said sincerely. "But won't Egon be here soon?"

We heard movement downstairs.

"Sooner than we thought," I said.

I threw on some clothes and gave Stig a towel because his shorts were still in the living room. As nonchalantly as we could, we went downstairs, Stig leaning heavily on me for effect rather than necessity.

"What's going on?" Egon looked up.

"I fell off the ladder," Stig said simply.

"Was the ladder in the bedroom?" Egon asked sarcastically.

"I had to lie down I was in so much pain," Stig lied.

"Can you work today?" Egon asked as politely as he could considering he didn't believe a word of it.

"Yeah, I'm just bruised." Stig turned to show him.

Egon picked up his shorts and threw them to him. "Put your clothes back on." When he stood up I noticed the outline of a not unsubstantial weapon in Egon's shorts and the telltale spreading stain. He had either seen or heard what was going on, or he had one helluva vivid imagination.

Stig noticed, too.

"I think I might stay like this a little longer," Stig said.

"As you please," Egon was miffed.

"No need to act like you got the rag on," Stig said. "There's plenty for you if you got the guts to take it." With that he grabbed Egon's crotch and squeezed. Egon pushed his hand away like he'd been burned.

"That's up to you, mate," Stig shrugged and patted his ass. "But it can be yours anytime."

I twinged with jealousy. Stig would never be mine for more than a quick grope but, still, on our wedding night I expected some sort of commitment.

"It could have been you, mate," Stig said to Egon. "Except you've always been too scared. Those crap photos of your wife and daughter. Don't you think I found out long ago that's your sister and her kid. Why pretend, mate? You slobber over me behind my back. You can fire me if you want 'cause it's your builder's license, but I'm gonna tell you something first. From now on, every morning when I come to this job I'm gonna have me some fun before we start. I'm gonna do it on my own time,

but I'm gonna do it every day. Or, at least as often as he wants
it." He pointed to me.

"Every day," I managed to croak.

"And if he'll let you, you can join in. You don't mind if he
joins in, do you, mate?" Stig asked.

He was so polite about it I could scarcely refuse.

The stain on Egon's shorts was spreading. But he made no
move. After a long pause, Stig grabbed his shorts and gingerly
pulled them up over his butt.

"Okay, back to work."

Stig gave me a long tongue-lashing and a wink before he
headed outside. He slapped me on the ass and told me to get
some sleep.

Over the next few days and weeks as the job slowly crept to
completion Stig blossomed under our morning fuck sessions. It
was the third day before Egon appeared at the door to watch
and another before he hauled out his rock-solid cock and jerked
off as he watched Stig bury his own cock to his balls in my ass.
Two days later he tentatively put his cock in Stig's mouth. His
education proceeded at a slower pace but he was learning.

Stig bought me a bigger and better chili plant. And then, one
day, the job was complete. Egon and I both fucked Stig that day.
He wanted it. It was the first time. As I watched I could see how
suited to each other these two were. The dark complementing
the light. It would take time but it would come. I felt like an
intruder that day.

Stig leaned over to kiss me. "Don't be sad," he said. "It was
the only way I could think to do it."

I bought a ladder and propped it against the window. It was
there for two weeks after they left. Then I took it away.

YOU MISSED A SPOT

Ryan Field

Kenneth J. Schenck was tall and lean and strong. His black hair was cut short; if you looked close you could see the beginnings of white specks popping up near his temples. He had a heavy dark beard, with five o'clock shadow surfacing almost two hours after a clean shave. When he stretched his forearms the muscles were long and sinewy. They were so well defined and prominent you could actually see the peaks and valleys where one muscle ended and another began. All this was a combination of genetics and his job in construction, and he was very proud of both.

He rented a nice house on Union Street, in the little town of Lambertville, New Jersey, and he was hoping to buy something soon. But all the money he made seemed to disappear on large payments for his black, extralarge extended pickup truck (with custom gold lettering on both sides that read KENNETH J. SCHENCK CUSTOM BUILDING). When Kenny built or renovated something it was unsurpassed.

When I met him, his wife had just left him for another man, mostly, as I later learned, because they didn't have enough sex to suit her. He placed an ad in the local newspaper for a part-time housekeeper. Kenny had decided it was cheaper to pay someone to wash his dirty underwear than it was to keep buying new pairs.

I answered the ad on a Friday morning in late June, and we agreed on an interview the next morning. I made it clear that I was in college and could work any hours he needed during the summer months, but come September I'd have a full-time schedule and he'd have to work around it. He also mentioned that the house was slightly messy, and I told him not to worry about it. But nothing could have prepared me for what I saw that morning.

You couldn't see the kitchen counter. It was covered with hard-crusted dishes, and pots and pans with burn marks on the bottom. The sink was filled with dirty glasses and wet garbage that smelled like sour milk. On the dining room tabletop there were newspapers and empty fast-food bags; half-filled soda cans and water bottles lined the end tables in the living room. When Kenny led me toward the sofa I had to push a pair of dirty sweat socks off to the side to sit down. He sat in a leather chair opposite me and spread his long, hairy legs as wide as they would go.

"I need someone to come in and keep house on Monday, Wednesday, and Saturday," he said. He held his chin in his palm and kept staring at the ceiling. Maybe the ripped jeans and skimpy black tank top I'd worn that morning had been a mistake. I knew he must have noticed that half of my tight, tanned ass was hanging out and ready for some guy to slip a hand up and grab a piece. I just figured I'd better show him right from the beginning that I liked to dress like a slut and that I wasn't going to change for anyone. "Ah, I mean, if those days are okay with you that is," he added.

I smiled. He was still staring toward the ceiling when I noticed that I could see his white briefs through the opening of his short pants. "Well, I guess I should start today then. From the looks of things around here it's not a minute too soon either. And my name is Rick." I'd only been joking, but when he lowered his head and creased his brows I was sorry I'd made the comment; he knew the place was a mess and didn't need me to tell him.

"Ah, well," he said, "I'm not much of a housekeeper. My wife left me and my son, and I work in construction and don't have the time to deal with any of this."

"You have a son?" I asked. I was good when it came to cleaning, but taking care of a child was not part of the plan.

"Ah, yeah," he said. "But he's usually with his grandparents. You won't see him much."

While we discussed money and when I'd get paid, I noticed his strong hairy legs; his hands were large and flat when he pressed them against his bare knees. When he spoke his voice was soft, but deep and strong, too. It occurred to me that Kenny, though he had to be at least fifteen years older, was the man of my dreams...rough and messy, a guy who worked in construction, a man with blisters on his palms and big strong legs that could leave black and blue marks on the backs of my thighs. "If you want me, I'll be happy to start today, Kenny."

"Ah, that would be good," he said. "I have to go out for a while to look at a new job, but I'll be back by three." His expression was so pensive, with his mouth turned down at the corners and his eyebrows creased, as though he hadn't smiled or relaxed in years.

We both stood and Kenny reached out to shake my hand. His

grip was rugged and when he squeezed my palm I felt the lips of my ass twitch and tighten. "Don't worry about anything. I'll have this place in great shape by the time you get back."

I worked hard that first day, sniffing his dirty underwear and sweat socks before I tossed them into the washer, vacuuming every room, and organizing the small kitchen so that you could actually see the sink and countertop once again. And when he came home that afternoon he smiled and placed his hands on his hips as though he were in shock. "I can't believe you did all this in one morning," he said.

"Well, it really wasn't all that bad," I said, shrugging my shoulders with the bold lie. Then I lowered my eyes and smiled. "It was just a little messy, but you're a busy man who doesn't have time for unimportant things like house cleaning. That's what I'm here for."

He paid me for a full day's work, thanked me too many times, and while I slowly walked out the front door I had a feeling he was staring at my ass the entire time. The next week I began a regular routine of showing up on Mondays, Wednesdays, and Saturdays, always making sure I wore something very skimpy and tight. On the third Saturday I decided to wear a pair of tight white shorts you could practically see through, a loose-fitting black tank top that scooped down so low you could see my nipples, and a pair of black boots with a chunky three-inch heel. A slut suit for sure; the last time I'd worn that outfit to a bar, three guys from out of town bent me over the hood of my car, spread my shaved legs, and took turns fucking my brains out.

When I went into the house that morning Kenny was still sitting at the kitchen table sipping a cup of coffee. "Hey, Rick. I'll be around today while you work. I'm finally getting around to fixing that back door that won't open and close right. Hell, I'm in construction, and my own house is falling apart."

I slowly turned and bent down to tighten my boot lace so he could see my ass. "Cool, would you like me to make you breakfast?"

He raised his hands in the air. "Oh, no, just this coffee and I'm going to start working, but thanks."

I stood and leaned against the counter, but when I pressed my ass up against it I felt something strange; as though I'd backed into a mound of soft clay. When I reached back to touch my ass I realized I'd just backed into a glob of something soft and sticky. I looked at my hand, now smeared with warm, purple grape jelly.

"Oh, shit," Kenny said, holding his fist to his lips, "My son must have forgotten to clean that up this morning."

I turned around and showed him my ass. "Is it really bad?"

"Ah, well, it's kind of all over the place," he said.

At first it occurred to me that I could ask him to help me clean it off; he could get my ass all wet and soapy; I wanted his big strong hands rubbing and stroking me. But then I had a better idea. "Do you mind if I just slip out of these shorts and work in my underwear today? I can toss them into the washing machine and they won't stain."

"Oh, my, well, I guess that's okay," he said. But he was staring at the ceiling again, as though the thought of me walking around in my underwear was too much to handle.

So I slipped out of my shorts as quickly as I could and stood there wearing nothing below the waist but a white silk thong and a big smile. I had to concentrate as hard as I could to not get a full erection and act as though I were just another guy changing his clothes in the locker room. I turned toward the sink and began to rinse the stained shorts with cold water. My bare ass was now facing him; I spread my legs a little and arched my back when I reached for the dish soap. "You're sure this is okay?

If I'd known I'd be working in my underwear today I would have worn something a little more conservative."

"Ah, well, I guess I'd better get to work on the back door," he said.

When he stood he banged his big knee into the Formica table and knocked it out of place. He couldn't look at me and didn't seem to know where to put his hands. He wore loose tan shorts, a white T-shirt, and his usual construction boots with white socks that morning. As he walked toward the laundry room where the back door was located I said, "If you need anything or want anything just let me know."

"Sure thing," he said, but I suspected he couldn't get away from my nude ass fast enough.

About an hour later, while I was down on all fours washing the kitchen floor, I heard a loud bang and then a yell. And then Kenny came rushing through the kitchen and crossed over to the sink. He'd banged his right index finger with the hammer and needed to run it under cold water.

I jumped up and rushed toward him. "Is it bleeding?"

"No," he said, "I just hit it pretty hard."

I turned on the cold water, gently grabbed his hand, and said, "Let me take a look." I shoved it under the ice-cold water and began to massage and relax his hand. "Is that better?"

"Oh, yeah," he said. "That feels really good."

His fingers relaxed and I began to massage the entire hand, working my way up his rock-hard forearm. "You'll feel better in a few minutes," I said. But he didn't reply. Instead he leaned forward and reached for my ass with his left hand. He placed his palm right on my ass crack and grabbed a handful. While he squeezed and jerked my asscheeks I arched my back and continued to massage his thick fingers. A moment later I pulled his hand from the sink, pressed his wet, bruised finger to my lips, and began to suck it gently. While I sucked and rolled my tongue up and down the base of his right index finger, his left middle finger found my tight pink hole. He moved the thong string to one side and began to work the tip into my hole. I spread my legs wider and sucked harder on his finger. With one hard thrust he slid his thick finger all the way up my wet hole; I sucked hard on his other finger and began to moan with my eyes closed. He slowly circled the inside of my ass, exploring all the right places. My nipples became rock hard and my cock went rigid and began to jump on its own.

"How's that?" he whispered. His breath was hot and smelled like spearmint.

But I could barely utter a word. My mouth fell open and all that came out was, "Ahhhhh...to the left a little; you missed a spot."

He laughed, and then probed to the left with his finger. I moaned and begged for more. But he needed to get off badly so he pulled his finger out of my ass and immediately began to drop his short pants. They fell to his ankles and he stepped out of them and kicked them across the floor. He wore pale blue boxer shorts; a huge cock with a large round head popped from the open fly. From experience, I knew and understood that because he was such a straight-acting construction dude (what I liked most about him) he'd probably keep his boots on and wouldn't bother to undress completely (some of the guys I'd had in the past only pulled down their zippers and bent me over). But I also knew they liked me to be completely naked and on my knees in front of them. So I stripped down to nothing right there in the middle of his kitchen.

"Ah, well," he said. "You have a great chest and a really thin waist." He cupped both my pecs in his palms and began to squeeze and play with them as though molding clay, pushing them up together to form cleavage. I moaned again and pressed my palms against his wide chest when he leaned forward to bite my chest muscles.

"I work my chest hard at the gym," I said. I didn't mention that I starved myself to keep a twenty-nine-inch waist or that I did leg squats until my legs were raw so my ass would bubble and bounce like a basketball.

"And not a hair anywhere," he said.

"I'm not very hairy," I lied. I didn't bother to mention I shaved every last inch of my body so guys like him could get off.

When he was finished playing with my tits I went down on my knees. I spread my legs, leaned forward, and sucked his nine-inch hammer all the way down my throat. It tasted salty; he'd been sweating while fixing the back door. His dick smelled a little like aged cheese and wet towels. I sucked gently, but with intensity, and never missed a beat. He spread his legs and stood as though he were about to take a piss. The head of his cock was about to explode; I could tell he hadn't been sucked off in quite a while. I reached down between my legs and began to jerk my own cock while I continued to slurp away on his. I had a mission: keep it wet and suck it with the same rhythm.

In the beginning I'd been hoping to suck him off for a few minutes, but to eventually finish with him fucking my ass. But he was so excited and so ready to shoot a load down my throat I didn't have the heart to break the momentum (the wife probably never sucked him off; if I had to guess I'd say he'd never had a good blow job). Though my ass was begging for a big dick that day, I was thoroughly enjoying the taste of his salty precum. But more than that, I hadn't swallowed a full load of juice in a while so my motives were slightly selfish, too.

"I'm getting real close. Is it okay if...?" he began to ask, ready to blow his load down my throat. He didn't have to ask, but I liked that he'd been considerate enough to check.

I nodded, still sucking, that it was fine with me. It wasn't always easy finding a guy who could actually cum in my mouth. So many usually like to get sucked off and then jerk off all over my lips. I don't mind licking the cum off their cocks after they've jerked off, but sometimes it's nice when a guy just shoots a load down your throat without touching himself.

While I jerked my cock I began the final, speedy sucking techniques I'd mastered. And he began to moan, "Yes...oh, yeah." His legs started to quiver and he grabbed my head in the palms of his hands. I gently pressed one hand to his strong thigh and rubbed it while the head of his big dick began to swell against my tongue; I stopped jerking myself off because I didn't want to cum before him.

"Here it comes," he whispered. His eyes were closed and his knees began to bend.

I quickly cupped his bull-sized balls in my hand; he blew his cream into my mouth so hard and fast I actually felt it hit the back of my throat. At that point I touched my cock and shot a full load all over the tile floor. After I came I pressed my palms against his hairy thighs and continued to suck out every last drop. He wasn't one of those sensitive types who has to pull out the minute he orgasms. Kenny liked depositing every last drop into my mouth. From the way he continued to moan and sigh, I think the after-sucking was the best part for him.

Finally, when his dick was semisoft against my tongue he pulled out and I gave it a few final licks to make sure I hadn't let a drop go to waste. He reached down and took my elbow in his palm so that I could stand again. "Ah, Rick," he said, "I never expected that." His voice was soft and deep; I reached down and grabbed his limp cock and balls and gently massaged them.

"Was it okay?" I asked, giving him a helpless, innocent look.

"Ah, well, that was pretty good," he said.

I smiled. "Why don't you go lie down on the sofa and I'll get a wet rag and wash between your legs. It will be relaxing."

His eyes bugged and his eyebrows arched at the thought of this. "Okay," he said. "But don't get dressed yet. Stay naked. I like to see you walk around like that in the house." He reached around and cupped my ass with his hand.

I leaned forward and whispered, "Only if you promise to fuck me in an hour or so."

"Ah, well, I think I can take care of that," he said. Then he smiled and gently slapped my ass.

VERTIGO

A. Steele

What do you think? It's a lot better than that closet you call an office now, huh?" Marv, Conrad's boss, grinned and threw his chubby arm wide, inviting Conrad to appreciate the view with him.

"Sure is." Conrad knew his own smile was tepid, at best. It *was* a great view. Only a few office buildings, all lower than this one, stood between him and the bay. It would be even greater when a nice thick pane of glass stood between him and the forty-foot drop.

"They need to know how you plan to arrange your desk and stuff," Marv said with bubbly enthusiasm. "Gotta pull the cables." He walked across the plywood subfloor, right to the edge of the roughed-out room. "You'll want your desk here, yeah?" he asked, pointing to a spot about six feet from the gaping, glassless hole.

Marv looked up from his study of the floor and seemed surprised that Conrad hadn't followed him. "What are you doing?

Get over here."

His gaze left Conrad. Thus, he missed the spasm of terror that crossed the younger man's face. "Rafe," Marv called to one of the guys gathered next to the elevator shaft. "You got the floor plans handy?"

"You bet. Hang on one sec," answered a husky-deep, deeply Southern voice. To his crew the foreman said, "Why don't we break for lunch? Pick me up a gyro, would'ya, Jim?"

Conrad's attention flicked to the fellow left behind as the rest of the plastic-hat pack trooped down the stairs. Marv—short and plump by the kindest of descriptions—looked positively dwarfed by the very tall, very black man who ambled over to stand beside him.

"What did you wanna see, Mr. Shane?" Rafe asked. With the grace of a dancer, he dropped to one knee and unrolled a set of blueprints on the floor.

His hard hat was white, the same dirt-streaked, hard-worn white as the T-shirt that stuck to his body like a second skin, showing off perfect muscles in his back and shoulders. There was a pack of cigarettes rolled up in the tee's cuff, which probably accounted for that wonderful, molasses-over-gravel voice. Gold shone in Rafe's ear, making his complexion seem especially dark in comparison.

"I want to show Mr. Wilcox his swanky new digs," Marv said, falling to his own knees with a lot less grace than the foreman had done. He didn't seem to care if his expensive linen slacks got soiled. "This is his office we're kneeling in."

Rafe lifted pale, hazel eyes to Conrad. His gaze lingered long on Conrad's khaki-covered legs, the bulge of his groin, his narrow waist and broad shoulders. Years of competitive swimming had given Conrad a body he was proud of, but he still found himself sucking in his stomach and flexing his pecs for the handsome man.

When his hazel eyes finally made it up to meet Conrad's green ones, the corner of Rafe's black-plum lips lifted into an arrogant smirk. "I can't think of anyone's office I'd rather be kneelin' in," he said. His voice held a cock-thickening combination of innuendo and amusement.

Marv chuckled good-naturedly, always quick to share a joke. Though Conrad didn't think his happily married, two-point-five kids, minivan-owning boss knew *what* the joke was.

"C'mon over and have a look, Mr. Wilcox," drawled Rafe. The way he stressed the syllable *cox* was downright illicit.

Conrad bit his lip and peeked at the open space behind Rafe and Marv. Then he set his shoulders, focused all his attention on the gold glint in Rafe's earlobe—Conrad couldn't help but wonder what else was pierced—and quick-stepped the distance required to join them.

Death gaped six feet away.

His own crouch wasn't as elegant as Conrad might have wished, but he was too anxious for the hard, splintered security of the floor to do anything but lunge toward it. Sweat slicked his hair, ruining the immaculately gelled black spikes.

Rafe's expression appeared thoughtful as Conrad dropped down beside him.

While Marv blathered on about lighting options and cork versus slate flooring, Conrad shut his eyes and stole a few calming breaths. The scent of manual labor and Perry Ellis cologne rushed into his nostrils. God, he loved that cologne. His ex, Michael, had worn it too, but it hadn't smelt quite so musky-sweet on him.

He opened his eyes again to find Rafe's face less than a foot away. The foreman's thigh was hot against his own. This close, the irises of Rafe's eyes were an incredible striation of gold and gray and brown. His nose was thin, right until the end where

heavy nostrils flared, and his mouth was so full it looked puckered, as if waiting to be kissed.

Rafe's tongue darted out—shocking pink—to slick along his
lower lip.

"Well?"

Marv's voice broke the spell. Conrad jerked his head back.
Jesus! Had he really been about to lock lips with a complete
stranger in front of his boss? "Pardon?" he asked Marv, having
no idea what the original question had been.

Marv shook his head, making his sparse brown hair wave.
"I said, did you want to use this space"—his thick finger tapped
the blueprint—"for a built-in or a closet?"

"Uh..." Actually, at the moment, Conrad couldn't give a flying fuck. He'd sprung a hard-on that could slice through steel.
Cut it out, moron, he told himself. *This is important.* He was
Callingwood Graphic's new head designer, and he was being
asked to help with the design of his own office. It was everything he'd been working toward since he'd graduated five years
before. *So never mind the window of doom or the eminently
fuckable basketball star beside you.*

Conrad took a good look at the plans. "Um. I wouldn't mind
a built-in here," he said, pointing to the alcove on the right of
the door. "If we could balance it with another one here." He slid
his index finger over an inch. "Is that possible?"

Marv looked to Rafe, which meant Conrad had to look at
Rafe, too. Christ, the man was sexy. Deep, almond-shaped eyes.
High cheekbones. Skin so dark it looked like espresso coffee...
and that mouth!

"Yeah. We *can* do that." Rafe cocked his head to study the
plan. Then he reached down to take Conrad's hand and move
it over a tad. His palm was almost twice the size of Conrad's
own. Conrad's cock lurched. "But it'll involve either creating a

weird jut-out into the hall, right here, or losin' a foot and a half
of floor space inside." Rafe gave Conrad's fingers an intimate
squeeze as he lifted his hand away. "Plus, changin' around walls
would require another round with the architect."

Conrad dragged his attention back to the blueprint and attempted to knee-shuffle sideways. Rafe was really buggering up
his concentration. A big finger hooked through the belt loop at
Conrad's lower back, halting his escape attempt.

"Oh, yeah. Of course," Conrad said, feeling foolish, feeling
flustered. *He* should have seen that. Was Rafe's hand creeping
down to his ass? "Well—"

"I could always make you a built-in...here," said Rafe, running a ragged fingernail across the wall-to-wall window. "I'll
make it low, but it'll still cut into some of that view you so ad-
mire." He shot Conrad a wink.

Conrad *really* wanted to kiss him now. That was a perfect
solution. With a partial wall in front of the window he wouldn't
feel like he was walking into death's abyss every time he opened
his office door.

"No need to go through the architect for that," Rafe went on.

"That sounds—"

"Are you joking?"

Conrad's eyes leapt to Marv. His boss was shaking his head
vigorously. Wave. Wave. "What's the point of having a floor
length..." His Blackberry chirped, and Marv's voice trailed off
as he unclipped the phone from his belt to glance at the display
screen. "I've got to take this," he said, standing up. "Do whatever you like, Wilcox, but I think messing with the view would
be a shame." He pushed a button and walked away to gain some
privacy.

"I was going to put a credenza there, anyway," Conrad said,
smiling up at Rafe. Even kneeling, the foreman was a head taller

than him. "So, yeah. If you could build something, I'd really appreciate it."

Rafe didn't answer right away, he was busy tracking Marv's progress. When Conrad's boss ducked into the stairwell, Rafe's hand finished its descent to Conrad's asscheek.

Conrad gasped as he was hauled flush against about two-hundred-and-sixty pounds of muscle.

"I can you help you with that phobia," Rafe whispered against Conrad's ear. Hot breath washed his cheek, right before strong teeth closed over his earlobe.

"With... Oh, Christ...what are you doing?" Rafe's tongue was in his ear and his fingers were lowering the zip on Conrad's pants. Normally, Conrad would be more than happy to roll around on the floor with a prime piece like Rafe. But his boss could be back any second. Not cool. "Stop it."

"With your fear of heights," Rafe elaborated, doing the opposite of stopping. He reached inside the now open zipper and proceeded to jack Conrad off through his white jockeys. His tongue tickled its way along Conrad's jaw.

"How'd you—"

"You looked like a deer caught in the headlights when he asked you to come over." Rafe chuckled and nipped at Conrad's Adam's apple. "A pretty, dark-haired, green-eyed deer." Now his lips moved up to hover above Conrad's own. His hand pumped faster. "You were so pale I thought you were gonna pass out," Rafe said, flicking his tongue into Conrad's mouth.

Before he'd even thought about it, Conrad was sucking on the strong, pink muscle. His balls drew up tight. "Christ, man, you've gotta stop," he groaned. In an act of incredible willpower, he tore his mouth away and twitched his hips back.

Rafe's eyes glittered. He took his hands away from Conrad's body long enough to push his hard hat off. Then he grabbed the bottom of his shirt and hauled that off, as well. The cigarette pack landed with a crinkly clatter somewhere behind them.

Conrad swallowed hard as Rafe's body was revealed. Except for small, fragrant tufts of black under his arms he was completely bald, from the top of his head to the ripples of his stomach. And yes, there was a matching gold hoop in his left, dime-sized, java-chip nipple.

"Fuck me, you're beautiful." Conrad couldn't help but lean forward and take the pretty brown, gold spangled button between his teeth.

"Later," Rafe said. "I'm gonna fuck you later." His long fingers tangled in Conrad's damp, spiky black curls, holding him close for a long second as Conrad gnawed on his nipple. Eventually, he pulled him away. "Right now, I just wanna see you come." Rafe held his gaze as he shimmied the khakis down Conrad's hips.

"Marv's—" Conrad started to protest.

"Gone downstairs," Rafe said. He slipped a forefinger below the elastic of Conrad's underwear. A quick tug and Conrad's cock sprang out, rosy red and granite hard. "Pretty boy," Rafe sighed. He spit into his palm and then wrapped his hand around the quivering shaft. With his other hand, he picked up his discarded T-shirt and draped it around the root of Conrad's penis. It hung there, limp, like a flag of surrender.

"I had a boyfriend a while back," Rafe said conversationally. "Was so scared of heights he couldn't even climb a ladder."

The hard and fast fist on his cock made Conrad's answer a bit less than coherent. "What'd you...oh...God...do?" He wrapped his arms around Rafe's neck, biting at the salty ridge of his collarbone.

"You know Communico's eighty-seven-floor monstrosity down on Randell Street?"

"Yeah." Conrad's hips rolled.

"Well, when it was just being built, and there were only concrete floors and steel supports, I hauled his ass up to the top."

Just as Conrad felt the first telltale clench in his stomach, Rafe clamped down tight on the base of his dick. "Fuck. Please!" Conrad gasped.

"I told you—fuckin' comes later. Listen to my story." His lips ghosted over Conrad's mouth. "I licked…" Rafe licked. "And sucked…" As he sucked Conrad's lower lip into his mouth, Rafe's hand resumed its up and down motion, but now the pace was much too slow. "And fucked him into submission." He unwound one of Conrad's hands from his neck and pressed it to the front of his jeans.

Conrad moaned at the feel of Rafe's hard, hard cock pushing against his palm.

"You see," Rafe said, picking up his pace incrementally, "I wouldn't let him come, 'til he'd put on a safety harness and hung his head out over the side of that big, nasty buildin'."

Conrad fucked Rafe's hand for all he was worth. He was so bloody close. "An-and he did th-that?" he managed to get out.

Rafe's chuckle was pure arrogance. "Course he did. I'm a great lay." He flipped his shirt over the crown of Conrad's cock. "Go ahead and come now, pretty boy. I hear the guys comin' back."

Now that he mentioned it, Conrad could hear them, too. The concrete stairwell amplified the tromping of work boots. The sound got louder with every second that passed. *How much time do I have?* he wondered, with a vague sense of panic. The answer was, enough. He had enough time.

When Rafe gave his balls a tug and shoved his tongue down Conrad's throat, Conrad shot all over that dirty T-shirt. His hands scrabbled for purchase on Rafe's slick back. He thrashed and moaned.

The footsteps got closer.

Almost before he was finished spurting, Rafe had wiped Conrad off and done up his khakis. Rafe tucked the slimed shirt into the waistband of his jeans. It drooped, covering the ridge of his impressive erection. "It's Saturday," he said, his voice mellow. He shifted back on his heels and smoothed the rumpled blueprints. They'd somehow ended up kneeling on top of them.

It blew Conrad's mind that the man could sound so damn calm. He swiped his hands through his hopelessly messed-up hair and tried not to look like he'd just come. "So?"

"So..." Rafe smiled. "The boys leave earlier on Saturday—around five." He rose to his feet with the same feline grace Conrad had admired before. "Me? I ain't got a family, or nothin'. So I'm thinkin'..." He held out a hand and, with no apparent effort, hauled Conrad to his feet.

Conrad looked up. Way up. He'd known Rafe was tall, but he hadn't realized...

The first of the construction workers rounded the corner. "Hey, Rafe," the man said. "Jim's got yer gyro down in the van."

Rafe lifted a languid hand to show he'd heard. "So I'm thinkin'," he leaned over to whisper again, "that maybe I'll stick around for a few hours. Watch the sun set from up on the roof. Tie up some...stuff."

"What d—"

Conrad's cell sang the opening bars to AC/DC's "Hells Bells." He fished the phone out of his pocket and saw Marv's name blinking on the screen. "Shit. Hang on." He stepped out of Rafe's shadow and brought the phone to his ear. "Hey, boss," Conrad said, all false bonhomie. "Where'd you get to?"

Rafe stooped to pick up his smokes and then wandered over to lean against the empty window frame. Conrad's skin pebbled in horror. He whirled away. "At three-thirty?" Conrad asked Marv. He checked his watch. "Okay. I'll meet you there." He turned back around, forcing himself to look only at Rafe, and not at the empty space behind him. "Marv had to leave," he said, with a wry smile. "Wish I'd known."

Rafe smiled, too. "I kinda liked not knowin'." He came forward, holding out his hand. "I'm afraid I've gotta get back to work, Mr. Wilcox."

Conrad shook his hand, feeling a little nonplussed at the sudden formality. But then, the construction crew was all around them, now.

"I hope to see you again soon, though," Rafe said. He turned his body a bit to brush Conrad's knuckles against his still-stiff cock. "Real soon."

Conrad sat in his car and drummed his fingers against the leather-covered steering wheel. The sinking sun cast the building's dark shadow right across the street. It licked the hood of his Volvo. Conrad craned his head out the driver's side window. That roof looked about ten miles high, though he knew it was only sixty feet or so.

He pulled his head back in and resumed drumming. Rafe was worth a lot. No doubt. But was the man worth *this?* "That is the question," he intoned, in a solemn, hammy voice.

A piercing whistle startled a few chickadees from the tree beside him. They wheeled up and around, complaining. Besides Conrad, they were probably the only creatures who'd heard the sound. This street, in the heart of the business district, was quite deserted at seven-thirty on a Saturday night.

"You comin' up, er what?" Rafe hollered.

"Er what," Conrad mumbled. He sighed and got out of the car. "Why don't you come down?" he yelled back, cupping his hands around his mouth to amplify the words.

Rafe stood on the edge of the roof, looking like a pagan god. Sunlight cast a fiery halo around his shirtless body.

After a long, charged silence Conrad got the answer he'd pretty much been expecting.

"No. Get up here."

Just the sound of Rafe's voice had him hard again. Conrad gave himself one more second to reconsider. "Fuck!" he growled.

The steel door leading onto the roof sprang open as Conrad reached for it.

"Got tired of waitin'," Rafe said. He grabbed a fistful of Conrad's shirt and hauled him through the doorway to crush him back against the concrete-brick wall.

The air left Conrad's lungs in a rush. "How'd you know I wouldn't chicken out?" he wheezed.

Rafe used his handhold to wrench the shirt right over Conrad's head. "I didn't. I was comin' down to you."

"Oh." *Oh!*

"But you're here now."

As soon as Conrad's mouth was clear of the fabric, while his arms were still tangled up high, Rafe's lips slanted over his. There was nothing of the slow tease about him now. Rafe was heat and want, grappling with Conrad's clothes, tongue fucking his mouth, grinding his cock into Conrad's hip.

Conrad gave up wrestling with his stupid shirt. He just sagged limp in Rafe's grip and ground back, riding the bigger man's thigh like it was a pony.

"I've been thinkin' about you all day, kid," Rafe broke away to say. He freed Conrad's arms and tossed the shirt aside. Then he directed Conrad's hand to the buttons of his tab-top jeans.

"Wanna see how *hard* I've been thinkin'?"

Fuck, yeah. "I do." Conrad sank to his knees and pulled the buttons apart. The rapid-fire *prrrrt* sound made his mouth water. When he saw that Rafe wasn't wearing any underwear, more saliva pooled under his tongue. And when he realized that Rafe didn't have any hair there, either... "Jesus," he breathed, swallowing the flood.

Rafe fished out his cock. His long, thick, *long* cock. It was so dark that his fingers looked pale against it. "You want this?"

Conrad couldn't look away from the damned thing. He supposed, in the part of his mind still capable of rationalization, that Rafe's penis was simply proportionate to his overall size. After all, he'd had black lovers before, knew the whole "horse" myth was just that—a myth. But... "Jesus," he said again.

"Hey." Rafe pinched Conrad's chin, lifting it. "I asked you a question." He tapped his cockhead against Conrad's lips. "Do. You. Want. This?"

"Yes." Conrad strained against his grip, reaching with his tongue when Rafe didn't let him get any closer.

"Yeah?"

"Yes!"

Rafe turned and strode away. He stopped about three feet from the roof's edge. "Then come and get it."

Shit! Conrad had managed to forget that part of the deal. "Look," he said. "I'm okay with being acrophobic. It's no biggie. Just come back, okay? You were going to come down anyway, right? We'll go to my place, have a nice..."

"No." Rafe had bent over to undo his boots. He straightened and toed them off. "Next time, we'll fuck like rabbits in your safe little bed." He stood on one leg to take off his sock. "Today..." Other leg. Other sock. "...We're gonna fuck right here."

Conrad held his breath as Rafe peeled his jeans down.

"You can crawl, if you have to," said Rafe. He sat down and then stretched himself out on a dark brown blanket that Conrad hadn't even noticed. "In fact..." A slow, sexy smile spread across his face. "I think I'd like that."

Well, he was already on his knees. "To you. No farther. Right?" Conrad asked, his voice shaky.

Rafe pumped his cock as he waited. He didn't bother to answer.

Conrad crawled forward, inch by agonizing inch. If he could have figured out how to get there flat on his belly, he'd have been doing that. When he made it to the blanket his teeth were chattering so hard he couldn't speak. Oddly enough, his cock was still stiff. Still throbbing.

"There's my boy," said Rafe. He rolled onto his back and opened his arms.

Conrad leapt on him, kissing and biting his way down that perfect brown body to that *perfect* brown cock. He swallowed as much as he could—almost three quarters. Spit ran down his chin as he bobbed.

"Whoa. Slow down."

"Fuck you," he lifted his head to groan. Then he ducked down again, working harder, sucking deeper. Rafe's scent was sweat and sex. So good. He tasted like salted tequila. Also good.

Rafe laughed and sat up. He tossed Conrad onto his back like he weighed nothing. "No. Fuck you. Which is why you gotta slow down." He looked down at Conrad with what could only be called predatory intent. "You are so pretty, kid," he sighed, running his hands over Conrad's torso. Rafe gave both pink nipples a gentle tweak. "I wanna see all of you."

He suited action to words and made quick work of Conrad's loafers, socks, and pants. When all that remained were his white briefs, Rafe shifted himself between Conrad's legs. His strong, wet tongue followed the underwear's downward progress. It swirled into Conrad's belly button, slicked over the hollows of his hips, gave his cock a single, unsatisfying lollypop lick, and then slithered down his inner thighs. His knees. His calves.

By the time his underwear was off, Conrad was a writhing, moaning mess.

Rafe spread Conrad's legs apart and began a tortuous return journey, interspersing tongue play with love bites as he worked his way back toward Conrad's groin.

"C'mon, c'mon, c'mon," Conrad grunted, trying to get a handhold on Rafe's smooth head and shoulders to haul the man up his body. There wasn't one. "Would you quit screwing arou– Ahhh, fuck!" He couldn't finish the sentence because Rafe had reached the apex of his thighs and, in a lightning-fast move Conrad was completely unprepared for, shoved his knees back against his chest. That wicked tongue thrust hard into Conrad's ass.

"Fuck!" Conrad cried again. He gave up trying to pull Rafe up his body, reaching for his own cock, instead. This was too much. He had to come.

Rafe caught his hands before he had a chance to put them to good use, and held them firmly against the blanket. His tongue probed and lapped. Conrad's head thrashed. "Jesus Christ, would you just fuck me already?" he hollered. When he heard Rafe laugh he could have happily killed the man.

"Well...but...here's the thing," Rafe said, crawling up farther between Conrad's thighs. His mouth stayed on Conrad's flushed skin. As he moved, he spoke, punctuating his words with bites. "We haven't...made as much...progress...as I'd hoped...to." When he got to Conrad's nipples he rasped his chin across the sensitive peaks and smiled.

Conrad dry-humped his sternum. "What do you mean?"

Rafe let go of Conrad's hands to rear up above him. "I

mean..." His attention wandered while he searched the roof to his left.

Conrad almost wept with relief when Rafe pulled a tube and a condom from the rumpled blanket.

"I mean," Rafe said again. He smoothed the latex over his cock and squirted out a dollop of K-Y onto his fingers. "I'd like to move closer to the edge, pretty boy." One long finger slid into Conrad.

Conrad bit his lip and bore down on the intrusion. Then there were two. "I'd rather not," he gasped. He gasped again when he was suddenly empty.

Rafe looked down to swirl his cock around Conrad's sphincter. "Yeah, I get that," he said, his voice smoky. "I do." He pushed...pushed...until the blunt head popped inside.

When Conrad tried to raise his hips and bring him in deeper, Rafe leaned forward, curved his arms under Conrad's shoulders and then, easy as pie, lifted him into his arms. He held Conrad's weight up high, preventing him from sliding down his cock. The man really was inhumanely fucking strong.

"Just a little bit closer," Rafe whispered. His arms trembled, but Conrad wasn't sure if it was from the strain or from the fact that Rafe was as anxious to hurry this along as he was.

When Rafe began to knee-walk forward Conrad couldn't protest, because every move sent that wonderful, thick cock farther into his body. "Okay. A little bit."

"Good boy." Rafe's smile was tender when he kissed him. Conrad squeezed his eyes shut and passionately kissed him back. He didn't know how far they traveled, and he didn't care. The delicious ache of Rafe's cock stretching his ass was a helluva distraction. When Rafe was buried as far as he could go, he abruptly laid Conrad down against the sticky, tar paper roof. His cock retreated and then stroked deep.

"Oh, yeah," Conrad moaned. He set his feet and thrust back, encouraging Rafe to quicken the pace.

Rafe's breathing was strained, his balls smacked the curve of Conrad's ass. He peppered kisses on Conrad's temple, cheek, and mouth. "Look at me," he said.

Conrad did. Rafe looked amazing. His pupils were huge and his lips were curled back in a primal sneer of pleasure.

"I can't last much longer." Rafe twisted one hand in Conrad's hair and dropped the other between their bodies to circle Conrad's cock. "You about ready?"

What a stupid question. Conrad had to laugh. "Man, I was ready down in the car."

Rafe grinned. "Keep your eyes open," he said. His hips began to snap, each thrust skidding Conrad a few inches higher. His hand moved to the same frantic rhythm as his hips.

"Oh, God," Conrad groaned. "I'm gonna…"

Rafe thrust once more. The skin on Conrad's back burned at the friction. Suddenly, there was air instead of roof under his head. Rafe pulled hard on his hair, bending his neck back.

Adrenaline ricocheted through Conrad's body at the exact same moment that his cock began to pulse. Conrad clung to the lifeline of Rafe's shoulders, sobbing. His orgasm's intensity seemed directly proportionate to the panic he felt. He'd never come this hard. Rafe hilted one last time and held himself still. The feel of that big cock jerking in his ass cranked Conrad's pleasure up another notch. His body bowed. His hips lifted, and his head fell back even farther. Conrad screamed Rafe's name to the skewed horizon. Vertigo warred with ecstasy. And he came, and came, and came.

The built-in credenza was gorgeous. Polished maple stained coffee-black, almost the exact same shade as Rafe's skin. Conrad

swiveled in his desk chair, leaned back and plopped his shoes
on top of it. He admired the view for a second before his eyes
dropped to the note that had been tucked into the credenza's top
drawer.

> *I'm working late tonight on the RDA building.*
> *(Downtown—9th Ave) Don't keep me waiting.*
> XO

Conrad pressed the slightly rumpled, Perry Ellis-scented paper against his lips. "I won't," he murmured.

In the two months they'd been seeing each other Rafe had
"encouraged" Conrad to conquer his fear on a number of
occasions and locations: the Skyview Bridge, Trenton Park's
ferris wheel, hanging over the balcony of Rafe's twelfth-floor
apartment.

The RDA building was thirty stories high, though. Much,
much higher than any of those. Conrad's stomach rolled in fear.

His cock swelled in anticipation.

AN OFFICE ROMANCE

William Holden

I t was a quick, unconscious glance that started it all, just a simple look that turned into a stare, a self-indulgent fantasy. A
solitary moment in time became something more. It pulled me
in. All I could think about was the stranger outside my window
on the twenty-seventh floor. I became attached to him, relying
on his presence to get me through the day.

My life as an accounting manager in international finance
can be summed up in one word—repetitive. Calculating and
analyzing numbers until my eyes grew blurry, I was saved by
two compensations: my salary and my office. It was a corner
location with floor-to-ceiling windows with breathtaking views.
I could watch storms come in across the horizon miles before
they actually hit the city. I often sat there staring out the window
when I should have been working.

I first noticed Frank when I was on an early morning confer-
ence call with a client from Germany. I was in the middle of a
complicated explanation, when I saw something move outside

my twenty-seventh-floor window. I quickly glanced at the new high-rise condominium complex going up across the street and saw a man walking across a steel beam. He appeared as confident and sure-footed as if he were walking on solid ground. I lost my train of thought as I watched him move with grace high above the concrete surface below. Every few minutes I let my eyes drift in his direction.

The rest of that morning I spent being shuffled between meetings. At midday, with the office quiet, I locked myself in my office to enjoy a quiet hour of eating a salad with Philip Glass playing in the background. As I sat there listening to the rise and fall of the tempo, Frank walked into view. I watched him as he moved effortlessly across the metal beam. He stood in the center and raised his hands over his head. His hands moved in small circles as if motioning to someone above him. A large metal cable soon emerged from above. He grabbed the cable and slowly pulled it, one hand over the other, guiding it downward.

Strands of jet-black hair, wet with his sweat, hung out of the yellow construction hat. I watched the muscles in his light blue T-shirt tighten and relax as he continued to pull the cable. He paused, still gripping the cable tightly. He looked down and then out across the street, as if he had felt my eyes upon him. I quickly looked down at my lunch, hoping he hadn't seen me staring at him. I kept my head down as I began to eat my salad.

I wanted to look up, to continue to watch him. I felt like a child who had almost been caught doing something bad. The feeling excited me all the more. Seconds felt like minutes as I waited, trying to analyze my next move. I couldn't take it. I looked up. His firm, hard body moved in the reverse direction, guiding the cable as it was brought back up. A large metal beam soon came into view. He let go of the cable and moved his hands onto the beam, steadying it in the gusting wind. It soon moved over his head. My eyes moved instinctively to the dark circles of sweat under his arms. The fabric of his shirt blended from a light blue to a deep royal at his armpits.

I imagined the warm scent radiating off his body as he continued to reach upward, holding the beam in his large hands. The edge of his shirt soon pulled free from the binding of his tan work pants, and I focused on his newly exposed skin. His torso was the same deep bronze as his arms and face. A small, thin trail of dark hair lay wet against his stomach. I felt a pang of desire deep inside. I licked the Italian dressing off my lips as I imagined running my tongue through those sweat-dampened hairs. The urge to touch him churned and knotted inside me before moving into the nerves of my cock.

I reached down to adjust my lengthening dick and let my hand linger between my legs. My finger ran up and down the thickening shaft trapped within my pants. As I thought of unzipping and masturbating in front of him, a jolt of nervous excitement rushed through me. I could feel my armpits getting damp. I raised my arm and lowered my head. I took a deep breath and closed my eyes, enjoying the scent of my body as the warmth of my skin activated the deodorant.

A primal urge erupted in me. I moved my face further into my pit and grabbed hold of the damp material with my teeth. I sucked on the cloth trying to extract my body's flavor from the fabric. I looked out across the street with a small amount of sweat-dampened fabric still in my mouth. He was looking back in the direction of my building. I didn't stop, nor did I try to hide my actions. At that moment I didn't care if he could see me; in fact, I wanted him to. I wanted him to see what he was doing to me.

I watched as he looked forward. Then his movement stopped. It appeared as if he was focusing his attention directly into my office window. A smile crossed his face and at that moment I knew he could see me. I pushed deeper into my pit and took another deep breath. The sweet smell of desire invaded my senses as I let him watch me. I let my arm fall and rested it in my lap. I raised myself briefly to make room for my fully erect cock. He looked at his watch then back at me. He raised his hand and took off his hat. His hair hung in wet streaks around his face. He shook his head, releasing some of the sweat, yet all the while remaining sure-footed on the steel beam.

We looked out at each other; him from his hot, open-air office, and I from my comfortable air-conditioned one. He smiled and nodded his head in a backward motion as if signaling me. Words suddenly became unnecessary. I knew what he wanted. I stood up and walked to the window. I could see the movement in his eyes now and I watched them move down my body, then stop. I looked down and realized he was looking at the large, swollen bulge in my pants. He ran his tongue across his lips and looked back up at me. I could feel him wanting me. My body trembled with nervous energy as I thought about him touching me, kissing me, fucking me.

He slipped a hand under his T-shirt. I watched the impression of his hand move underneath the material. He raised his arm up and slid his hand into his armpit. He looked at me and smiled. My pulse ripped through my body as I saw the tips of his fingers appear out of his sleeve. He pulled on the opening, exposing the sweat-soaked hair that covered his armpit. His fingers ran through the mass of hair, pulling and tugging on it, teasing me into a fit of passion. I slapped my hand against the window and rested my head on the heated glass, desperate to get closer to him as he continued to taunt me with his body.

He suddenly stopped what he was doing and removed his hand from underneath his shirt. He looked at me, then off to the left, then back at me. I could see a seductive smile appearing from across the distance. He turned away from me and began to leave. My heart stopped. I pounded on the glass trying to get his attention, to get him to stay a bit longer. I turned my head and pressed it as close as I could get to the window, trying to absorb every moment I could of his body as he walked farther away from me. Soon he was out of sight.

I hit my head on the window several times and closed my eyes against the empty view. I could feel the sexual tension rushing through my body, trying to find a release. I touched myself, wanting relief, but realized it wouldn't be the same without him to look at.

As I stood there trying to burn the vision of him forever into my mind, I felt the faintest of vibrations coming through the panes of glass. It became stronger. I opened my eyes and looked out and then down. He was rising up in a construction bucket, looking up at me with a grin.

My breath stopped as I watched him rise, his eyes caressing my body. He stopped for a moment when he became eye level with my crotch. I looked down at him. His hand touched the glass as if trying to get to my cock. I pressed it against the glass. The pressure forced my precome to the surface, dampening the material of my slacks. He licked the window as if licking the moisture from my cock. His tongue was large and spread out across the glass. I wondered what it would feel like in my mouth, sliding, twisting, and rubbing against mine.

He pushed the button inside the bucket and began to climb once more. His hands touched the glass, and we stood face-to-face at last. Less than an inch separated us, but that inch seemed infinitely thick. His dark masculine features stole my breath: the small black hairs on his jawline forming his soon to be five o'clock shadow, his full lips inviting me to kiss him, and his deep green eyes ripping away my clothes to pierce my body. I wanted nothing more than to feel his body next to mine, to feel his breath against my face as we lay naked on the floor of my office. We stood motionless, staring into each other's eyes. The sexual energy between us seemed to penetrate the glass that kept us apart.

I placed my hand against the window. He placed his over mine. A smile lit up his face and caused the most beautiful dimples to appear. I touched my face and then pointed to his as I mouthed the words, "You are beautiful."

"Thank you." He spoke slowly so I could follow the movement of his lips. "You are, too. I'm Frank."

"I'm David," I mouthed back to him.

He raised his eyebrows quickly and winked at me before stepping back from the window. Blood rushed through my body as I watched him pull his shirt up over his head. My desire for him grew as his bronzed, hairy chest was exposed to me. He dropped the shirt in the floor of the bucket and raised his hand above his head and leaned on the window. I could see the beads of sweat forming in the mass of dark hair of his armpits. I watched as one formed and rolled down the side of his body. I licked my lips, wishing I could taste him.

He motioned with his head for me to follow his lead. I stood back and removed my tie and then began to unbutton my shirt. I watched as his eyes moved quickly over my body as each button was released. His smile grew as I let my shirt drop to the floor exposing my smooth, hairless torso. He pressed his body to the glass. His large erect nipples flattened against the window. The sweat of his body matting the hair left swirls of damp streaks across the glass.

He moved his left hand down and groped the window in front of my crotch. I slowly unzipped my pants, teasing him with the thickness that lay beneath. He began to mouth something, but I couldn't make out what he was saying. His throat appeared to be strained as he spoke again; all I could hear was a deep muffled sound. His chest rose and fell quickly.

He pounded on the glass as if begging me to remove my pants. I slipped off my shoes, my socks damp in the cool air of the office. I undid the clasp of my pants and let them fall around my ankles. My light gray briefs were stretched to their capacity. A large damp spot covered the left side where the head of my cock rested. I pulled them down and released my swollen cock. It fell against the window with a loud, wet smack as precome splattered across the glass.

Frank leaned down and ran his tongue up and down across the glass that separated him from my cock. I pushed myself closer against the glass and rubbed my precome into my hairy balls. He licked his lips as he stood back up to face me.

I grabbed my cock and began stroking it. It lengthened even more in my grip as I continued to devour Frank's body with my eyes. With one arm resting on the glass above his head, he ran his other hand over his chest and down to the edge of his pants. He undid the button of his pants and then slowly moved the zipper downward. I tried to imagine the sound of the metal teeth of his zipper as they released. My body trembled in response.

He motioned with his hands for me to kneel down. I did as he asked. He raised one foot to the edge of the bucket and untied the lace of his work boot. He removed the boot and wiggled his socked toes in front of me. I took a deep breath hopelessly wanting to smell the scent of his feet through the pane of glass. He reversed his position and removed the other boot in the same manner.

He slid his pants down and tugged each leg out of them. He stood in front of me in a pair of white, tight-fitting boxer briefs.

His legs were thickly muscled and covered in the same thick black hair as his chest. The whiteness of his briefs was beautifully exaggerated by the deep coloring of his skin.

He moved closer to the window, and the bulge of his crotch expanded as he became more excited by our actions. It filled the pouch and pushed on the thin, ribbed material. I could see the entire outline of his cock, including the thick overhang of foreskin. I licked my lips as he moved in closer.

I could see the pulsing veins through the material of his underwear as they rushed more blood into his expanding shaft. Dampness appeared and spread across the material. He slipped his hand inside and tugged on the end of his cock. His fingers came out wet and covered in a thick layer of precome. I watched as he moved them into his mouth, savoring his own sweet, salty flavors.

I reached down between my legs and began stroking my cock again. My fist instantly became wet with my excitement as Frank pulled off his underwear. His thick, uncut cock fell heavily between his legs. Precome formed in the folds of his skin and hung loosely in the wind. He wrapped his hand around the head of his cock and milked the precome from the layers of skin before smearing it over his shaft. He leaned into the window with one arm above his head, his hips pushed farther back and his legs spread apart.

He gripped his cock and began stroking it in long, slow rhythmic movements. The thick foreskin and covered head of his cock were positioned directly in front of me. I watched with growing urgency as the large, pink mushroom head of his cock was pushed in and out of the thick folds of its skin. His piss slit widened and he held it open for me. I could see the soft, moist tissue deep inside of it. My tongue slipped out of my mouth almost unconsciously, wanting to slip inside. I saw the muscles in his body tighten just as a stream of thick precome poured out of the slit. He ran the head of his cock across the glass in front of me, leaving a thick trail of dampness behind it. I ran my finger along it, following the flow back and forth as we continued to masturbate.

I stood back up and rested my arm above my head as he had done. Our arms almost seemed to touch one another in our need to get closer. We leaned our foreheads together and looked into each other's eyes as the motion of our hands increased below us. My pulse quickened as I saw Frank's breathing becoming stronger and more pronounced. Sweat poured out of his pores, soaking his body to a glistening shine in the sun.

I felt the pressure inside me build, that one-of-a-kind feeling when your body first crosses the no-turning-back line. My body trembled. I heard myself groaning. And then even through the thick pane of glass, I could hear Frank moaning in intense pleasure. We smiled at each other with the realization that we were going to come together.

I grunted. Frank groaned. Our bodies began to tremble. Our overheated bodies pressed tightly against the window trying desperately to make contact. Our eyes locked on to each other's and wouldn't let go. My knees buckled as I shot my first load onto the glass. Frank winced, and his eyes rolled back in his head as he lost his load against mine. He quickly looked back at me as if not wanting to miss a moment of our brief time together.

We continued to stare into each other's eyes as we went on coming. We collapsed toward the ground and came face-to-face with our come dripping down both sides of the window. As if we each knew what the other was thinking we ran our tongues across the glass, licking and tasting our own come. Our tongues and come seemed to blend together. As his eyes stared deeply into mine, I tried to imagine my come as his, his come as mine.

He smiled at me and pressed his lips to the glass. I did the same. We kissed with the barrier between us. Both wishing for something more but knowing it was not possible.

An hour later, I was tired and spent and knew no work was going to get done for the rest of the day. I decided to pack it in and go home.

As I left the building and headed down the street I saw Frank coming toward me from the opposite direction. We looked at each other, and he reached out and ran his finger down my arm. My body melted remembering what we had shared on the twenty-seventh floor during our brief office romance.

SANDHOGS

Kiernan Kelly

Already blistering hot at seven in the morning, the sun bakes my ass inside my flannel work shirt and jeans. I can feel sweat dripping down my spine, collecting at the small of my back, pooling in my armpits, dampening my crotch. Standing in front of the Check-In/Check-Out board for City Tunnel No. 3, where I'm supposed to meet Sonny's kid, I'm dressed for fucking December, not August. But down in the tunnels the temperature never gets much above fifty-five degrees, even when the city is being fried to a crisp under the summer sun six hundred feet above my head.

Sonny was a good guy, Pop's best friend. Before he died, I promised Sonny I'd take his son down the first time, and I'll know the minute the cage starts to descend into the shaft whether or not he's got the stuff it's going to take to make it in this business. The money's good, which is the only reason a lot of men stay at it. Still, most sandhogs are second or third generation. It's in our blood, but even then it's not for everybody.

Takes something special in a man to be a sandhog, to spend your
life drilling holes underneath the ground like a mole. Breathing
in dust all day, knowing that it's going to fuck up your lungs;
knowing that there's a good chance that you might go down
and not ever come back up, but still showing up for your shift.
I only hope Sonny's kid doesn't puke or shit his pants before we
hit bottom.

Walking toward me is a younger version of Sonny, what he
must have looked like when he first put on his hard hat forty
years ago. Six foot at least, broad shoulders, thick neck. No
gut—that'll come later after a few years spent drowning his fears
in pitchers at O'Malley's after work, if he makes it. For the time
being his stomach is flat, hips lean. He's wearing a dark blue
flannel shirt and stiff jeans that look brand new. Enjoy the feeling while it lasts, kid. They're going to be covered in mud and
soaked in sweat by quitting time.

"I'm Billy," he says, holding out his hand for me to shake.
It's big, like the rest of him, but soft. Not a single fucking callus,
although his grip is strong. Well, that'll change soon enough.
Those smooth palms will be sprouting blood blisters by the end
of the day.

If he lasts that long—most don't. They'll go topside at lunchtime and never come back. Billy tried college but hated it, and
decided to follow in his dad's footsteps. We'll see if this is just
another thing he quits.

"Ready to go?" I ask, looking into Billy's dark blue eyes. I'm
still sizing him up, looking for weaknesses, for anything that'll
give me a clue as to whether he's going to make it or be crying
for his mama before noon. I see nervousness masked by Brook-
lyn cockiness, a cool I-dare-you-to-fuck-with-me flash in his eyes
and a tight, thin smile on his lips. Well, you can't fool me, kid.
Don't bother with the tough-guy attitude—I know better. I've

seen too many boys like you go down, full of piss and vinegar, only to come up an hour later shaking and puking on the toes of their brand-new rubber boots. "Okay, then. Let's go. Flip your tag," I order, nodding toward the Check-In/Check-Out board.

Billy takes a minute to find his name on the pegboard. Under each man's name is a double-sided hangtag. Green side means you're topside, red means you've gone down into the belly of the beast. We have to flip the tags on the way down and when we get back up—it's the law. In reality, it's the only way the contractor will know which bodies to look for if something goes wrong down there, although I refrain from mentioning that tidbit of information to Billy. No sense in having him shit his pants before we even get down.

I lead Billy over to the cage, the narrow, metal-grated elevator that will take us into the shaft. This is it, the moment of truth. Once the cage gets deep enough where the surface is so far above your head that you can't see the sky or feel the air moving, a man is forced to be truthful with himself. It's in that moment that he finds out if he's got the balls for this kind of work.

Standing shoulder to shoulder with Billy in the tight confines of the cage, I can smell him. He's sweating, but not from fear. Fear has a unique odor, sharp and biting, that oozes out of a man's pores along with his perspiration. But Billy doesn't reek of fear—it's something else entirely. A musky scent that's familiar, that makes me take a quick look at the crotch of his jeans.

I'll be dipped in shit if he doesn't have a fucking hard-on. He's not afraid—he's excited. Good for you, Billy-boy. Any man who can get a boner from the idea of being stuffed six hundred feet underground with a couple of thousand tons of rock and earth hanging over his head has promise. Maybe he's going to make it after all.

I can't help but be impressed by the size of his bulge. Damn, the boy has talent there under his zipper. I can imagine it springing free into my hand, thick and hot, its fat, rosy head already wet with precum. No shaving for Billy-boy—he'll have a thick thatch of hair at his cock's root, inky black. I want to bury my nose in it, feel those crisp curls against my cheek.

No, I can't let myself go there. Sex, especially sex with the son of Pop's best friend, a kid still wet behind the fucking ears, is something I shouldn't be thinking about right now. Letting your mind wander when you're in the tunnels can get you killed. Not to mention that my brother sandhogs would probably geld me with a sledgehammer if they ever found out that I'm into men. Got to stay focused, but damn, it's hard. Then again, so am I, thinking about Billy's cock.

The cage rattles and groans, slowly lowering us into the darkness of the shaft, and I force my thoughts back to where they should be—on the job. The trip down will take four minutes—and you have no idea of how long four minutes can be until you spend it being dropped feetfirst into the bowels of the earth. I find myself rooting for Billy. I want him to make it. Hold on, Billy-boy, here we go. Keep it together, now.

An image of Billy's cock, stiff and slick, balls hanging heavily behind it, flashes into my mind. Yeah, think happy thoughts, Billy. I know I am.

Halfway down the shaft, he curses softly under his breath. His eyes dart toward me, wide, his Adam's apple working double time as he swallows repeatedly.

"Don't look up," I yell over the grating metallic scream of the cage, wrapping my fingers around his forearm. His muscles are tense and as hard as stone under my hand. Lifting weights, doing chin-ups and push-ups has kept him in shape, bulked him up. He's strong enough to wield a sledgehammer, or keep a jackhammer under control. Strong enough for the work that needs to get done, if he can just keep his cool. "Don't think about it. We're almost there."

The fear fades, and he nods, takes a deep breath, lets it out slowly. I can feel his muscles relax under my hand. Good boy. That's when I know for sure that he's going to be okay. He'll make it, tough it out. He's got sandhog blood.

We finally hit bottom, stepping out of the cage into the bell-out area. Assigned to work breaking up rocks the tunnel boring machine spits out, we pick up a pair of sledgehammers and hop the railroad car that will take us to the rock face at the head of the tunnel. It's hard, backbreaking, sweaty work, but it sure as hell ain't rocket science. Billy's got a strong back. He should do fine.

The morning passes without incident. Billy proves to be a hard worker, swinging his sledge tirelessly against the rock, breaking down the larger pieces so they can be carried back up to the surface on the conveyer belts.

After an hour at this, his flannel shirt is plastered to his body, soaked from both sweat and the water that constantly drips down from the rock ceiling. Under the pretense of supervision, I stand back and watch Billy's muscles move fluidly underneath the wet material, rock-hard biceps bulging as he smashes the rock into gravel. Billy's thighs are powerful, his ass firm as it clenches under his jeans. I wonder if he'd look as good naked as he does under those wet clothes. Some guys don't, but I imagine that Billy would look even better in his skin.

It's the best show I've seen all week, and I'm almost disappointed when the lunch whistle blows.

"Lunchtime. Good, I'm starving," I holler over the roar of the machinery. True enough, but it's not food that I want. I'm hungry to take a bite out of Billy's tight ass, to suck his cum out through his dick until he whimpers, but unfortunately that's not on the menu.

"I smell like a fucking sewer," Billy says, taking a quick whiff of his armpit after he drops his sledge. Personally, I'm into the smell of a hardworking man, musky and strong, the odor of male. I wouldn't mind burying my face in his hairy pit, taking a lick, but Billy doesn't seem to have the same appreciation for it. He screws up his face, waving a hand in front of his nose.

"Get used to it. We all wear the same cologne down here— Eau de Sandhog," I laugh. "C'mon, let's go eat." I try to ignore the fact that my cock is filling again. As I turn away I readjust myself, hoping Billy hasn't noticed that I've been sporting wood for the better part of the morning. Damn, what is it about this boy that has me so fucking turned on?

His body is hot, that's the reason, and I know it. No use lying to myself. He's not a pretty boy, but then I've never been attracted to sweet little twinks. I don't want to change diapers—I want to fuck. I like my men beefy, men who can take what I've got to give and give it right the fuck back. The kind of guys I don't have to be afraid of breaking when I ride them.

Billy fits the bill. Clean shaven when we met at seven in the morning, his jaw is already covered by a blue-black shadow and smudged with dirt and grease. His eyes are deep set under thick dark brows that are trying to meet in the middle but don't quite make it across his wide forehead. Billy's nose is strong but slightly twisted, as if it might have been broken a time or two. The prettiest part of his face is his mouth. Full and lush, his lips are the kind made for kissing, the sort that make a man ache to taste them.

Billy is all Man, with a capital M, from his short-cropped black hair to his size 14 boots. Everything in between is rock solid and slathered in testosterone, exactly made to order for a guy like me. I can't seem to keep my eyes off him, or keep my mind from doing things to him that would make a porn star blush.

It's going to be a long fucking afternoon.

I lead Billy away from the conveyer belt and the clouds of dust and rock that choke the air, into one of the dark, narrow side tunnels. It's even colder there, away from the heat generated by the machinery and the bodies of the men who work them, but it's relatively quiet and dry.

The only light comes from the beams on our hard hats, weak yellowish rays that illuminate dust motes floating in the air. I flick on a portable lantern and set it down on an empty oil barrel, shedding a little more light on our impromptu café. Settling down on a pair of wooden crates, we crack open our metal lunch boxes and dig in. Regardless of my current state of horniness, sandhogging is hungry work and I'm starved. I wolf down two bologna sandwiches and half a thermos of coffee without pausing to take a breath between bites.

Billy's even faster than me, inhaling a foot-long hero made up of some unidentifiable deli meats, and draining a pair of Cokes in no time flat. I don't think I saw him chew once. He's like a snake, swallowing his food whole.

"Want some coffee?" I ask when I see Billy watching me with a greedy look in his eye. I'm out of anything edible, but the kid looks like he's hungry enough to chew rocks. I cock an eyebrow when Billy stands up, looking down at me. He's not saying anything, just staring at me like I'm a breaded pork chop or a piece of fried chicken.

"You've been watching me all day," he finally says, hooking his thumbs into his front pockets. I can't help but notice that his hands frame the bulge at his crotch, which is now temptingly at eye level and no more than a foot away from me. Look but don't touch, I have to remind myself. I want to reach out and give him a squeeze, feel the meat that pushes against his zipper, but instead I jerk my eyes upward to meet his.

"That's my job. To make sure you don't get dead on your first day."

"That's not what I meant and you know it. You've had a fucking hard-on all day. I've seen it. Shit, I felt it every time you brushed against me. You're queer," he says quietly. It's not an accusation, there's no venom in his voice; but that he's up and said it in the first place presents me with a huge problem.

I feel like I've been slammed upside the head with a major case of what the fuck, bringing me to my feet. I thought I'd kept it on the down low, keeping what I'd been thinking all morning to myself. The last thing I need is for this kid to spread rumors around the tunnel. That gets around and I'll find myself without a job before I can blink, and probably beat-to-shit to boot, union or no union.

Billy is my height, and I find myself standing nose to nose with him in the dim cavern. I open my mouth to lie, deny, and slam the closet door shut once and for all, but before I can get a single word out Billy traps my face in those big hands of his and plasters his lips to mine.

Old habits die hard. I've spent too many years hiding who I am from the others, pretending to be someone I'm not. Instinctively, I push him away, my hands curling into hard fists, ready to plow one into his face. I'm breathing hard, and a war rages inside my head. I can't deck the new guy—he's Sonny's kid. Plus, he's right about me—I don't want to fight him. I want to fuck him.

Instead of punching Billy, I push him back against the wet rock wall, pinning him there, my hands splayed flat against his broad chest. I can feel his heart hammering under my palms. His muscles harden under my fingers as he tenses, ready to fight back, ready to do some damage.

But something besides his muscles has grown hard, too. I can feel his cock as I lean against him, my body weight helping to hold him back against the wall. It bites into my groin like an iron poker. Every bit of my resolve bleeds out of me and I groan as I grind my crotch against his, rubbing our cocks together under the rough denim of our jeans. Smashing my mouth against his, I muffle the sound, my tongue pushing past his surprised lips.

His mouth tastes cool and sweet from the Cokes, his tongue soft and warm. Bristly whiskers scrape my cheeks; the kiss is deep and wet. Coming alive between the wall and me, Billy's hands pull at my shirt, jacking it free of my jeans. They slide up underneath the material, tracing the knobs on my spine. His fingers burn like fire, driving me crazy. I want more. Now. No turning back.

"Fuck, Billy! You feel so good," I whisper hoarsely. Got to keep our voices down, keep the moaning and groaning down to a minimum. Can't let anyone in the main tunnel hear us.

"Touch me," he growls. I feel his teeth biting down on my shoulder through my shirt, hard enough to leave a mark. I can feel it all the way down to my toes.

Sliding my hands around his hips, I cup the ass I've been dreaming about all morning. His butt is solid, his muscles clenched as I squeeze his cheeks in my palms. Pulling us together until there's no air between our bodies, he's close enough for me to feel his body heat through the fabric of our clothing.

Not enough. I need skin-to-skin contact, need to feel his flesh burning under me. Tearing at his flannel shirt, I'm frustrated by the buttons. I'm too keyed up, too eager to bother wasting time unbuttoning them. Frantically, I rip it off over his head, dropping it carelessly onto one of the crates. Holding his arms above his head, I indulge myself in my earlier fantasy, dipping down to explore his hairy pit. His scent is strong, sweat laced with lust, and as I run my tongue through the forest of black hair it fills my mouth with the taste of man.

Billy's chest is furry, covered in short black curls that funnel into a thin line, creasing his stomach and snaking down under his waistband. His nipples are large, golden brown, and peaked into tight, whitened nubs. Bending, I take one between my teeth, nipping until he moans and presses down on my hard hat, urging me lower.

"Suck me," he orders. I've never been partial to taking orders from anyone; it goes against my grain. But in this instance, I'll make an exception. I want him too badly to care about a bruise to my ego. Let him order me. Yes, sir. I hear and obey.

It only takes me a moment to unhook his belt buckle and open his fly. Grabbing the waistband of both his jeans and his boxers, I wrench them down to his knees in one smooth movement. Freed at last, his cock slaps against my cheek, every bit as long and thick as I'd imagined it would be. I can smell his musk, feel the trail of wetness his dick leaves along my jaw.

Unbuckling my belt, I free my own cock before the sticky precum that I can feel gathering on its head soaks through my underwear to my jeans.

Billy's cock has a large head, rosy red and perfectly shaped. His shaft is thick, heavily veined; his balls are swollen. Just as I'd suspected, Billy's pubic hair nests his cock in a thatch of crisp black curls. Cupping his sac in my hand, feeling the weight of his balls in my palm, I open my mouth wide and go down on him, sucking him into the back of my throat.

"Oh, fuck!" Billy hisses through his teeth. His hips rock, feeding me more of his length, almost more than I can take. Damn, but the boy is fucking gifted. My mouth is stuffed full; my tongue swirls over the fat head of his cock, lapping up his musky taste. My lips burn as they slide over his velvety skin, from root to tip and back again.

It's still not enough. I want to taste more of him. Releasing him, ignoring his grunt of protest, I grip his hips and urge him to face the wall. "Give me your ass," I growl, finally giving an order of my own. He obeys, bracing his arms against the slick rock wall and spreading his legs as wide as his jeans, still bunched up at his knees, will allow.

Oh, but his ass is a thing of beauty. Rounded, firm young flesh, dusted with black hair that runs thicker at the crack, it's an ass made for licking, for biting, for fucking, and I want desperately to do it all, and all at the same time. Given the circumstances however, I'm forced to hurry things along. Lunchtime must be almost over, and we wasted a lot of time eating sandwiches instead of each other.

My fingers pry his asscheeks apart, revealing his dark, cinnamon-colored hole. Ringed in dark fur, his anus clenches as I exhale a warm breath over it. "God, what an ass," I moan before flicking my tongue out for my first taste. His heady, pungent flavor fills my mouth with that first quick lick, and I savor it for a moment before my tongue darts in again to explore the ridged texture of his asshole.

Billy bends over farther, giving me better access. His hand is moving over his cock, jerking off as I tongue-fuck him. My lips pull at his asshole, as if I'm trying to suck him inside out. I'm driving him crazy, I can tell.

"Put your finger in my asshole, Dale," he begs, wiggling that fine fleshy butt against my face. "Fuck me!"

Oh, I want to fuck him all right. I want to slide my cock up his tight ass so deeply that it brushes the roof of his mouth. I want to fuck him balls deep, feel my hip bones pound against the soft flesh of his ass. Instead, I push my finger into him, groaning as the fiery, silken walls of his anus mold themselves around it. "So fucking tight," I moan, wrapping the fingers of my left hand around my cock.

I slide my finger into him repeatedly, up to the knuckle, my other hand mirroring the rhythm over my dick. A little spit lubes him nicely, and I push another finger in next to the first. Billy's ass has a death grip on my fingers, making me want more of me inside him. A two-finger fuck is better than nothing, but I'd love to work my whole hand into that tight space, fist-fuck him up to my elbow. Not enough time now for anything but what I've already got going. Besides, I'm going to cum soon. I can feel my balls winding up for the pitch, ready to shoot.

So is Billy. "I'm gonna cum," he says, his voice hoarse and throaty.

I jump to my feet, slipping my fingers out of his ass on the way up. I want to watch him cum, watch him watching me. I want to jerk him off as he paints my belly with his juice, and I want the favor returned in spades. I want a lot, but I don't think Billy will mind my demands in the least.

Belly to belly, our hands wrapped around each other's cocks, we jerk each other in fast, strong strokes. My breath is hitching now; I can feel my orgasm winding its way through my scrotum, setting my belly and balls on fire. Then it's here, my teeth grinding and my muscles contracting as I cum hard and fast, thick white ribbons spurting over Billy's hand and stomach.

"Oh, God! I'm cumming!" Billy screams, his voice tight and rising several octaves higher with each syllable. I jerk the last drop from his cock, still breathing hard from my climax as Billy reaches the end of his own.

We stand together for a few minutes, hard hats clanked against one another, waiting for our breathing and heartbeats to slow down to normal. God, I hope nobody heard us, especially Billy's last shriek. The boy's a screamer, and while I do love men who let me know that I'm working it, vocalizing is a bad thing when we're on the job. Lunchtime quickies will have to be kept quiet—maybe next time I'll gag him. The thought is intriguing, and I almost wish he hadn't drained me so completely. I wouldn't mind giving a ball gag a try on Billy-boy. Doesn't really matter. I don't have the time or the equipment now anyway. Maybe I'll pack a little something extra in my lunch box tomorrow.

That there will be a next time goes without saying. There will be, no doubt about it. There's no fucking way on earth that I can work side by side with Billy and not want to fuck him blind at lunchtime. Dinnertime. Maybe breakfast. The thought makes me smile.

"There's the whistle," I say, breaking away from him, pulling up my pants. We dress in hurry. I don't want Billy to be late from lunch on his first day on the job.

"Dale..."

"Yeah?"

"I'm gonna like sandhogging," Billy says with a cheeky grin. "The fringe benefits rock."

I laugh, swatting his ass. "Come on, kid. Get a move on. We're going to be late."

By the time we reach the end of the side tunnel, we've both got our game faces back on. Just two more sandhogs back from lunch, ready to bust our butts doing what we do best.

Yeah, I think, watching Billy heave the heavy sledgehammer up over his shoulder and bring it crashing down on a large piece of granite, *he's going to do just fine.* He's a sandhog. It's in his blood.

ABOUT THE AUTHORS

GAVIN ATLAS currently lives in Houston, Texas. He has been published in *Honcho* and his story "The Last Adventure of Blast Boy" will appear in *Superqueeroes* (Haworth Press). His e-book *Claiming Danny* is available from Forbidden Publications. He would like to thank wonderful handy-bear Robin Vieno for his invaluable aid with construction work authenticity. Gavin also thanks his boyfriend, John, for being a terrific fellow. Gavin can be reached at www.GavinAtlas.com.

LAURA BACCHI writes erotica and erotic romance. Her stories can be found at Ruthie's Club, Loose-Id, Samhain, and Amber Allure, and she is a member of ManLove Romance. For more about Laura and her work, please visit www.laurabacchi.com.

A native Californian, **BEARMUFFIN** lives in San Diego with two leather bears in a stimulating ménage à trois. His erotica has appeared in many gay publications. He now writes for *Honcho* and *Torso*. His work is featured in several anthologies from Alyson and Cleis Press.

DALE CHASE has been happily writing male erotica for nearly a decade, with more than one hundred stories published in various magazines and anthologies including translation into German. Her first literary effort appeared in the *Harrington Gay Men's Fiction Quarterly*. Her collection of Victorian gentlemen's erotica, *The Company He Keeps*, will be published by Haworth Press. A native Californian, Chase lives near San Francisco and is at work on a novel and a collection of ghostly male erotica.

DALTON is a writer and sexual adventurer who lives very happily with two longtime companions in the upper Midwest. A fan of all things sexual, Dalton has experienced everything from kinky and gay to plain vanilla and straight as well as all fetishes, kinks, lifestyles, and pleasures. "I feel that to be truly human a person must fully express themselves in a sexual manner. As a person grows and changes, their sexuality must also and so continuing exploration is critical to a fulfilled life." A trained journalist, Dalton's work can be found on the Web and in print going back to the late 1980s under a variety of names.

LANDON DIXON's writing credits include *Options*, *Beau*, *In Touch/Indulge*, *Three Pillows*, *Mandate*, *Torso*, *Honcho*, *Men*, *Freshmen*, and stories in the anthologies *Straight? Volume 2*, *Friction 7*, *Working Stiff*, *Sex by the Book* and *Ultimate Gay Erotica 2005* and *2007*.

RYAN FIELD is a thirty-five-year-old freelance writer who has had many short stories published in anthologies and collections.

He lives and works in both Los Angeles and Bucks County, PA, and is currently working on a novel.

JEFF FUNK has written hundreds of choral works published by Warner Bros. Publications, with more than 1.7 million copies in print. His stories appear in *Dorm Porn 2*, *Tales of Travelrotica for Gay Men Volume 2*, *My First Time Volume 5*, *Ultimate Gay Erotica 2008*, and the forthcoming *Superqueeroes*. As an actor, he appears as Crawling Man in the horror film *Return in Red*. He lives in Auburn, Indiana.

T. HITMAN is the nom-de-porn for a full-time professional writer whose work routinely appears in a number of national magazines and fiction anthologies. "Sooty" is an homage to his home, a small bungalow set on a large plot of land in a rural corner of New England, which he and his amazing partner of the past half-decade rescued from a diabolical developer. The house has been restored, and his partner, who swings a mean hammer, looks hella hot in his trusty tool belt.

WILLIAM HOLDEN has been writing gay erotica for more than six years and has served as fiction editor for *RFD* magazine. Currently residing in Atlanta, he is by day a librarian specializing in LGBT issues. He continues to spend his evenings and weekends hanging out in gay clubs around the country gathering ideas for his next story. He can be contacted at wholden2@mac.com.

DAVID HOLLY's stories have been printed in a variety of gay erotic publications, including *Guys*, *First Hand*, *Manscape* and *Hot Shots*. His work has also appeared in *Dorm Porn 2*, the second volume of *Travelrotica for Gay Men*, *My First Time* and other anthologies.

KIERNAN KELLY lives in the southeastern United States, writing m/m erotic romance while drinking margaritas served by thong-clad cabana boys. Okay, in reality, Kiernan lives chained to a temperamental Macintosh, drinking coffee and writing m/m erotic romance while dreaming of thong-clad cabana boys. Sigh. You can find a complete listing of Kiernan's work at her website www.kiernan-kelly.com, along with several free reads and giveaways.

BARRY LOWE is a Sydney writer whose plays have been produced worldwide including *Homme Fatale: The Joey Stefano Story*, *The Extraordinary Annual General Meeting of the Size-Queen Club*, *The Death of Peter Pan*, *Seeing Things* and *Rehearsing the Shower Scene from* Psycho. He also cowrote the screenplay to *Violet's Visit*. His short stories have appeared in *The Mammoth Book of New Gay Erotica*, *Flesh and the Word*, *Best Date Ever*, *Boy Meets Boy*, and others. He is also the author of *Atomic Blonde: The Films of Mamie Van Doren*.

AARON MICHAELS is a short fiction writer whose work has appeared in numerous publications, including *Animal Attraction* published by Torquere Press in August of 2007 and *Screaming Orgasms and Sex On the Beach* edited by Shanna Germain for Pretty Things Press.

STEPHEN OSBORNE has had stories published in many anthologies, including *Best Date Ever*, *Dorm Porn 2*, *My First Time Volume 5*, *Travelrotica for Gay Men 2* (all available from Alyson Books), and *Unmasked*, an erotic superhero anthology from Starbooks Press. A former improvisational comedian, he now resides in Indianapolis with two cats and Jadzia the Wonder Dog. He's been known to go to parties and make out with straight guys. Hey, they started it.

G. RUSSELL OVERTON is a historical researcher for a consulting firm in Lansing, Michigan. He has produced a number of works, both fiction and nonfiction, has two novels in pre-publication, and was a contributor to *Paws and Reflect: Exploring the Bond Between Gay Men and Their Dogs*. His fields of study in history include pre-Revolutionary Russia and Native Americans in the nineteenth and twentieth centuries. His fictional style is to create romantic adventure, unbounded by the dictates of political and cultural agendas, for readers of gay and lesbian literature. Contact him at ro1898@yahoo.com.

ROB ROSEN is the author of *Sparkle: The Queerest Book You'll Ever Love*, and the forthcoming Haworth Press novel, *Divas Las Vegas*. His short stories have appeared in such noted anthologies as: *Mentsh, I Do/I Don't: Queers on Marriage*, *Best Gay Love Stories 2006*, *Truckers*, *Best Gay Love Stories: New York City*, *Best Gay Romance*, *Superqueeroes*, *My First Time: Volume 5*, *Son of PORN!*, *Best Gay Love Stories: Summer Flings*, *Ultimate Gay Erotica 2008*, and *Best Gay Romance 2008*. His erotic fiction can often be found in *MEN*, *Freshmen*, and *[2]* magazines. Please visit www.therobrosen.com.

A. STEELE has written for Torquere Press, Starbooks Press, and Ruthie's Club.

LOGAN ZACHARY is a mystery writer living in Minneapolis, MN. Growing up watching "Dark Shadows" instead of taking his afternoon nap, he quickly found the world of books. The Hardy Boys and Nancy Drew grew into Agatha Christie and Stephen King. He is an avid collector of signed books and a devoted movie fan. His two dogs keep him busy when not writing, reading, or enjoying a good or even a bad movie. He can be contacted at LoganZachary2002@yahoo.com.

ABOUT THE EDITOR

NEIL PLAKCY is the author of the mystery novels *Mahu, Mahu Surfer*, and *Mahu Fire*, and coeditor of *Paws and Reflect: Exploring the Bond Between Gay Men and Their Dogs*. His erotica has been featured in many anthologies, including *Men Seeking Men, My First Time 2, Travelrotica for Gay Men, Best Gay Love Stories: New York City, Best Gay Romance, Treasure Trail, Cowboys, Hot Cops, Ultimate Undies*, and *Fast Balls*.